# Nostradamus Ate
# My Hamster

## Robert Rankin

## W F HOWES LTD

This large print edition published in 2002 by
W F Howes Ltd
Units 6/7, Victoria Mills, Fowke Street
Rothley, Leicester LE7 7PJ

First published by Doubleday 1996

A catalogue record for this book
is available from the British Library

ISBN 1 84197 534 6

Typeset by Palimpsest Book Production Limited,
Polmont, Stirlingshire
Printed and bound in Great Britain
by Antony Rowe Ltd, Chippenham, Wilts.

# Nostradamus Ate My Hamster

This book is dedicated to
a very good friend of mine
Graham Theakston
the now legendary director
of *Tripods*. Let's see
you direct *this one*, sucker!

It also owes a debt of thanks
to Mr Sean O'Reilly, without
whose strange dreams it would
never have been possible.
Thanks, Sean.

A WORD TO THE WISE

This book contains certain passages
that some readers might find deeply
disturbing. Due to the questionable
sanity of the author and the convoluted
nature of the plot, it is advised that it
be read at a single sitting and then
hidden away on a high shelf.

# Nostradamus Ate
# My Hamster

# CHAPTER 1

# OH LITTLE TOWN OF BRENTFORD

All along the Ealing Road the snow fell and within The Flying Swan a broad fire roared away in the hearth.

Neville the part-time barman whistled a pre-Celtic ditty as he draped the last tired length of tinsel about the lopsided Christmas tree. Climbing down from his chair, he rooted about in the battered biscuit tin which stood upon the bar counter. Herein lay the musty collection of once-decorations and the wingless fairy that had served The Swan well enough for some fifteen Christmas-times past. Neville considered that the jaded pixie still had plenty of life left in it, should The Swan's Yuletide revellers be persuaded to keep their malicious mitts off her.

Drawing the elfin relic into the light, Neville gently stroked the velvet dust away. She was a sad and sorry specimen, but tradition dictated that for the next two weeks she should perch upon her treetop eyrie and watch the folk of Brentford making the holy shows of themselves. Being a practising pagan, Neville always left dressing the tree until the very last night before Christmas.

1

That its magic should work to maximum effect.

Clambering once more onto his chair, the barman rammed the thing onto the treetop, thinking to discern an expression of startled surprise, and evident pleasure, flicker momentarily across the wee dolly's countenance. Climbing carefully down, Neville stepped back to peruse his handiwork through his good eye.

'Blessed be,' said he, repairing to the whisky optic for a large measure of Christmas cheer.

The Guinness clock above the bar struck a silent five-thirty of the p.m. persuasion and an urgent rattling at the saloon bar door informed the barman that at least two of the aforementioned revellers, evicted a scant two hours before, had now returned to continue their merry-making. Neville drained his glass and smacked his lips and sauntered to the door.

Click-clack went the big brass bolts, but silently the hinges.

Upon the doorstep stood two snowmen.

'Looks like filling up out,' said one.

'God save all here,' said the other.

'Evening, Jim, John,' said Neville, stepping aside to allow The Swan's most famous drinking partnership entry. Jim Pooley and John Omally (both bachelors of the parish) shook the snow drifts from their shoulders, rubbed their palms together and made towards the bar.

Neville shambled after, eased his way behind the counter, swung down the hinged flap, straightened his dicky-bow and assumed the professional position.*

With stooped-shoulders back and head held high, he enquired, 'Your pleasure, gentlemen?'

'Two pints of Large please, Neville,' said Pooley, slapping down the exact change. Neville drew off two pints of the finest.

Jim raised his glass to his lips. 'Yo ho ho,' said he, taking sup.

John took sup also and account of the tree. 'Our good woman the fairy has made her yearly phoenix rise from the biscuit tin, I see.'

'Christmas,' said Neville in a voice without tone. 'Who can odds it, eh?'

John and Jim drew upon their pints, the snow crystallizing on their shoulders to steam away by the heat of the blazing fire. 'You have *The Act* booked, Neville?' Omally asked.

Neville gave his slender nose a tap. 'The Johnny G Band. Northfield lads. Oldies but goodies and things of that nature.'

Omally made a face. 'I've heard of these fellows. Buffoons to a man.'

'The brewery,' said Neville. And that was that.

Outside the snow continued to fall and a stagecoach-load of travellers enquired the route to Dingly Dell.

The saloon bar door swung open to admit a flurry

---

* Not to be confused with the *other* professional position.

of white, an ancient gentleman and a snow-covered dog. 'Good-evening, Neville,' said Old Pete, hobbling to the bar. 'A dark rum, if you please, and something warming for young Chips here.'

The barman thrust a glass beneath the optic and with his free hand decanted a ladle of mulled wine into the dog's personal bowl. Old Pete pushed the exact change across the polished bar top and accepted the drinks.

'Deepening out?' asked Neville.

The ancient gave a surly grunt. 'Christmas,' he said. 'Who can odds it? Norman not here yet?'

The part-time barman shook his brylcremed bonce and took up a glass to polish. 'He'll be along.'

Christmas Eve at The Flying Swan always had about it an almost religious significance. It fell somewhere near to the ritual of the high mass. There was the arrival, the blessing, the hymns, the taking up of the offering, the communion of souls and the big goodbye. You had to have your wits about you to pick up on all the subtle nuances though.

Pooley, having made his arrival, now made the first blessing. 'To Christmas,' he suggested, raising his glass. 'Another Christmas, nothing more, nothing less.'

Omally clinked his glass against his fellow's and drained it with feeling. 'Nothing more, nothing less,' he agreed. 'Two more of similar please, Neville.'

4

Old Pete hefted a colourfully wrapped parcel onto the countertop as the barman did the business. 'It's a goody this year,' he confided to the drinkers.

Regarding the *offering* part of the high mass, it had become something of a tradition amongst The Swan's patrons to reward, upon this special night, the year-long endeavours of their barman. That Neville should actually have survived intact another year behind the counter of The Flying Swan was a meritorious something in itself. And with the passing of time the unhealthy spirit of competition had entered this tradition and the drinking populace now vied with one another to produce the most original, exotic or extraordinary gift.

Using Christmas as a theme (it being available and everything), the plucky Brentonians chose to bombard their pagan barkeep with trinkets of a Christian nature. The irony of this was never lost upon Neville, although it had others bewildered.

Last year he had received, amongst other things, a full-length bath towel, printed with the image of The Turin Shroud, which did little to enhance the post-tub rub down; several more nails from the true cross, that didn't match any of the others he already had in his drawer; an aftershave bottle containing The Virgin's tears and a genuine piece of Mother Kelly's Doorstep (this from a dyslexic).

Every gift, however, was inevitably overshadowed

by that borne in by Norman Hartnell* of the corner shop. Norman's present was usually the high point of the evening.

Pooley and Omally made nods and winks towards Old Pete and patted at bulges in their jackets.

Neville presented further pints and the patrons sat, took in their cups and discoursed upon the doings of the day.

Overhead, a heavily laden sleigh, jingling with bells, drawn by six reindeer and bearing a Shaman clad in the red and white of the sacred mushroom, swept off in search of good children's stockings. The snow fell in cotton wool balls and crept up towards the bench mark on the Memorial Library wall. Several more revellers blew in from the blizzard.

Roger de Courcey de Courcey, production buyer for a great metropolitan television company, staggered towards the bar, bearing upon his arms a brace of evil-looking hags. These had displayed themselves at the Christmas bash (with him half gone in *Pol Roget*), as a veritable deuce of Cindy Crawfords. But the snow had been sobering him up.

'G and Ts,' said Roger, his Oxford tones raising hives and bouncing off the baubles.

'Doing it for a bet then, Roger?' Neville asked.

* Not to be confused with the other Norman Hartnell.

'Care for a couple of paper bags, while you're about it?'

Roger winced, but went 'haw, haw,' said 'typing pool,' and 'well away'.

'And the sooner the better,' said Omally. 'I hope you have a licence for them.'

The two hags tittered. One said, 'I fink I need the toilet.'

Old Pete moved away to a side table, taking his dog with him. The Memorial Library clock struck six.

In dribs and drabs the Yuletide celebrants appeared, patting snow from their duffle-coats and discarding their fisherman's waders beside the roaring fire.

At length Johnny G made his arrival. He was small, dark and wiry. But he walked without the aid of a stick and appeared to have all his own teeth. Small details, but none the less encouraging to Neville.

Booking an *Act* is a bit like buying a used Cortina from Leo Felix. You never quite get what you think you have got but it's hard to tell just how you haven't.

Publicans accept that when they book a band to begin at eight and play until eleven, they have entered into an agreement which is, for the most part, largely symbolic in nature. If, by half-past eight, even one of these professional players has turned up and actually possesses his own PA system and a full complement of strings to his guitar, the publican considers himself one bless'd of the gods. Should two or more musicians arrive and commence to play before another hour is up, then the publican will probably contemplate suicide, reasoning that he has now seen everything that a man might ever hope to see in a single lifetime. Or possibly more.

Johnny G strode manfully from the three-foot snow fall, bearing an aged guitar and a thirty-watt practice amp. 'Corner all right, guvnor?' he asked.

Neville nodded bleakly. 'And slacken your strings. We have an opera singer comes in here and the door still has its original glass.'

Johnny nodded his small dark head as if he understood. '"Blueberry Hill", "Jack to a King", that kind of business?'

'That kind of business.' Neville looked on as Johnny braved the elements once more to dig his equipment from the rear of the GPO van he had 'borrowed' for the evening.

Much ink could be wasted and paper spoiled in writing of Johnny's equipment. Of its history and ancestry and disasters that nightly befell it. But not here and not on such a night as this. Suffice it to be said, that some thirty-five minutes and three near-fatal electrocutions later, he had completed its elaborate construction. He seated himself behind an obsolete Premier drum kit, slung a war-torn Rickenbacker across his shoulders and a harmonica harness about his neck and was definitely ready for lift off.

'Johnny G *Band*?' asked Neville, suspiciously.

'Five piece,' said John. 'Vocals, guitar, drums, harmonica and kazoo.' He called a hasty, 'One-two,' into the mic and a scream of feedback tore about the bar, rattling the optics and putting the wind up young Chips.

Neville gave his head another shake. 'Christmas,' said he. 'Who can odds it?'

In four feet of snow and a little way up the road, Tiny Tim pressed his small blue nose against the window of Norman's corner shop and took to blessing the Woodbine advertisements.

Each and every one.

Within The Swan, Christmas Eve was now very much on the go. The cash register rang musically, if anything somewhat more musically than the Johnny G Band, and the patrons were already in full song.

There appeared to be some debate regarding exactly which songs they were fully singing and it was generally left to those of loudest voice and soundest memory to lead the way.

Old Pete had turned his back upon the young strummer and now applied himself to The Swan's aged piano. Those who favoured Yuletide selections from the Somme joined him in rowdy chorus. Johnny strummed on regardless, oblivious to the fact that the jack plug had fallen out of his guitar and that no-one was really listening anyway.

A merry time was being had by all.

Omally was doing the rounds of the local womenfolk, smiling handsomely and pointing to the mistletoe sewn into the brim of his flat cap. He gave Roger's hags a bit of a wide berth though.

Young Roger had already phoned for a minicab, donned a disguise and repaired to The Swan's bog. Here he was apparently conversing with God down the great white china speaking tube. Pooley stood beneath the tree, miming *The Wreck of The Hesperus*.*

Neville moved up and down the bar, dealing with all-comers, as the roaring voices of the various singing factions ebbed and welled according to who had been called to the bar or caught short. The Johnny G brigade, composed mostly of those to whom drunkenness brought charity, came greatly into its own during periods when Old Pete, whose bladder was not what it used to be, took himself off to the bog. But it fell into disarray upon his reinvigorated returns. The Guinness clock ate up the hours and crept towards ten, the traditional time for Neville's present openings.

Outside, in answer to a thousand schoolboy prayers (Christmas being, as all drunkards will knowledgeably inform you, a time for children), local transvestite, Will Shepherd, washed his frocks by night.

* ★ ★ ★

* Don't ask!

10

A minicab driver fought his way in from the cold, togged out in heavy furs and snow shoes of the type once favoured by Nanook of the North (he of the 'yellow snow' fame). He enquired after a certain Mr de Courcey de Courcey, but none felt inclined to arouse the lad who now lay snoring peacefully beneath the Christmas tree.

The short-sighted driver, who had had his fill of Christmas anyway, ordered himself a triple Scotch and soon fell into conversation with two hags, who appeared to his limited vision as nothing less than a deuce of Cindy Crawfords.

Old Pete, who had exhausted his repertoire, was now downing a yard of rum at the expense of a well-heeled punter. Omally was braving the elements in the rear yard with The Shrunken Head's temporary barmaid, who had lost her way in the snow. And it was toward this direction that Jim Pooley danced at the head of an inebriated conga line, composed for the most part of under-age females.

Johnny G had given up the unequal struggle against both the spirited opposition and the ranks of free pints lined up on his amp. He lay slumped across his drum kit, mouthing the words to a song his mother had taught him back in Poona and blowing half-heartedly into a crisp-muffled kazoo. The holly and the ivy were doing all that was expected of them and it certainly did have all the makings of a most memorable night.

Neville stacked another tray-load of drinks and wiped away a bead of perspiration which had unprofessionally appeared upon his professional brow. He looked up towards the Guinness clock. Nearly ten, the counter gay with gifts, but where was Norman?

'Pints over here, please,' called Old Pete, proffering a bundle of newly acquired money notes.

The second hand on the Guinness clock completed another circuit and the hour was struck. Although no-one actually heard it, the signal echoed mystically about the saloon bar, halting the singers and drinkers and talkers and revellers in mid-swing and silencing them to a man. Or a woman. Or Will Shepherd.

'Merry Christmas to you all,' called Neville the part-time barman. And the folk of The Swan, with their drinks in their hands took to flocking about him at the bar.

Omally excused himself from his near-naked and frost-bitten unofficial bride-to-be and stumbled in through the rear door, gathering up Jim Pooley, whose women had deserted him and whose keyhole eye had snow blindness.

'Three cheers for Neville,' quoth Omally, and the cry went up.

Neville cleared his throat, made a brief speech of thanks, blissfully devoid of time-wasting and sentiment, rubbed his hands together and to much applause applied himself to the nearest parcel. It contained an elegant set of cufflinks with matching tie clip, wrought from discarded beer bottle tops. It was a present from Wally Woods, Brentford's foremost purveyor of wet fish.

'Nice one,' roared the crowd. 'Very tasteful.'

Wally accepted these ovations modestly. 'It was nothing,' he said.

'Correct,' agreed the crowd. 'We were being sarcastic.'

The second gift was something of an enigma, being an item which appeared to be neither animal nor vegetable nor mineral. There was much of the mythical beast to it, but even more to suggest that its antecedents lay with the sprout family. Neville held it at arm's length and ogled it with his good eye. He rattled it against his ear and cocked his head on one side.

The crowd took to murmuring.

The bearer of this gift stepped hurriedly up to the bar and whispered words into Neville's ear. Neville's good eye widened. 'Does it, be damned?' said he, rapidly removing the thing to below counter level. 'Most unexpected,' adding, 'just what I always wanted.'

Pooley's present proved to be of extraordinary interest. Once naked of its newspaper wrappings it displayed itself as a square black metal box, approximately six inches to a side, with a slot at the top and bottom.

Neville shook it suspiciously.

'It's a thing patented by my grandaddy,' said

13

Jim, 'called *Pooley's Improver*. It converts base metal into gold.'

'Well now,' said Neville, making what is known as an 'old-fashioned face'. 'That's useful.'

'And fully practical.' Jim popped a copper coin into the top slot. Grinding sounds, suggestive of gears meshing, issued from the box and within but a moment or two, something which had every appearance of a golden sovereign dropped into Neville's outstretched palm.

Neville held it between thumb and forefinger and then took a little bite at it. 'Tis genuine,' said he. 'My thanks, Jim. Here, hang about, what is that funky smell?'

The beer-steeped air of The Flying Swan had suddenly become permeated by a ghastly odour, suggestive of rotting eggs or the-morning-after-the-big-Vindaloo bathroom.

'My goddess!' Neville drew back in alarm. 'It's this coin!'

The Swan's patrons dragged themselves into a broad crescent, amid much nose-holding, drink-covering, coughing and gagging. 'Get that thing out of here, mister,' shouted someone. A kindly soul, eager to help, swung wide The Swan's door, only to vanish beneath an avalanche of snow. Neville hurled the stinking object into the street and a rescue team of helpers dug out their companion and rammed home the door.

Neville gave Pooley the coldest of all fish eyes.

'There are certain flaws in the process,' Jim

explained. 'The grandaddy never did get around to ironing them all out.'

Neville folded his brow, fanned his nose with a beer mat and pushed the offensive black box aside.

The crowd moved in once more.

Neville unwrapped a Santa's grotto composed of used pipe cleaners. 'Mine,' said Old Pete, patting his Fair Isled chest. A *Miss Magic Mouth* inflatable love doll, that no-one would own up to, a flagon of sprout gin, which many did, and all bar John Omally wished to sample. A hand-painted facsimile of The Flying Swan. Beaten 'pewter' tankards, bearing incongruous words such as *Heinz* upon their planished brims. Boxes of cabbage leaf cigars and several objects of evident antiquity which would have had the late and legendary Arthur Negus reaching for his reference books.

Someone had even created an extraordinary likeness of Neville from the thermostat and components of a 1963 Morris Minor.

Neville opened each parcel in turn and beamed hugely at every disclosure. He was, as the alchemists of old would have it, in his element.

'Next round on the house and supper is served,' he called, as The Swan's Christmas catering staff appeared from the kitchen bearing the traditional groaning trays.*

These were loaded to the gunwales with rugged

---

* Trays don't really groan. It's a lie.

15

mountains of baked potatoes, chorus lines of turkey legs and passing-out parades of mince pies.

Old Pete availed himself of the barman's hospitality and returned to the clapped-out piano, striking up a rousing 'We Wish You a Merry Christmas'.

Those capable of joining him between chewings and swallowings did so as and when.

In the midst of all this feasting and merrification, the saloon bar door suddenly flew open to reveal a stunning figure in black. Black hat. Black coat. Black strides. Black boots. Black sunspecs also. He bore an enormous parcel (black wrapped), and stood in the doorway, dramatically silhouetted against the all-white back drop.

Many of the uninformed instantly recognized this apparition to be none other than the angel of death himself. A miserly fellow, who knew the ghost of Christmas past when he saw it, hastily took a dive for the Gents.

'Merry Christmas,' called Norman Hartnell. For it was he.

The crowd cleaved apart as the shopkeeper stepped forward, struggling manfully beneath the weight of his burden. Pooley and Omally offered assistance and the parcel was conveyed with difficulty to the countertop.

'For me?' Neville asked.

Norman nodded. 'Compliments of the season,' said he.

The part-time barman plucked at the swarthy

wrappings, which fell away to reveal a gilded casket of such magnificence that all present were cowed into awe-struck silence.

The thing was wondrous and that was a fact, wrought with cunning arabesques of gemstones and inlaid with many precious metals. A corona of golden light surrounded it and this bathed the faces of the assembled multitude to a nicety. By gosh.

Neville ran a hand gently over the fantastic object. 'Incredible,' he whispered. 'Incredible, Norman. Whatever *is* it?'

Norman flicked a snowflake from a Bible-black lapel. 'I believe it to be nothing less than the now legendary lost ark of the covenant. I dug it up on my allotment. I thought it might amuse you.'

'*Amuse me?*' Neville nodded numbly. 'I don't know what to say, Norman. I mean it's . . . it's well . . . it's . . .'

'Nifty,' said Norman. 'And not at all Christmassy.'

'No indeed.' Neville viewed the casket. 'How does it open? Does it open? Have you opened it?'

'Handles. Don't know, and no,' said Norman, answering each question in turn. 'Two little handles, on the side there. On the little doors. You could give them a pull, Neville. Just to see what might happen.'

'Yes,' said Neville, taking hold of the handles. 'Just to see what might happen.'

Away in the distance and high upon the Chiswick flyover, three wise men on camels, who had been following a star, took sudden account of a blinding beam of golden light that rose from the Brentford area.

'Now, whatever do you take that to be?' asked one.

'Looks like a pub,' said another. 'Sort of atomizing and being sucked into the sky.'

The third wise man blew into his frozen mittens. 'Christmas,' he said, 'who can odds it, eh?'

And who could?

CHAPTER 2

'And?' said Russell.
'And what?' said Morgan.
'And what happened next?'
'Nothing happened next. That's the end of the story.'
'Neville opened the ark of the covenant, which Norman had dug up on his allotment and The Flying Swan atomized and got sucked into the sky?'
'That's it.'
'And you were actually there when this happened?'
'Of course I wasn't actually there. If I'd been actually there, I wouldn't be here now to tell you about it, would I?'
'I suppose not. But if you weren't actually there, how can you be sure it really happened?'
'You don't have to actually be somewhere to know something happened, Russell. I wasn't actually there when they built Stonehenge. But I know it happened, because Stonehenge is there to prove it.'
'But surely The Flying Swan is *not* there to prove it.'

19

'Well, that proves it then, doesn't it?'

Russell let this percolate a moment or two. 'Are you sure?' he asked.

'Of course I'm sure. I can't see what more conclusive proof you could need. If The Flying Swan *was* still there, then it couldn't have happened. It isn't, so it must have. QED.'

'QED?'

'It's Latin, it means "so there, you bastard".'

'Incredible,' said Russell. 'And when exactly did this happen?'

'A couple of years back.'

'A couple of years back? Then you must have seen The Flying Swan. Did you ever meet Pooley or Omally?'

'Longer ago then. They used old money. Perhaps it was twenty years ago. I'm not sure.'

'I thought you *were* sure. You said a moment ago you *were* sure.'

'Sure it *happened*. I'm not altogether sure of the exact date. But then I'm not altogether sure of the exact date they built Stonehenge. But it's there and The Flying Swan isn't and that proves it.'

Russell shrugged. 'I suppose it does,' he said. 'Although—'

'Although, *what*?'

'Although, well, I mean I'm not certain I believe *all* of it. I could believe *some* of it. Like Neville and Pooley and Omally. But, well, the ark of the covenant, surely that's just ripped off from the Indiana Jones movie.'

20

'I think you'll find it's ripped off from the Old Testament.'

'Yes, well, I know that, of course.'

'But if you are prepared to believe in Pooley and Omally, you must be prepared to believe in all those adventures they had.'

'Well,' said Russell. 'They *could* just be tall stories, you know. Like urban myths.'

'*Urban myths?*'

'As in "almost true". Anyone could make the mistake of believing them.'

Morgan took to much head-shaking. 'Pooley and Omally are *not* urban myths. The Flying Swan was *not* an urban myth. An author called Rankin wrote all about them.'

'Perhaps he was just making it up,' Russell suggested. 'To entertain people.'

'*Making it up?* What, make up a story about The Flying Swan and all its patrons being atomized and sucked into the sky?'

'It's just possible,' said Russell. 'Don't you think it just possible that this Mr Rankin might have made *some* of it up? He could have based his characters on real people and set his stories in a real place. But then invented The Flying Swan and all the fantastic stuff. Let's face it Morgan, no offence meant, but nothing ever happens in Brentford. Nothing ever *has* happened and nothing ever *will* happen.'

Morgan rolled his eyes. 'Of course things happen, Russell. They happen all the time. It's just that they never happen to you.'

21

'You're right there,' said Russell.

'And do you know why?' Morgan did not wait for a reply. 'It's because you're too nice, Russell. You're too polite to the customers. You work too hard. You're too damn honest and you never go out and get pissed. You never take any risks. How could anything ever happen to someone like you?'

'I could get run over,' said Russell. 'Anyone can get run over.'

'Not you, you always look both ways.'

'Well, I don't want to get run over.'

'Trust me,' said Morgan. 'Perhaps things don't happen the way they used to happen. But all the things I told you happened, happened. They just did. That's all.'

Russell sighed. 'Incredible,' he said. And rather nicely he said it.

The voice of Frank, the manager, entered the tea room through the Tannoy speaker. It said, 'Get back to work, Morgan, and stop winding Russell up.'

Morgan put the cups in the sink. He didn't wash them up, because it wasn't his turn. It was Bobby Boy's turn. But Bobby Boy was off sick. Bobby Boy had a stomach bug caused by drinking from a cup that hadn't been washed up properly. It had been Morgan's turn on that occasion, but Morgan had been off sick. Since then things had got a little complicated and now there were an awful lot of cups in that sink. Russell had to bring a fresh one from home every morning. His mother was beginning to pine for the lack of cups. But it wasn't Russell's turn to wash up, so there wasn't much he could do about it. Although he really wanted to.

Morgan and Russell emerged from the darkness of the tea room into the light of description. Russell was undoubtedly the taller of the two, due to Morgan's lack of height. But for what Russell gained in the vertical plane he lost in the horizontal. Morgan was by far the fatter. And the balder. Where Russell had hair to great abundance, dark hair, and thick (and curly), Morgan had his baldness. And his spectacles. And his moustache.

Russell didn't have a moustache. Russell was cleanly shaven. Although he had cut himself a few times that morning. On his spots. Morgan didn't have any spots.

Morgan had perspiration stains beneath his armpits. But no spots. He had once owned a dog called Spot though. It had been a spaniel. But it wasn't a spaniel any more, because it hadn't looked both ways and a bus had run over it. Perhaps in dog heaven it was still a spaniel, but not here. Here it wasn't anything. Except a memory, of course. A happy memory.

Russell had no memories of Spot the dog. He had never met Spot the dog. Spot the dog had met his tragic demise years before Russell had ever met Morgan. In fact, Russell was not altogether sure that there had ever been a Spot the dog. It was just possible that Morgan had made up

23

Spot the dog in order to sound interesting. But, of course, Russell was far too polite to suggest such a thing.

So here they were. The two of them. Russell the taller, the hairier and the nicer. But Morgan without the spots. Both were roughly the same age, early twenties, both unmarried, both working as they did, where they did.

And where was that? Exactly?

Where that was, was Fudgepacker's Emporium, a prop house in Brentford. On the Kew Road it was, in the deconsecrated church that had once housed the piano museum.

And what is a prop house?

Well.

A prop house is a place you hire props from. Theatrical props. Theatrical *properties*. For the film and television industries mostly. Things. All sorts of things.

You see, when you make a movie you have to hire everything. You begin with nothing. Nothing but money. Then you hire. You hire a scriptwriter and a director and actors and technicians and sound men. And a best boy, naturally. Where would you be without a best boy? But you also have to hire everything that will be put on the film sets.

Everything.

The carpets, the furniture, the cups and saucers, the fixtures and the fittings. And so all over London there are prop houses. They tend to specialize.

24

Some do guns, some do cars. Costumiers do costumes, of course, because you have to hire all those. And some do antiques. Some do pictures. Some do modern furnishings. Fudgepacker's?

Well.

Fudgepacker's does the weird stuff. The really weird stuff. The stuff you couldn't hire anywhere else.

If you need a pickled homunculus, an eight-legged lamb, a hand of glory, a scrying stone, a travelling font, a thundersheet, a shrunken head, the skull of the Marquis de Sade, Napoleon's mummified willy, a tableau of foetal skeletons re-enacting the battle of Rorke's Drift . . .

Then Fudgepacker's is, as Flann would have it, *your man*.

The company was founded and still run by Ernest Fudgepacker. And that is *the* Ernest Fudgepacker, seminal Arthouse B Movie maker of the late Fifties and early Nineteen Sixties. Director of *I Bleed in Your Breakfast, Sherlock Holmes Meets the Princess of Pain, Bound to Please, Love Me in Leather, Surf Nazis Must Die*\* and *Blonde in a Body Bag*.†

Hollywood hadn't been ready for Ernest.

Shepperton hadn't been ready for Ernest.

The censor had been ready for him though.

Ernest retired from directing. It was Hollywood's

---

\* A different version.

† A Lazlo Woodbine thriller. And a bloody good one.

25

loss. And Shepperton's. Though the censor didn't seem too fazed.

Fudgepacker opened his emporium in nineteen sixty-three, to coincide with the assassination of President Kennedy. He reasoned that, should his guests ever be asked at some future time whether they could remember where they were when Kennedy was shot, they would say, 'Why yes, we were at Fudgepacker's opening party.'

Where he got all his mysterious stock from no-one knows, because he's not telling. But he was right on target back then. Ken Russell was making the good stuff and Hammer films were knocking out the classics. But that was then and times are not so clever now.

Movies change with the times. Movies reflect the times.

And the best of times are always in the past.

Morgan returned to the packing bench and Russell to the office. Once Fudgepacker's had owned to a staff of twenty, now there was just the four. Morgan and Russell, Frank the manager and Bobby Boy. Although Bobby Boy wasn't there very often. Stomach trouble, or he was looking for another job. Probably the latter, as Bobby Boy wanted to be an actor.

Morgan was certainly looking for another job. He wanted to be a spy or an explorer. Russell, however, was *not* looking for another job.

Russell liked working at Fudgepacker's. Russell

liked old Ernie. Ernie was a character. Russell even liked Frank the manager and no-one ever likes a manager.

Russell returned to his desk, but he couldn't bring himself to sit at it, he paced up and down before the window. Outside the day was dull, the sky gasometer-grey. The waters of the Thames were grey. Grey cars drifted along the grey Kew Road, going nowhere.

Russell put a bit more spring into his pacing.

'Don't do that,' said Frank. 'It reminds me of my first wife.'

Russell sat down. 'Frank,' he said, 'did you ever drink in The Flying Swan?'

'Don't think I know the place. I once lit Sophia Loren's cigarette, though. Did I ever tell you about that?'

'You mentioned it in passing, yes.'

'Beautiful woman,' said Frank. 'They don't make women like her any more. I was prop man at Pinewood then. Happy times.'

'Are we expecting any customers today?'

'Trevor Jung phoned, said he'd be in later. He's working on a pilot for a new TV sitcom.'

'There's always room for another sitcom,' said Russell.

'They don't make sitcoms like they used to. That Wendy Craig was a beautiful woman. I never lit her cigarette though. I think I helped her into her coat once, or perhaps that was Thora Hird.'

27

Russell clapped his hands together. 'I think I'll rearrange the office,' said he.

'No,' said Frank.

'Then I'll go and dust the grimoires.'

'No.'

'All right. I'll polish the funerary urns. They could do with a buff.'

'No.'

'I could wash up the teacups.'

'*No!*'

'But I want to *do* something.'

'You are doing something, Russell. You are sitting at your desk awaiting a customer. They also serve who only stand and wait, you know. Or in your case, sit.'

Russell made a sorry face. Things had been much better before Frank became manager. Frank with his love of rosters and paperwork. Russell hated inactivity, he liked to be up and doing, he couldn't bear to waste time. It was Frank who had instigated tea breaks. He dictated exactly who did what, and when. It was a very inefficient system. But Frank *was* the manager and there was nothing Russell could do about it.

'So, I'll just sit here?' Russell said.

'Just sit there, yes.'

And so Russell just sat there, drumming his fingers on the desk.

And absolutely nothing happened.

28

Nothing whatsoever.

Which was strange really, considering the immutable laws which seem to govern these things. According to these immutable laws, something should definitely have happened right about now. And something *big*. Big enough to cover all the foregoing dullness and chit chat, or if not actually *happened*, then at least offered a strong hint of humungous happenings to come.

Possibly something along the lines of . . . Unknown to Russell, great forces were even now at work. Great forces that would change his world for ever, in fact change everybody's world for ever. For Russell was about to take the first step on a journey that would lead him into realms where no man had ever set foot before. Or such like.

But nothing did.

So Russell just sat there drumming his fingers. It did occur to him, however, that it might be interesting to find out whether there was any truth to the tale Morgan had told him. He could spend his lunchtimes and evenings asking around Brentford, to see if there really had been a Neville and a Pooley and an Omally and a Flying Swan. And if there had, then whether any of the fabulous tales told of them were actually true. It was something to do. It would be interesting. Yes.

'Can I give the floor a mop?' asked Russell.

'No,' said Frank.

# CHAPTER 3

# THE CONTENTS OF BOX 23

B ack in the Nineteen Fifties, when the world
was still in black and white, policemen were
jolly fresh-faced fellows who all looked like
Dixon of Dock Green. They were firm but fair,
these fresh-faced fellows, and the felons whose
collars they felt put their hands up without a
fuss and said things like, 'It's a fair cop, guvnor,
slap the bracelets on and bung me in the Black
Maria.'

So, no change there.

In those monochrome days, before the advent
of crime computers and international networks,
'information received' was stored away in big
box files on a high shelf in the chief constable's
office. There were always twenty-three big box
files. The first twenty-two dealt with the everyday
stuff, tip-offs regarding forthcoming sweetshop
robberies, or those suspected of sneaking through
the back doors of the local cinema without paying. Box 23, however, was an altogether different plate of pork. This contained the odd stuff,
the stuff that didn't quite fit, reports of curious phenomena and mysterious uncatagorizable

material.* Remember that these were the days when the strolling beat-bobby was a well-respected figure in the community. Folk talked to policemen back in those times, sent them cards at Christmas and polished their bikes during Bob-a-Job week.

There was never much that could be done with the contents of box 23 and once the box was full these were taken out, bound with black ribbon and stored away in the basement. My Uncle John told me that there was always more stuff in box 23 than in any of the other boxes.

This went on until the early Sixties when the systems were updated. Filing cabinets were installed and a directive circulated that all reports which would formerly have been consigned to box 23 were now to be stored in a file marked X†. These were to be gathered together at the end of each month and sent to a special department at Scotland Yard. The name of this department, however, could not be wrung from my Uncle John, who told me that it 'didn't matter', and 'it was a long time ago and I can't remember anyway.'

It is to be assumed that someone in a position of authority was taking a great interest in the substance of these reports which ranged, in Uncle John's words, 'from the bloody whacky to the downright strange'.

A friend of mine, who was once in the TA,

* This is all absolutely true by the way. My Uncle John was a policeman.

† Also true, I kid you not.

told me that something similar goes on in the armed forces. And that when you join up and sign the Official Secrets Act you also have to sign a document swearing that should you witness any unexplained phenomena (he presumed this to mean UFOs), you must report these immediately to your commanding officer and say nothing of it to other ranks unless you are authorized to do so. The words IN THE NATIONAL INTEREST apparently feature prominently throughout this document.

So, what's it all about then, eh?

Good question.

There is a school of thought that the governments of the world have known all about so-called UFOs for years. That President Truman was taken to a secret American airbase in the late Nineteen Forties to be introduced to alien entities. That the aliens have struck a deal with those who rule our lives and are allowed to abduct a limited number of humans each year for study and experimentation in exchange for advanced technology. It is suggested that micro-chip technology would never have reached its present state without 'outside help' and that the Roswell alien autopsy footage is, in fact, genuine and part of a concerted effort on the part of world governments to prepare us for some rather high-profile alien involvement due to come our way in the very near future.

It's pretty unsettling stuff and made all the more unsettling by the fact that it does seem to have the ring of truth to it. But, as those in authority will reliably tell you, belief is not proof. And until something huge happens and the mothership drops down onto the White House lawn, those who suspect what governments know to be the truth, and broadcast these suspicions to the public at large, will continue to be labelled paranoid conspiracy theorists.

My Uncle John did, however, tell me one tale about the contents of box 23. It is a story so fantastic that its telling might well cast doubt on Uncle John's sanity and therefore question his reliability concerning all the foregoing. But it is a great story, so I have no hesitation in telling it here.

The temptation to embellish the tale is a difficult one to resist, but I have done so, adding only an ending of my own, clearly labelled to avoid confusion. Those of a nervous disposition or prone to night terrors are advised to skip over this ending and go straight on to the next chapter which is all about Russell and so pretty safe.

## UNCLE JOHN'S TALE OF BOX 23

To set the scene, the year was nineteen sixty and Uncle John had recently moved to Brentford to serve as a constable with the force, based then in the old police station, now demolished, on the Kew Road near to the Red Lion. Uncle John came from Shropshire and the year before he had married Aunt Mary, my father's sister.

They moved into one of the new police flats just off Northfields Avenue. These were fully furnished and we used to go up for Sunday lunch and a walk in Lammas Park with Uncle John's dog Frankie.*

The story begins in the summer of that year, when the normally law-abiding borough of Brentford had unaccountably been struck by a mini crime wave. The crimes started in a petty fashion but grew and grew. Seemingly unrelated, they spanned a vast spectrum and were so audacious that they soon had the Brentford bobbies in something of a lather.

First reports involved doorstep milk bottle theft, these went on for weeks. The culprit was sighted on several occasions and described as a stubby ginger-haired youth in grey school uniform. A simple enough matter on the face of it. Uncle John was dispatched to the local primary school to give the pupils a looking over. No stubby ginger-haired youth was to be found. A truant perhaps? No truant fitted that description and in a small town like Brentford where everyone knew pretty much everyone, heads were scratched and gypsies blamed.

The next crimes involved shop-lifting. A young blond woman in a 'modern' pink coat walked into the ladies-wear shop in the high street, snatched up

* Aunt Mary being a big Frankie Vaughn fan at the time.

an armful of summer frocks and took to her heels. Later in the day she repeated the performance, swiping a pop-up toaster from Kays Electrical, a number of chocolate bars from the tobacconists and a hock of ham from Barlett's butcher's shop.

More was to follow.

A tall gaunt man, with black sideburns and a centre parting, helped himself to the contents of the cash register at The Red Lion when the landlord wasn't looking. And The Red Lion was almost next door to the police station.

The Brentford bobbies were not best pleased.

The crimes continued and they followed a pattern. A stranger of distinctive appearance would arrive from no-where, carry out a series of crimes all in a single day, then vanish away never to be seen again.

The eyes of the Brentford constabulary turned towards Ealing. Obviously these criminals were 'out-borough' denizens of the new council estate a mile up the road. Day trippers of evil intent. Uncle John was sent up the road to talk to the boys at the South Ealing nick.

No joy. The descriptions did not match those of any known offenders. And Ealing was a small town and everyone knew everyone there. And the folk talked to the policemen and nobody knew anything about anything.

Odd.

And the crimes continued.

A fellow resembling Father Christmas, with a

big broad belly and a long white beard, held up the Brentford post office with a gun. *A gun!* This was nineteen sixty! Now the Brentford boys in blue were very upset.

And now a certain individual appeared on the scene. He had been sent by Scotland Yard.

Nothing surprising there. A gun crime. A post office hold up. In situations such as this you called The Yard.

The chap from The Yard was known only as The Captain, although as far as Uncle John knew, and as far as I have been able to ascertain, there is no such rank as captain in the police force. Odder still, the chap from The Yard, although listening to all the reported crimes, appeared to be more interested in the contents of box 23 than anything else. He took the box into his own custody, commandeered the chief constable's office for an hour or two and then returned to the front desk. Uncle John recalls to this day his words. They were: 'You have one of *those* at large in the borough. This must be handled discreetly.' Back then 'one of those' generally meant a homosexual.

It was Uncle John's time to clock off then, so he clocked off. When he clocked on again the next morning a number of rather strange things were going on at the police station. Some chaps in tweed suits were milling about at the front desk along with several squaddies. The squaddies were armed with Remington rifles. Uncle John had served in the war and he said that he did not recognize the insignias

36

worn by the squaddies. In fact, he even took the trouble to visit Walpole library and look them up. The insignias were of no listed regiment.

Also there were several official-looking cars parked outside the police station and Uncle John swears that a cabinet minister, well known at the time, sat in one of them.

Uncle John had just cause to wonder exactly what was going on. And so he asked and was told in no uncertain tones to mind his own business and do exactly what he was told. And then he was issued with a pistol.

There is a degree of vagueness concerning exactly what happened next. There was a lot of driving about in police cars and he was stationed at the end of an alleyway and told to shoot anyone who was not a policeman who came running down it. Uncle John was somewhat alarmed by this and, although he had shot a German officer in a tool shed somewhere on the Rhine in 1944, he was not at all keen to let fly at what might well prove to be an innocent bystander. Even if the bystander was, in fact, running at the time.

The next thing Uncle John recalled in any great detail was a suspect. *The* suspect being brought into the police station. And the fact that *the* suspect did not resemble any of the suspects involved in the various unrelated crimes. Especially he looked nothing like the Father Christmas character who'd held up the post office.

The suspect was marched into the police station.

37

Uncle John says that he was more like carried and that he bobbed about in a peculiar fashion and seemed in a very agitated state.

Then Uncle John and several of his colleagues were told that they must go to a certain address and search the premises. And this they did.

Uncle John said that it was one of the weirdest experiences he'd ever had, although not as weird as the one he would have shortly afterwards. An ordinary terraced house it was, two up, three down. But it was packed. Packed with clothes. All kinds of clothes of every size. Children's clothes, adults' clothes, male and female. But big clothes and little clothes. And all shapes and sizes. And all the clothes the reported felons had worn were there. The child's grey uniform, the blond woman's pink coat, the gaunt man's clothes, the Father Christmas man's outfit, the lot.

This was evidently the now legendary thieves' kitchen. There was a gang of them. The apprehended suspect was probably the leader. And the stolen goods were all there, the pop-up toaster, piles of money. And more. There were strange things. Artificial legs. A glass eye. Obviously this robber band owned to a few disabled members. It was all quite dramatic.

But it was bugger all compared to what Uncle John witnessed back at the police station. The suspect had not been taken to the cells, he was being interviewed in the chief constable's office. And Uncle John knew that if you climbed up on a box in the back corridor you could see in through a little hatch and look down into this office.

I don't know how he knew this, but he did know it, so he lost no time in shinning up and taking a peep.

What he saw was to remain with him for the rest of his life.

The Captain and several of the squaddies had the suspect held down across the chief constable's desk. They grasped him by the hands and feet and the suspect was screaming. One of the squaddies pushed a handkerchief into his mouth and The Captain pulled at the man's clothing. He was undressing him. As my uncle looked on, The Captain pulled down the man's trousers to reveal a pair of artificial limbs.

My uncle was amazed, this man was an invalid, he didn't have any legs.

Then the jacket was pulled from him and his shirt. The man's arms weren't real. They were false arms with false hands. The man was a total amputee.

My uncle says that The Captain was shouting. He shouted, 'You see, he's *all* of them. *All* of them.' And it was only later that my uncle realized what it meant. This man was *all* the criminals. He was the child and the woman and the tall man and the fat man, and who knows who else. He obviously owned a collection of different-sized arms and legs. He could make himself as tall or short as he wanted, depending upon which he wore. My uncle worried about the arms and hands though. He'd seen false legs in action, Douglas Bader flew Spitfires wearing false legs. But how could false arms and hands work? But somehow they did, this man was obviously one master of disguise and one most extraordinary master criminal.

As Uncle John looked on, he saw The Captain unstrapping the man's false arms and legs. The man was really struggling, like a lunatic. He spat out the handkerchief, but a squaddie rammed it back in again. When the arms and legs had been removed the man didn't struggle quite so much, but he writhed about. It was quite horrible to watch apparently, but Uncle John said that it was all too fascinating to turn away from. Although he wishes he had now.

What happened next was really freaky. One of the squaddies was holding onto the man's hair and it came away in his hands. It was a wig, but when it came away it brought the man's ears along with it. They were false ears. And when the squaddie tried to put the wig back on, he knocked off the man's nose.

The Captain was worrying at the man's vest and he ripped that open to expose a number of buckles and straps and these he began to undo. The man's shoulders came off next, they were just rounded pads. His chest was a sort of stuffed bra affair and when The Captain tore off the man's underpants, his genitals were made of rubber.

Things got somewhat out of control then. My

uncle recalls seeing a squaddie pulling the handkerchief out of the man's mouth, bringing with it the
teeth and lips. The skin of the face appeared to be
latex and it came off like a mask, revealing a hard
dark material that might have been wood.

A rib cage, that was obviously wood, got yanked
away. Inside was a lot of stuffing, like a Guy Fawkes
dummy, and within minutes the entire frame was
disassembled, leaving absolutely nothing.

There was no man inside there, not one little
piece of a man.

And that is basically the end of the story as my
uncle told it. He swore it was true and that he
saw it happen with his own eyes. He was a retired
policeman and I for one find it hard to believe that
he made it up. I've never heard anything like it
before and I don't pretend to know what it means.
But that's it.

Further questioning on my part turned up a
very little. The bits and pieces, of what amounted
to nothing more than a dummy, but which had
undoubtedly been a struggling man moments
before, were gathered up, put into sacks and taken
away. Uncle John had enough wisdom to mention
nothing of what he'd seen to his fellow officers. He
never saw The Captain or the mysterious squaddies
ever again. Nor did he wish to.

That's it.

# RANKIN'S ENDING
## (The one not for the faint hearted)

Of course The Captain and the mysterious squaddies of the unlisted regiment didn't know that Uncle John had witnessed all this. He had shinned down from his box and slipped back to the front desk. So when they came out of the chief constable's office, all looking somewhat green of face and carrying several large sacks, he was the first policeman they saw. So they said, 'Oi, you, Constable, give us a hand to get this evidence loaded.' And they stuck two of the sacks into his hands and marched him out to a waiting van.

He loaded the sacks in and returned for another two which he also put into the back. There was a lot of talking going on and no-one was looking at him. So Uncle John thought, Well, nobody is ever going to believe a word of this when I tell them, so why don't I just dig into one of these sacks, take out the nose or a hand or something as proof and stick it in my pocket.

So that is just what he did. Or what he tried to do. He opened up the neck of one of the sacks and took a peep inside. It was stuffed with all this padding and straps and wooden bits and so forth, but right on the top was the mouth. The lips and the teeth. Uncle John was about to reach in, when the lips parted and the teeth moved and this little voice said, 'Help me, help me.'

Well, I warned you.

# CHAPTER 4

# CLOSE ENCOUNTERS OF
# THE THIRD REICH

Russell never went for lunch. He always waited until Frank went for lunch, then he did some tidying up. He really did want to get at those teacups in the sink. But he didn't want to offend Morgan, so he usually settled for a bit of dusting and rearrangement. Today he had planned to have a go at the religious relics. John the Baptist's mummified head needed a dose of Briwax and the phial of The Virgin's Tears had dried up again, so called for a quick squirt from the cold tap (which isn't dishonest if it's just 'topping up').

But untrue to form upon this day, Russell put on his waxed jacket with the poacher's pockets* and sallied forth into the streets of Brentford.

The Ealing Road first, he thought. If The Flying Swan ever *had* existed, then some trace of its whereabouts *must* remain. That was about as straightforward as you can get. People's memories tend to be uneven and unreliable, but as Jim Campbell says, 'Buildings are the pinions of

---

* A present from a doting aunt.

history.' If a building had once existed, some trace, no matter how small, probably would remain.

Well, it might, for Goddess' sake!

It's a very short walk from Fudgepacker's to the Ealing Road. You just turn right at The Red Lion. Most of the properties are old. Victorian at the very least. There are two pubs there, The Bricklayer's Arms and The Princess Royal. Further up there's The New Inn; so that makes three. Not bad in two hundred yards. But this *is* Brentford. And Brentford had the only football club in the country with a pub on each of its four corners.

Russell reasoned that should there be a gap somewhere, or a new building looking somewhat out of place, there was potential. So he marched up the Ealing Road. He couldn't trudge, Russell, nor could he plod, marching was all he knew. Or jogging. Well, jogging was good for you, and you have to look after your health.

Russell would have jogged, but he was investigating, so he marched instead.

Past the corner tobacconist's, and the bookies, and the greengrocer, to The Bricklayer's.

Russell looked up at the pub in question. It was solidly built. A Victorian frontage, local glazed tile, fiddly bits, window boxes. Dug in, it was. Built to last, and last it had.

'If The Flying Swan really was along here,' said Russell to no-one but himself, 'the folk who run this pub must know about it.'

Russell came to an abrupt halt before the door.

Because here a great problem presented itself. Russell did not go into pubs. It was quite simply something he did not do. As a non-smoker, the very smell of pubs appalled him. And as virtually a non-drinker, there was little point in him going into them anyway.

Although regular pub-goers will tell you that all the most interesting people are to be found in pubs and that the heart of a town is its finest tavern, this is not altogether true.

Pub-goers actually represent a tiny percentage of any given town's population*. Curiously enough, exactly the same percentage as regular church-goers. And regular church-goers will tell you that all the most interesting people are to be found in churches (and so on and so forth).

Russell dithered. This was probably all a waste of time anyway, perhaps he could just interview passers-by, get himself a clipboard and tell them he was doing a survey. That would be for the best.

Russell turned to walk away. But then he stopped to pause for further thought. It was no big deal going into a pub. If he came out stinking of cigarette smoke it hardly mattered, his clothes would be going into the wash at the end of the day anyway. He was being a real wimp about this. If Morgan were to find out, he'd never let him hear the last of it.

* Apart from one or two notable exceptions. Penge, Orton Goldhay, etc.

'Right,' said Russell, squaring his shoulders and taking a breath so deep as might hopefully last him throughout his visit. Up to the door, turn the handle, enter.

Russell entered The Bricklayer's Arms.

It was really quite nice inside. It didn't smell *too* bad. The furniture was all mellow browns and greens, glowing softly in that light you only find in pubs. The saloon bar was low ceilinged and narrow, a few high stools ranked before the counter and on these sat lunch-time patrons: secretaries from the office blocks on the Great West Road, young bloods in suits with mobile phones. A couple of old boys slung darts in the general direction of a mottled board, a number of trophies glittered in a case on the wall. Ordinary it was, what you might expect, anywhere.

Russell approached the bar. The young bloods made him feel somewhat uneasy. He was in jeans and a sweatshirt, they wore professional suits. Perhaps he should go round to the public bar.

'What'll it be then, love?' The barmaid caught Russell's eye. And most winsomely she caught it too. A tall narrow blonde of a woman, constructed to Russell's favourite design. Wide blue eyes and a big full mouth that was full of big white teeth.

The words 'a Perrier water' came into Russell's mind, but 'a pint of best bitter,' came out of his mouth.

'Coming right up.' The barmaid turned away, with a sweep of golden hair and a click-clack of high heels. Russell spied out an empty stool at the end of the counter and climbed onto it. Why had he said *that*? A pint of best bitter? Russell didn't even like best bitter, Russell *hated* best bitter. But Russell knew exactly why he'd said it. Real men didn't drink Perrier water. Blonde barmaids liked real men. Russell liked blonde women.

'There you go,' said the barmaid, presenting Russell with his pint. He paid up and she smiled warmly upon him. As she brought him his change she said, 'Funny you should drink bitter, I thought my luck had changed.'

'Pardon,' said Russell.

'My horoscope in the paper this morning said love may come in the shape of a tall dark stranger.'

'Indeed?' said Russell, warming to the idea.

'A tall dark stranger who drinks the water of life.'

'Eh?' said Russell.

'Only water of life in this place is Perrier water,' said the barmaid. 'Still, I'll keep looking, you never know, do you?'

'No,' said Russell, as she turned away to serve a young man who had recently entered the pub, and who stood by patiently waiting (and listening).

'What will it be then, love?'

'Perrier water,' said the young man.

Russell buried his face in his hands.

'If you've had too much, mate, go home and sleep it off.'

Russell unburied his face.

The landlord glared him daggers. 'I pop out the back for half an hour and that blonde tart gets all the customers drunk. That's the last time I hire an ex-contortionist go-go dancing sex-aid demonstrator.'

Russell made a low groaning sound.

'And don't you dare chuck up,' growled the landlord.

'I wasn't,' said Russell. 'This is my first pint, I've only just come in.'

'Well, watch it anyway.'

'I will,' promised Russell, and the landlord went his way.

Russell sipped at his beer. It tasted ghastly. Russell gazed about the bar. It was all so very normal. Everything about Brentford was so very normal. Russell felt certain that it always *had* been normal, always *would* be normal.

There had never really been some golden age, when local lads battled it out with the forces of evil and saved the world from this peril and the next. It was all just fiction.

The landlord shuffled by with a trayload of empties.

'Excuse me,' said Russell.

'You're excused,' said the landlord. 'Now bugger off.'

'I wondered if I might ask you a few questions.'

'You might,' said the landlord. 'But I doubt if you'd get any answers.'

48

'It's about The Flying Swan.'

'Ah,' said the landlord, and it was as if some golden ray from heaven had suddenly been turned upon him. He drew himself up from his slovenly slouch and beamed a broad grin at Russell. It wasn't much of a grin, being composed of nicotine-stained stumps for the most part, but it lacked not for warmth and enthusiasm. 'The Flying Swan, did you say?'

'I did say, yes.'

'So what would you like to know?'

'I'd like to know whether it ever really existed.'

'Really existed?' The landlord slid his tray onto the bar counter and thrust out his chest. It wasn't much of a chest, being scrawny and narrow, and the shirt that covered it was rather stained, but it lacked not for pride and confidence. 'Of course it really existed, you're sitting in it now.'

'I'm *what?*'

'This is it.' The landlord did further grinnings, he turned his head from side to side, displaying sparse sideburns and ears from which sprouted pro-digious outcroppings of hair. 'I'm him,' he said.

'You're who?'

'Neville. Neville the part-time barman.'

'You never are.' Russell all but fell off his stool. 'You're Neville? I mean . . . well, I don't know what I mean. My goodness.'

'Pleased to meet you,' said the landlord, extend-ing his hand for a shake. Russell took the grubby item and gave it one.

49

'I'm Russell,' said Russell.

'And how many are there in your party, Mr Russell?'

'I, er, sorry?'

'Will you be wanting to hire the upstairs room? We provide costumes.'

'Costumes?' Russell asked.

'For re-enactments, of course, cowboy night, that kind of thing. Will there be any Americans in your party?'

'Americans?'

'We had a coachload in last year. They brought their own costumes, but we had to charge them for that anyway. It's all in the brochure. I'll get you one.'

'Phone call,' said the blonde barmaid, leaning over the counter. Russell could smell her perfume. It smelled like pure bliss.

'I'm talking to this gentleman,' said the landlord.

'It's the brewery, about *that* business.'

'Shit,' said the landlord. 'If you'll just excuse me, sir, I'll be right back.'

'Yes,' said Russell. 'Fine, yes. Well, yes.'

The landlord dropped back into his slouch and in it he slouched away.

Russell took a big pull upon his pint. This was incredible. The first pub he'd gone into. Incredible! Instant success! And Neville was here and everything. True, he didn't look exactly how Russell had imagined him to, nor did the pub

50

look quite right either. But you couldn't expect everything. The number of times he'd walked right by this building and he'd never known that *this* was The Flying Swan. Incredible!

Mind you, it didn't mean that the rest of it was true, but it meant something.

'Brilliant,' said Russell, taking another pull. He smacked his lips, perhaps the bitter wasn't all *that* bad. It was an acquired taste probably. He'd try a pint of Large next. He'd never been sure exactly what a pint of Large was, but they sold it in The Flying Swan. And this *was* The Flying Swan.

'Brilliant.' Russell finished his pint. And as he lowered the empty glass to the counter, a strange feeling came over him. It wasn't so much a feeling of satisfaction that he had accomplished the task he'd set himself so swiftly and successfully. It was a different kind of feeling. It was the feeling that he was about to be violently sick.

'Oh my God,' burbled Russell, clapping his hand over his mouth and making for the Gents. Where *was* the Gents? Through that door over there. Russell made for that door at the hurry up.

He stumbled through it, found the cubicle, entered same, slammed its door shut behind him and transferred the pint of best bitter from his stomach into the toilet bowl. Oh dear, oh dear.

Russell gasped and gagged, his hands upon his knees. Beer really wasn't his thing. If only he'd gone for the Perrier water instead. A very clear image of a naked blonde ex-contortionist go-go dancing sex-aid demonstrator filled his mind as his stomach continued to empty.

Cruel fate. But just deserts.

Russell ran through the full repertoire of throwing-up techniques. It was a long time since he'd done that and he'd forgotten just how terrible it was. The stomach cramps, the tear-filled eyes, the bits in the back of the throat, the bits that came out of your nose.

At length the worst had passed and Russell was able to straighten up and draw breath.

You always feel *so good* afterwards, don't you?

Russell didn't.

He flushed the pan, left the cubicle and availed himself of the wash hand basin. Presently some semblance of normality returned. Russell perused his reflection in the cracked wall mirror. Not a pretty sight. His eyes now resembled those of the late great Peter Lorre and his face was a most distressing shade of beetroot red.

'I think I'd better go back to work,' said Russell.

And then he heard a noise.

The noise was that of shouting. Ranting really. Ranting and raving, in fact. And ranting and raving in a foreign tongue.

There was a little window open above the urinal. And the ranting and raving was coming through this. Russell tiptoed over, stood upon his tipping toes and peered through the little window.

Outside was a small back yard which held stacks

of beer crates and the ruins of what once might have been a barbecue.

Beyond was a sort of shed. Probably a store. The ranting and the raving came from this.

Russell sighed and lowered himself to flat feet. Whatever it was, it was none of his business. He did *not* put *his* nose into other people's business. That was *not* his way.

Russell checked his reflection once more. His skin tone had now returned to almost normal. His eyes were still a bit poppy though. He'd leave quietly. Come back later for Neville's brochure. When he was feeling a bit more like himself. That would be for the best.

Russell left the Gents. The door to the rear yard was open a crack. The ranting and raving came through it. Russell shrugged. None of his business. Yet. It did sound pretty manic, perhaps someone was in trouble. Perhaps Russell could help. He was always eager to help.

'I'll just take a little look,' said Russell to himself. 'To make sure.' He opened the door and slipped out into the yard. The shed was a green clap-board affair, its door was closed, but its window was open. Russell crept up to the window.

What was that language? It wasn't French. Russell knew French, well *some* French. This was a bit like French.

Russell ducked down, slid beneath the window, then edged up, to peer into the shed.

And then Russell ducked back down again. And

a look of horror appeared upon his face. His face that had quite enough upsetting its normal cheery balance already.

He had seen that, hadn't he?

He had.

Seen that. Seen *them*.

'No,' whispered Russell. 'I'm sure that I could not have seen *that*.'

He eased himself up once more and took another look into the shed. There was little enough in there to be seen: a trestle table, a couple of chairs. Three men. Three men were in there. Two were standing before the table. To attention. The other was sitting behind it. This other was the one doing all the ranting. Russell took a big long look.

The two that were standing wore uniforms. German uniforms. Second World War German uniforms. Second World War SS Nazi German uniforms. They had their backs to Russell, straight backs. Cropped blond hair beneath smart caps. Jack boots.

The one sitting behind the table . . .

Russell's breath hung in his throat, his heart went bump, bump, bump, bump. The one sitting behind the table wore a light grey uniform, very sharp, well cut, he was small, hunched, thick set. A black swathe of hair hung over one eyebrow, a Charlie Chaplin moustache sat beneath the nose of the contorting face. The contorting face that could belong to no other being who had ever walked the earth, apart from the one it belonged to now. *Impossibly* now.

The contorting face of Adolf Hitler.

Russell sank down hard onto his bottom. This *wasn't* happening. This could *not* be happening. He must be drunk. Or something terrible had been slipped into his pint. He had to be hallucinating. That man in there could not, by any stretch of the imagination, possibly be the *real* Adolf Hitler. He simply couldn't, that was all there was to it. Russell felt suddenly faint and his hands began to shake. Have another look, just to make absolutely sure, sure that, well, sure of something. Russell took a very deep breath and hoisted himself back to the window.

And took another peep in.

It *was* him. It bloody well was. He was just as he looked in the old documentary footage. A bit smaller, but folk always look smaller in real life. Except for the tall ones, of course, although they *might* look smaller. It was just a bit more hard to tell.

Russell ducked down again and tried to think his way out.

But it *was* him. Actors never got him right, they always looked like Alec Guinness. Even Alec Guinness looked like Alec Guinness, but then he would, wouldn't he?

Russell's thoughts became all confused. Something had happened, something most odd. Had he entered something? Like some parallel world? The world of The Flying Swan, where the impossible was possible and this sort of stuff happened everyday?*

'It can't be him.' Russell gritted his teeth and assured himself that it couldn't be him. Well, it couldn't. That was all there was to it.

Russell stuck his head up and took another peep. And found himself staring face to face with the monster himself. The very personification of all that was evil in the twentieth century. Adolf Hitler.

'Aaaaagh!' went Russell.

'Achtung! Achtung!' went Adolf and added further words of German which meant 'Kill the spy!'

Russell didn't know what they meant. But he *knew* what they *meant*, if you know what I mean. Russell took to stumbling, staggering legs and turned on his heels and ran.

As he ran through the bar the landlord thrust a brochure into his hand, 'Discount on block bookings,' he said.

'Oh . . . oh . . . oh,' went Russell, running on, 'Oh my goodness, oh.'

* Actually Russell did not think this at all. This was a far too sophisticated concept for Russell to simply think up there and then. It's probably just been included for the benefit of the astute reader whose mind it *has* crossed. There's no telling, but that would be my guess.

# CHAPTER 5

W hen Russell got back to Fudgepacker's Emporium, which he did in a world-record time, he found Morgan sitting idly by the packing bench, smoking a cigarette.

'Morgan,' went Russell. 'Morgan, I . . . Morgan . . . oh.'

Morgan looked up at the quivering wreck. 'Whatever happened to you?' he asked.

'Morgan, I've been *there*. I've seen *him*. I saw him, he was there. What are we going to do? Oh dear. Oh, oh.'

'Russell are you all right?'

'No, I've been in this pub—'

'You're pissed,' said Morgan. 'Bloody hell, Russell, whatever came over you, you don't drink.'

'I'm not pissed.'

Morgan sniffed. 'You've chucked up, you pong.'

'Yes, I have chucked up, but I—'

'You'd better not let Frank see you in this state.'

'I'm not in any state—'

'Trust me, Russell, a state is what you're in.'

'But I've been *there*, I saw him.'

57

'What, heaven? You saw God?'

'Not heaven, the opposite of heaven. Though there was an angel there, but because I didn't drink Perrier water I didn't get to take her out—'

'Russell, you're gibbering. Are you doing drugs? You selfish bastard, you're doing drugs and you never offered me any.'

'I don't do drugs, I've never done drugs.'

'You're pissed though.'

'I'm not pissed. I'm not. You've got to come with me now. No, we daren't go back. We must call the police, no call the army. Call the SAS.'

'How about you just calming down and telling me exactly what happened?'

'Yes, right. That's what I'll do.' Russell took deep breaths and tried to steady himself. 'Right, I'm OK, yes.'

'So tell me what happened.'

'I went out to see if I could find whether there really was a Flying Swan.'

'Oh,' said Morgan, 'did you?'

'I did. And I found it.'

'Ah,' said Morgan, 'did you?'

'Yes I did.'

'Go on.'

'What do you mean "go on", aren't you amazed at that much already?'

'Not really, but do go on.'

'I met Neville,' said Russell.

'Yes?' said Morgan.

58

'What do you mean "yes"? I just said I met Neville.'

'Which one?'

'What do you mean, which one?'

'Is this why you're in all this state, because you think you found The Flying Swan and you think you met Neville?'

'No it's not, and I don't *think* I met him, I *did* meet him. But that's not it. What it is, is really bad. Really terrible. *He's* here, right now. He's here in a shed.'

'Neville is in a shed?'

'Not Neville, *him*.'

'I'm up for this,' said Morgan. 'Which *him* is in a shed?'

'A . . . Adolf H . . . Hitler,' stammered Russell. 'Adolf Hitler! He's here!'

'In a shed?'

'Behind The Flying Swan.'

'Behind The Flying Swan?'

'He's there. I saw him. What are we going to do? We should call the army, shouldn't we?'

'Russell,' said Morgan.

'Yes?' said Russell.

'I'm impressed.'

'Eh?'

'I'm very impressed.'

'What?'

'You've a lot to learn, but as a first-off I think you deserve at least nine out of ten for effort.'

'What?'

59

'I think where you've blown it,' said Morgan, 'is that you've set your sights too high. Hitler doesn't really fit the bill, what with him being dead and everything. You should have gone for someone else, someone feasible. Lord Lucan, you should have gone for. Lord Lucan hiding out in a shed.'

'*What?*' Russell said.

'But you also have to build up the plot. Rushing in and burbling "I've seen Hitler in a shed" does have a certain impact, but you have to build up to it.'

'I'm not building up to anything. This is all true. I saw him, I did. I did.'

'You didn't, Russell. You *really* didn't.'

'I really *did*.'

'In The Flying Swan?'

'In a shed out the back.'

'And which pub exactly *is* The Flying Swan?'

'The Bricklayer's Arms.' Russell still didn't have all his breath back. 'The Bricklayer's Arms. And I can prove it. I can. I can.' He rooted about in his waxed jacket and pulled a crumpled piece of card from his poacher's pocket. 'There,' he said.

Morgan took the card and uncrumpled it. 'The Bricklayer's Arms,' he read, 'alias The Flying Swan, famous pub featuring in the novels of blah, blah, blah.'

'It doesn't say blah, blah, blah, does it?'

'It might as well do.'

'You can't deny what's in print.'

'Really?' Morgan fished into the back pocket of

60

his jeans and brought out his wallet, from this he withdrew several similar pieces of card. 'Here you go,' said Morgan. 'The Princess Royal, alias The Flying Swan, The New Inn, alias The Flying Swan, The Red Lion, alias The Flying Swan. Even The Shrunken Head in Horseferry Lane, they *all* claim to be The Flying Swan. Do you know how many pubs claim that Oliver Cromwell slept there?'

'Did he sleep at The Flying Swan then?'

'No, he bloody didn't. Half the pubs in Brentford claim to be *the original* Flying Swan. It's bullshit, Russell. They do it for tourists.'

'But Neville?'

'Slouching bloke, rotten teeth, stained shirt?'

'That's him.'

'Sid Wattings, been the landlord there for years.'

'Eh?'

'Is that blonde barmaid still there? The one who can tuck her legs behind her head?'

Russell groaned.

'It's a wind-up,' said Morgan. 'I'm sorry, Russ.'

'Don't call me Russ. I don't like Russ.'

'It's a wind-up, *Russell*. If you'd told me you were going to look for The Flying Swan, I would have warned you not to waste your time. This Adolf Hitler you saw, how did he look?'

'He looked a bit rough, but he looked just like he did in the old war footage.'

'And you don't think that a bit strange?'

'No,' said Russell. 'That's the whole point.'

'It's not the whole point. It didn't occur to you

61

that he might have looked a bit older? Like *fifty years* older? Like he should have been at least one hundred years old?'

'Ah,' said Russell.

'Exactly, *ah*. This is where Sid's slipped up. Hitler was dying anyway at the end of the war, he had all sorts of stuff wrong with him. Yet the Hitler you saw was no older. What did he do then, drink the elixir of life? The water of life?'

Russell let out a further groan as the image of a Perrier bottle swam into his mind, followed by certain other images of an erotic nature, some of them actually involving a Perrier bottle. 'So it wasn't really Hitler?'

'Could it *really* have been Hitler? Ask yourself, could it *really* have been?'

'I suppose not,' said Russell.

'I'm sorry, Russ, er, Russell. You've been had.'

Russell made a very miserable face and turned his eyes towards the floor. 'I've made a bit of a prat of myself, haven't I?' he said.

'It's not your fault. That Sid's getting a bit sneaky. Perhaps the competition's getting too strong. Perhaps they've installed a Lord Lucan in a shed behind The New Inn. It's a good wheeze.'

'It didn't half look like Hitler,' said Russell. 'But I suppose you must be right. It *was* a wind-up. It couldn't really have been him.'

'Still,' said Morgan. 'Look on the bright side, Russell. You actually had a bit of an adventure.

It doesn't matter that it was all baloney. I bet it got your adrenalin rushing about.'

'It certainly did that.'

'So you've lived a little. For a brief moment you weren't reliable old Russell, who nothing ever happens to. For a brief moment you were actually having an adventure. And it felt pretty good, didn't it?'

Russell raised his eyes from the floor and for a brief moment, a very brief moment, they really glared at Morgan.

'I'm going back to the office,' he said. And back to the office he went.

# CHAPTER 6

# BACK TO THE FÜHRER

Of course Morgan had to be right, there was no possible way Adolf Hitler could really be in Brentford in the nineteen nineties, looking just like he did in the nineteen forties. Especially with him being dead and everything.

No possible way.

It's a big statement though, 'no possible way', isn't it?

There's always *some* possible way. It might be an *improbable* way, or a way considered *im*possible, or *im*plausible, or something else beginning with *im*.

For instance, *one* possible way springs immediately to mind and 'immediately' begins with *im*. If we return once more to the contents of box 23. And had we been given access to the one on the chief constable's high shelf in Brentford police station in May, nineteen fifty-five, we would have been able to read a statement placed there by a certain constable Adonis Doveston, which read thus:

I was proceeding in an easterly direction along Mafeking Avenue at eleven p.m. (2300 hours) on the 12th inst at a regulation 4.5 mph when

I was caused to accelerate my pace due to cries of distress emanating from an alleyway to the side of number sixteen. I gained entry to said alleyway and from thence to the rear garden of number sixteen. And there I came upon Miss J. Turton in a state of undress. This state consisting of a brassiere with a broken left shoulder strap, a pair of camiknickers and one silk stocking. She was carrying on something awful and when I questioned her as to why this might be, she answered, 'Why lor' bless you, constable, but wasn't I just whipped up out of me bloomin' garden by a bloomin' spaceship and ravished by the crew and when they'd had their evil way with me, then didn't they just dump me back here without a by your leave or kiss my elbow.'

I later ascertained that this statement was not entirely accurate, in that Miss Turton had in fact had her elbow kissed, also her eyeballs licked and the lobes of her ears gently nibbled. I accompanied the lady into her back parlour, took off my jacket to put about her shoulders and was comforting her, prior to putting the kettle on, when her father returned, somewhat the worse for drink.

Would it be possible for me to have the Saturday after next off, as I am to be married?

A straightforward enough statement by any reckoning, a simple case of alien abduction, no doubt.

Or was it?

Behind this statement was stapled another statement and on this was scrawled a few lines, these being Miss Turton's description of the alien crew:

Tall and blond, wearing grey uniforms with a double lightning-flash insignia and black jackboots.

A description that would fit the dreaded storm troopers of Hitler's *Waffen* SS. Those known as The Last Battalion.

Significant?

*Not* significant?

Well, it's bloody significant when viewed in the light of a certain scenario I am about to put forward, concerning how Adolf Hitler could turn up in Brentford in the nineteen nineties looking exactly the same as he did in World War Two.

You'll kick yourself afterwards for not seeing how obvious it is.

It is a fact well known to those who know it well, that towards the end of the Second World War, the Nazis had all sorts of secret experimental research laboratories, working on all manner of advanced weaponry. And had they been able to hold out for a few more months they would have completed certain dreadful devices to wreak utter havoc upon the Allies.

One of these was the sound-cannon. A sonic

energy gun constructed to project a low frequency vibrational wave that could literally shake apart anything within its path. Another was the *Flügelrad* (literally flying saucer), a discoid aircraft designed by Viktor Schauberger, powered by electromagnetic energy and capable of speeds in excess of 2000 km/hr.*

Let us take a trip back to one of those secret establishments, New Schwabenland in Antarctica, 'somewhere due south of Africa'. The year is 1945 and a fleet of U-boats has just arrived, having come by way of Argentina. On board are crack troops known as The Last Battalion, a number of the highest ranking Nazi party members and a certain Mr A. Hitler esquire.

They enter a vast hangar affair where several *Flügelrads* and other state-of-the-then-art craft are in various stages of completion.

It is a little after tea-time.

Adolf Hitler enters first, he is limping slightly, due to chilblains acquired on the long yoyage, allied to his verrucas and athlete's foot. He speaks.

HITLER: Someone get us a bleeding armchair, me
   Admirals† are killing me.
GOERING: And some sarnies, my belly's emptier

* The plans for these were actually found in Hitler's bunker and handed over to the CIA, whatever happened to them next is anyone's guess.
† Nazi rhyming slang. Admirals of the Fleet: feet.

67

than a Führer's promise. (Laughter from the officer ranks.)

HITLER: (Adjusting his hearing aid.) What was that?

GOERING: I said, praise the fatherland, my Führer. (Further laughter.)

HITLER: You fat bastard.

Now before we go any further with this particular drama, it might be well worth identifying the principal players, explaining a little bit about them and a few things that are not generally known about the German language.

Firstly Hitler. Well, we all know about him, don't we? Sold his soul to the devil at an early age, the rest is history.

Hermann Goering. One of Hitler's original henchmen, drinking buddy from their old bier-keller bird-pulling days. In charge of something or other pretty big, it might have been the airforce. What is known is that although he was a fat bastard, a really fat bastard, he was also a fop who used to change his clothes as many as five times a day. He probably sweated a lot and this was before the invention of underarm deodorants.

Heinrich Himmler. He was the little sod with the pince-nez specs who masterminded the extermination camps. Described as looking 'like a school teacher'. Sexual pervert and sadist. He'd have fitted in quite nicely at any of our public schools really.

Joseph Goebbels. Well, we all know him, he was the 'poison dwarf', in charge of propaganda, looked like Himmler only shorter.

Albert Speer. He was the architect who was designing the new Germany. Didn't seem to have much in the way of imagination, as the new Germany was going to look just like Old Rome. Curiously enough, Prince Charles' designs for a 'new London' mirror almost exactly Speer's vision of the new Berlin. I wonder if perhaps they are related.*

Regarding the German language, what most people don't realize is that it, like other languages, has regional accents. If we were to equate the German language with the English language and consider the way it was spoken by the players listed above, we would find: that Hitler spoke the German equivalent of broad Cockney; Goering, Yorkshire; Himmler, Eton and Albert Speer, Dublin!

Well, they speak English in Dublin (and for the most part better than we do).

So, if there's anyone left who hasn't been offended and is still prepared to read on, we rejoin the action back in the big hangar. Armchairs have been brought and sandwiches and Viktor Schauberger (who nobody knows anything about,

* Albert Speer was Prince Charles' uncle twice removed through the old Saxe-Coburg clan (allegedly). Prince Charles' great grandad was also called Albert.

but who a great deal of costly personal research on my part has revealed spoke very much like a Welshman) is getting down to business.

SCHAUBERGER: Indeed to goodness, yacky-dah and leaks, isn't it?

HITLER: What's this Zurich* on about?

HIMMLER: If I might interpret for you, my Führer, he is trying to explain the major breakthrough that he and his colleagues have precipitated, using the advanced technology supplied by our off-world allies.

HITLER: Our bleeding *what*?

HIMMLER: The chaps from outer space, my Führer.

HITLER: Foreigners? I hate bleeding foreigners.

GOERING: That's reet good, coming from an Austrian. (Laughter.)

SCHAUBERGER: 'Reet good's' Geordie, isn't it? Like 'away the lads'.

GOERING: Well, I'll go to the foot of our stairs. How's that?

SCHAUBERGER: More like it.

HITLER: Can we get this over with? I want to get me Aryans† off and rub some lard on me Yiddishers.**

* Zurich banker: wanker.

† Aryan roots: boots.

** Yiddisher's nose: toes (This is Nazi rhyming slang and therefore anything but politically correct).

70

HIMMLER: I will explain everything, my Führer. As you may or may not know, Mr Schauberger here has been working on the *Flügelrad* project.

HITLER: Yeah. Yeah. Disc-shaped aircraft, they've got as much chance of getting in the air as the allies have of winning the bloody war. (No laughter.)

HIMMLER: Well, my Führer, far be it from me to disagree with a man who is virtually a living god, but the craft have already been test flown, and with the aid of the technology given to us from certain 'allies' of our own, the craft not only flies faster than sound, but also faster than light, which is to say, faster than time.

HITLER: Do what?

HIMMLER: The fatherland has conquered time travel, my Führer.

HITLER: Well, bugger me backwards.

HIMMLER: Later, my Führer, but please allow Mr Speer to explain the details.

SPEER: My Führer, as you might have noticed, we have not got underway quite as rapidly as we might have liked regarding the building of the new Germany. It does have to be said that the knocking down of the old one is well ahead of schedule, thanks to the Allies (some laughter, a soldier is taken away and shot). But the actual rebuilding is reckoned to take, oh, about mmmm years.

HITLER: Speak up, how many years?

SPEER: mmmmm years.

HITLER: How many?

SPEER: About seventy-five years, my Führer. Sir.

HITLER: *How bloody many?*

SPEER: Say sixty. Sixty years, no problem. As long as –

HITLER: As long as *what*?

SPEER: As long as *we* win the war.

HITLER: Of course we'll win the war.

HIMMLER: Of course we will, my Führer. In fact we definitely will, have no fear of that. You see we can't lose now. Might I explain?

HITLER: Grunt.

HIMMLER: Thank you, my Führer. The plan is this. Two *Flügelrads* have been completed. One designed to travel back in time and the other forward. The one going back will take details of how we, ahem, lost all our previous military campaigns and deliver them to the generals in question *before* they actually fight the battles, so they'll win, see?

HITLER: (stroking chin) Nice one. I like that.

HIMMLER: The other will carry you forward one hundred years, so you can arrive at a predestined time and place to step from the craft into the glorious rebuilt Reich of the future.

GOEBBELS: You will appear according to predictions prophesied, as the new messiah, my Führer, stepping from the craft to rule the entire world.

HITLER: All right!

HIMMLER: We'll have an ambulance waiting.

HITLER: *What?*

HIMMLER: Medical science will have advanced one hundred years, my Führer. All your little aches and pains, we'll have them immediately sorted out for you.

HITLER: Even my piles?

HIMMLER: Even those.

HITLER: And my flatulence?

HIMMLER: Especially your flatulence.

HITLER: Well, let's not sit about here like a bunch of Russians*. Let's get in them old *Flügelrads*, I've a future world needs ruling.

HIMMLER: We're right with you, my Führer.

HITLER: No you bloody well aren't. You lot go back and sort out all the cock-ups.

HIMMLER / GOEBBELS / SPEER / GOERING: Aaawwww!

HITLER: That's show biz!

And so it came to pass. Or rather, it almost came to pass. If history is notable for at least *one* thing, then that *one* thing would be that the Germans did *not* win the Second World War. They came second, but they didn't win it. It must be supposed that the reason for this was that something went wrong with the *Flügelrad* that travelled back into the past. Himmler, Goering and Co. came to well deserved sticky ends and Speer never got a chance

* Russian fronts: er . . .

73

to oversee the building of the thousand-year reich. Tough shit!

But it all does fall into place rather neatly, if you think about it. There is no real proof that they ever found Hitler's body and for years rumours abounded that he escaped.

Where to?

Well, it's obvious, isn't it? Into the future, that's where. Off one hundred years into the future, to step from his craft as the new messiah into a reich-dominated world.

Except there isn't going to be one.

So what if, just if, his craft broke down on the way into the future? What if it crash landed in the nineteen nineties? And not in Germany? After all, the world spins around and if his coordinates were set for Germany and he landed too early, he could have ended up in England by mistake. In Brentford, in fact.

Well he *could*! It's possible.

So the close (very close) encounter Miss Turton had in nineteen fifty-five could have been with a Nazi *Flügelrad* pilot and an engineer, or someone, stopping off on the way to the future for a bit of 'how's-your-Führer' and Russell might really have seen Mr Hitler looking just like he did back in the nineteen forties.

I told you it was possible.

And I *did* tell you you'd kick yourself afterwards for not seeing how obvious it was.

Well, I *did*.

# CHAPTER 7

'**B**limey, Russell,' said Frank, 'you smell like sh—'

'Yes,' said Russell. 'I know, I was sick.'

Frank made delicate sniffings at the air. 'It's beer,' said he. 'Now, don't give me a clue, I'll get it. It's bitter.' Sniff, sniff, sniff. '*Best* Bitter. *Garvey's* best bitter. The Bricklayer's Arms. Am I right, or am I right?'

'You're right,' said Russell mournfully.

'Flavoured crisps often throw me,' Frank brushed imaginary dust from his jacket shoulders. 'But not cornflakes. I know my vomit. Elizabeth Taylor was sick all over me once, did I ever tell you about that?'

'I thought it was Greta Garbo who was sick all over you.'

'No, it was definitely Elizabeth Taylor, she'd been drinking stout.'

Russell sat down at his desk and put his head in his hands. And then he looked up at Frank and then he began to laugh. '*Stout?*' he said. 'Elizabeth Taylor had been drinking *stout?*'

'No, you're right,' said Frank. 'It *was* Greta Garbo.'

'Has anyone been in?'

'I've only been back five minutes myself. But no, no-one's been in. You've a memo on your desk, though.'

'A memo?' Russell perused his empty desk top. 'Where is it?' he asked.

'I threw it away,' said Frank.

'Why?'

'Because it was exactly the same as the one I got.'

'But it was addressed to me?'

'Yes, but it was the same memo.'

'So what did it say?'

'Yours or mine?'

'Mine.'

'Same as mine said.'

'So what did yours say?'

'None of your business, Russell.'

Russell sighed. 'Where is *my* memo?'

'In *my* waste-bin.'

Morgan now entered the office. 'I've just found a memo on my bench,' he said.

Frank said, 'Let's see it.'

Russell said, 'No, don't you let him.'

Morgan asked, 'Why?'

'Read it out,' said Russell.

Morgan read it out. 'To all staff,' he read. 'As you are well aware, business has been falling off in alarming fashion of late. To such an alarming fashion has it been falling off, that it has now reached a state of no business at all. Such a state

76

of no business at all is not a state conducive to good business in terms of profit margins and expansionism. Such a state of no business at all is more conducive to a downward curve into bankruptcy and receivership. Therefore you are asked to attend a meeting in my office at 3 p.m. to discuss matters. This meeting will be held at 3 p.m. in my office and you are asked to attend it, in order . . .' Morgan paused.

'Yes?' asked Russell.

'Well, it sort of goes on in that fashion.'

'Is that the same as the memos we got, Frank?'

Frank shrugged. 'More or less.'

'We're all going to be made redundant,' said Morgan.

'No, no, no.' Frank shook his head. 'It's just a temporary slump. The British film industry has temporary slumps. Things will pick up. I remember Richard Attenborough saying to me once—'

'It's nearly three,' said Morgan.

'Uncanny,' said Frank. '"It's nearly three and I'm pissed, Frank," he said. "Give us a lift home in your mini." His wife was a beautiful woman, didn't she marry Michael Winner?'

Frank took the phone off the hook (to give any incoming callers the impression the Emporium was doing lots of business), and the three men trudged off towards Mr Fudgepacker's office.

Russell definitely trudged, he did not have a jog or a march left in him. Frank was a natural trudger

77

anyway, and Morgan, who was easy about such things, was prepared to give trudging a try.

Geographically, the distance between the sales office and Mr Fudgepacker's office was a little more than twenty feet. But due to the imaginative layout of the place, the route was somewhat circuitous. About a five-minute trudge, it was.

So, while this trudging is going on, now might be a good time to offer a bit in the way of description regarding Fudgepacker's Emporium. As has already been said, it was housed within the deconsecrated church and, as has also been said, it contained many 'wonders'.

The visitor, entering by the fine Gothic doors at the front, will find a pleasant vestibule with a glazed tile floor and walls of York stone. Here is offered a taste of things to come. To the left stands a torture rack, *circa* 1540, a wax mannequin stretched thereon, its sculptured face expressive of considerable discomfort. Several suits of samurai armour are mounted upon stands. A row of human skeletons, two lacking heads, and a Dalek.

Through the vestibule and into the main hall. The word 'cavernous' springs immediately to mind. It is not a word you normally associate with the interior of churches, but it is appropriate here. From low tiled floor to high fan-vaulting, the space has been divided into numerous levels, constructed in finely laced cast-ironwork. And the name Escher now springs to mind, that amazing artist who drew all those wonderful pictures of

78

staircases that lead forever nowhere, yet somehow join onto one another in a never-ending, mind-boggling, continuity. Galleries and catwalks and stairways. And items. Items strung from the ceiling, rising from the floor, suspended between the catwalks, stacked along these walks and ways and housed in racks and cases, bags and boxes.

Stuffed beasts proliferate. A bear in battle with a tiger. A swooping eagle snatching at a piglet. A row of baboons clad in Regency garb standing to attention, glazed eyes alert. Pickled specimens also abound. Tall glass jars, many being the preparations of the famous Dutch anatomist Frederik Ruysch, who supplied curiosities to the collection of Peter the Great. Are the faces that stare out at you real? Were they once human? Yes, they are and were.

All human life is here, suspended in time. Preserved in formaldehyde. Here a diseased kidney. Here a distended bowel. Here a lung far gone with tumorous canker. Here a brain all—

'Here we are,' said Morgan.

'I'll knock,' said Frank. 'I'm the manager.'

'I'll just skulk then,' said Morgan. 'I'm the packer.'

'I'm the salesman,' said Russell. 'What should I do?'

'Just stand, I suppose,' said Morgan. 'But not quite so close.'

Frank did the knocking.

'Come in,' called the crackling voice of Mr

79

Fudgepacker. 'That is, enter those who are with-out. I'm inside, as it were, the one who's calling you to come in. It's me. Who *is* that?'

'It's us,' called Frank.

'Sounded like just the one of you. Did you all knock together?'

'I did the knocking,' called Frank. 'I'm the manager.'

'Oh, it's you Frank. Come on in then, if you're not in already. And I see that you're not. Enter.'

Morgan rolled his eyes. 'I've been sacked plenty of times before,' said he, 'but this should be a new experience.'

They entered.

Mr Fudgepacker's office was housed in the old belfry. The bells were gone, but the bats were still there. It wasn't a very big office, because it wasn't a very big belfry. There was room for about four coffins lying down, not that anyone had ever tested this. And they might well have, there were plenty of coffins downstairs, several with their original occupants.

The walls of this minuscule office were made gay with posters. Film posters. Film posters of the nineteen-fifties persuasion. *We Eat Our Young, I was a Teenage Handbag, Carry on up my Three-legged Bloomers, Mr Felcher goes to Town*, and others.

All banned. All Fudgepacker productions. All collector's items now.

The ruins of the great director sat behind his

cut-down desk. Again a word springs to mind, this word is 'decrepit'. Decrepitude is no laughing matter. Not when you were once young and vigorous, once bursting with life and virile fluids. Happily for Ernest Fudgepacker, decrepitude was no problem. He had always been decrepit. He looked very much today as he had forty years before. Rough. He was altogether bald, altogether pallid, altogether frail and thin, altogether decrepit. Weak and rheumy were his eyes and he had no chin at all. He had splendid glasses though, horn-rimmed, with lenses half an inch thick. These magnified his eyes so that they filled the frames. Russell lived in mortal dread that he might one day take his glasses off to reveal—

Nothing.

'Close the door,' croaked Mr Fudgepacker.

Frank struggled to do so, but what with the three of them now in and crammed up against the desk, this wasn't easy.

Mr Fudgepacker viewed his workforce, his magnified eyes turning from one to another. 'Eerily' the word was, if anyone was looking for it.

'Where's Bobby Boy?' asked Mr Fudgepacker.

'Off sick,' said Frank. 'Stomach trouble.'

'Something catching I hope. I enjoy a good illness. See this hand?' He extended a withered paw. 'The nails are dropping off. Doctor said I should have it amputated.'

'Good God,' said Frank. 'When?'

'1958, silly bastard. I told him, this hand will see

me out. And it saw him out too. And his successor. What's that horrible smell?'

'It's me,' said Russell. 'Sorry.'

'Don't be sorry, lad, nothing wrong with a horrible smell. I collect horrible smells. Keep them in little jars. Little black jars. What did I ask you lot here for anyway?'

'You sent us a memo,' said Frank.

'Ah yes,' said Ernest. 'And you bloody watch it, Frank, trying to distract me with talk of sickness and bad smells. Sucking up to me isn't going to help your cause.'

'Eh?' said Frank.

Morgan sniggered.

'Business,' said Ernest.

'Yes,' said Frank.

'We don't have any,' said Ernest. 'Any don't we have.'

'It will pick up,' said Frank.

Ernest sniffed. It was a quite revolting sound, like half a ton of calf's liver being sucked up a drainpipe. 'I'm not going to beat about the bush,' said Ernest. 'Prevarication never helps, if you prevaricate it's the same as if you dither. There's no difference, believe me. A prevaricator is a ditherer, plain and simple. And I've been in this business long enough to know the truth of that statement. When I was a boy my father said to me, "Ernest," he said. "Ernest, don't do that to your sister." He didn't prevaricate, see.'

'I see,' said Frank.

'So let that be a lesson to you.'

'Right,' said Frank.

'Well, don't just stand there, get back to work.'

'Oh right,' said Frank. 'Is that it then?'

'That's it,' said Ernest. 'Except that you're sacked, Frank, so you won't be getting back to work. Well, I'm sure you will be getting back to work, but just not here.'

Frank made tiny strangulated noises with the back of his throat.

'Are you going to have a heart attack?' Ernest asked. 'Because if you are, I'd like to watch. I had one once. Two actually, but I didn't get to see what they were like. I'd have liked to have filmed them. If you're going to have one, could you hold on until I load my camera?'

'You can't sack me,' gasped Frank. 'I'm the manager.'

'Oh,' said Ernest. 'Who should I sack then?'

'Sack Morgan,' said Frank.

'You can't sack me,' said Morgan. 'I'm the packer.'

'Oh,' said Ernest. 'Who should I sack, then? One of you has to go.'

'Sack Russell,' said Frank.

'Oh,' said Russell.

'No,' said Morgan. 'That's not right, Russell is the salesman.'

'If one of us has to go,' said Russell, 'then it had better be me. Last one in, first one out.'

'I agree with that,' said Frank.

83

'Right,' said Ernest. 'You're sacked then, Russell.'

'Thank you,' said Russell. 'I'm sorry that I have to leave, perhaps if things pick up, you'll take me on again.'

'No, no, no,' said Morgan. 'That won't do. Russell is just being Mr Nice Guy again. You can't sack Russell.'

'Why not?' Russell asked.

'Because Russell is the salesman. He takes the customers round, writes up the orders, supervises pick ups and returns and does the loss and damage reports. You can't sack Russell.'

'Oh,' said Ernest. 'Who should I sack then?'

'Sack Bobby Boy,' said Morgan.

'That's a bit unfair on Bobby Boy, isn't it?' Russell asked. 'With him not being here to speak up for himself.'

'Keep out of this, Russell.'

'I think Bobby Boy should have his say.'

'Bobby Boy, you're sacked,' said Ernest, 'wherever you are.'

'But—' said Russell.

'Be quiet, Russell, or I'll sack you too.'

'Oh,' said Russell.

'Well,' said Ernest, 'I think that all went rather well. Now back to work you lot.'

'But—' said Russell.

'What?' said Ernest.

'Could I wash the cups up?' Russell asked.

'Are you sure you can fit that in, with all the other things you have to do?'

'I'll try,' said Russell.

'Good boy, now off you go.'

'Thank you,' said Russell.

They squeezed outside and Frank shut the door.

'That was close,' said Frank.

'Yeah,' said Morgan. 'Thanks for putting my name forward.'

'You liked that?'

'No, I was being sarcastic.'

'I'm going back inside,' said Russell. 'If anyone has to go it should be me. Last in, first out.'

'I wouldn't do that if I were you,' said Morgan.

'Oh, and why not?'

'Because I met Bobby Boy at lunch-time and he's got himself another job.'

'Phew,' said Russell. 'Then I'm saved. Thanks a lot, Morgan.'

'Least I could do,' said that man.

The voice of Ernest Fudgepacker reached their ears, it called, 'Oh, and we'll have another meeting this time next week and if business hasn't picked up, I'll have to sack somebody else.'

'Do you mind if I say "fuck"?' Russell asked.

CHAPTER 8

'Grease,' says the old song, 'is the word,' but this is not altogether true. In fact, it isn't true at all. 'Stress' is the word. Stress. Stress. Stress.

In movies, the hero or heroine is put under stress. Hollywood scriptwriters understand this. They understand this because this is what Hollywood producers demand of them.

'Is the hero being put under stress?'

The reason for this is because a movie must not be 'plot-led'. The hero or heroine must take the initiative. Forces are up against them, but they must do all the doing. They have a goal that must be reached. You may argue that all movies aren't like that. But they are, you know. Pick any movie you like and think about the plot and the hero (or heroine). It's all to do with stress.

Hollywood thrives on stress.

Russell didn't thrive on stress. Russell hated stress. Stress was not Russell's thing. But stress he had and stress he was going to get lots more of.

He didn't get sacked the next week. Morgan

didn't get sacked the next week, nor did Frank. Although Frank really deserved it.

The reason none of them got sacked was because something rather unexpected happened. And what this rather unexpected something was, was a rather unexpected upturn in the fortunes of Fudgepacker's Emporium. And how this rather unexpected something came about was all down to Russell.

Who was under stress at the time.

'Under stress' and 'at the time'.

We've done a bit about stress, so now let's do a bit about time.

James Campbell once said (last week, in fact, at The George), 'The future and the past have a lot in common. This being that neither of them actually exists. Which leaves us with the present, whose round is it?'

'Yours,' I told him.

'It was mine last time,' he said.

'But that was in the past,' I told him, 'and the past does not exist.'

'Fair enough,' said James and went off to the bar.

Presently he returned, with just the one drink. For himself.

'Where is mine?' I asked him.

'Good question,' he replied, 'I believe, at the present, we're buying our own.'

An evening out with James is always instructive. Though rarely profitable.

But, time. Time is a bit of a bugger, isn't it? It doesn't really exist at all. It appears to be a series of presents, perhaps a never-ending state of presentness. But something *must* happen, because you definitely get older. Which is strange if you spend all your time in the present and never in the past or the future. Mind you, you have spent some time in the past, which used to be the present. But you've never spent any time at all in the future. Because when you get to the future, it turns out to be the present and by the time you've thought about it, it's already the past.

Russell never thought that much about the future, he was always happy with the present. Especially the birthday present, especially if it was a bicycle. Which it once had been, but that was in the past now.

It's all so confusing, isn't it?

Russell certainly didn't know that he was going to be instrumental in future events which would affect the present yet to come. As it were.

He wasn't happy when he got back to the sales office. He was mournful.

'Why are you mournful?' Morgan asked.

'I am mournful,' said Russell, 'because I do not want to be sacked.'

'You won't be sacked,' said Morgan. 'If anybody's going to be sacked, then that somebody will be Frank.'

'It bloody won't,' said Frank. 'I'm the manager.'

'I wasn't going to bring my wild card into play just yet,' said Morgan, 'but I think I will anyway.'

'Oh yes?' said Frank.

'Oh yes,' said Morgan. 'You may be the manager, but Ernest Fudgepacker is my uncle.'

'Shit,' said Frank.

'I should go,' said Russell. 'Last in, first out.'

'Will you shut up about that.'

'No, he's right,' said Frank. 'Don't stand in his way, he's doing the right thing. Forestall the ignominy of a sacking, Russell, go and hand your notice in.'

'All right,' said Russell. 'I will.'

Now, this is all wrong, you see. In Hollywood they wouldn't have this. In Hollywood they would say, 'The hero is under stress and now the hero must fight back. And win.' That's what they'd say. In Hollywood.

'I'll hand my notice in,' said Russell. 'It's only fair.'

'Quite right,' said Frank.

'Quite wrong,' said Morgan.

'You know what though,' said Russell, 'if we could do something to bring in some business, none of us would have to be sacked.'

'Good point,' said Morgan.

'You can't run a company without a manager,' said Frank.

'There must be something we could do,' said Russell. 'Something *I* could do.'

89

'What?' Morgan asked.

'Hand in your notice,' said Frank. 'Save the rest of us.'

'That wouldn't be fair to you,' said Russell. 'Putting you through all the misery, waiting for the axe to fall. No, handing in my notice won't help. I must do something positive, something that will help us all.'

'Are you taking the piss?' Frank asked.

'No, I'm dead straight. I'm going to think hard about this. Find a way to save Fudgepacker's. That's what I'm going to do.'

'It's five-thirty,' said Morgan. 'Knocking-off time. What would you say to a pint of beer?'

'Not in The Bricklayer's?'

'Not in The Bricklayer's.'

'I would say thank you, let's do it.'

The Ape of Thoth was a popular pub. A music pub. All kinds of bands had played there. Some had become quite famous since. The Who once played there, and Manfred Mann. Of course that is going back a bit. The Lost T-Shirts of Atlantis never played there, nor did Sonic Energy Authority, but you can't have everything. The landlord of The Ape was a Spaniard by the name of Luis Zornoza. Tall, dark and handsome, he was, and a bit of a ladies' man*.

Russell had never been into The Ape before.

* As Spike once said, 'One bit in particular.'

90

Morgan drew his attention to a sign above the bar. 'The Ape of Thoth, formerly The Flying Swan, welcomes you.'

A blond barmaid came up to serve them.

'I'll have a Perrier water,' said Russell.

'You'll have a pint,' said Morgan.

'Yes, you're right, I will.'

'Two pints of Special,' said Morgan.

The barmaid looked at Russell with wistful eyes. 'Pity,' she said.

'Look,' said Morgan, as the drinks were delivered. 'I know you'd like to help, Russell, but it really isn't your thing, is it? I mean you're a helpful fellow, but when it comes to *big* helpfulness, like making a *big* move, you just don't do that sort of stuff, do you?'

Russell sniffed suspiciously at his pint, then took a small sip. 'I'm not an idiot, you know,' he said. 'I am quite capable. I could *do* things.'

'Yes, but you know you won't. Chaps like you never do. No offence meant, but you just don't.'

'But I could, if the opportunity presented itself.'

'I think you have to make your own opportunities.'

'So you just said.'

'No, I didn't.'

'You did, and you said that too.'

'What?'

'Oh no.' Russell glanced about the place. Luis the landlord had gone off to the cellar with the blond barmaid and but for himself and for Morgan the bar was deserted. 'Quick,' cried Russell. 'Jump over the counter. Quick.'

'You're not going to rob the place? Russell, no!'

'Something's going to happen. Quickly, quickly.' Russell shinned up from the barstool and scrambled onto the counter.

'Have you lost all reason, Russell?'

'Quick, it's going to happen, I know it is.' Russell grabbed Morgan's arm and began to haul at him.

'What is? Oh shit.'

A vibration ran through the bar. A shudder. Optics rattled, ashtrays shook. The dartsboard fell off the wall.

'Earthquake!' cried Morgan.

'Not an earthquake, quickly.' Russell dropped down behind the bar, dragging Morgan after him.

'Oh my God!'

An icy wind sprang up from nowhere, became a mini-hurricane, snatched chairs from the floor and hurled them about the place.

'Keep your head down,' Russell shouted, but Morgan didn't need the telling. Tables whirled and twisted, splintered against the walls, beer mats and ashtrays, glasses and bottles filled the air, rained down from every direction.

And a blinding light.

It shot up before the counter, became a sheet of blue-white, expanding to extend from wall to wall, from floor to ceiling. Then it folded in upon itself with a sound like water vanishing down the plug-hole and was gone.

A tinkling of glass, a final thud of a falling chair and all became silent.

Very silent.

Unnaturally silent.

Russell got to his knees, brushing glass and beer mats from his shoulders. He peeped over the counter and gawped at the devastation.

'Is it over?' called Morgan, from the foetal position.

'I think it's just about to start.'

The sound was like an express train coming out of a tunnel, or a jet plane taking off, or a rocket being launched (which is a bit like a jet plane, though less like an express). Sort of 'Whoooooooosh!' it went. Really loudly.

The wall at the far end of the bar seemed to go out of focus and then to open, much in the fashion of a camera lens. As Russell gawped on he saw the light reform, blaze out, and a figure, a distant moving dot of a figure, running. Closer and closer. Though two dimensionally. It's a bit hard to explain really. Imagine it looking like a movie projected onto the wall. That's what it looked like. The figure running towards the camera. With a further much-intensified whoosh, the figure burst out of two dimensions into the third.

It was a woman. A beautiful woman. She wore an elegant contour-hugging frock of golden scales.

Cut above the knee, her stockings were of gold, as were her shoes.

And her hair.

She flashed frightened eyes about the bar. 'Russell,' she called, 'where are you?'

'I'm here.' Russell's gawp had achieved the status of a mega-gawp. But he said, 'I'm here,' none the less.

'I knew you wouldn't let me down. I knew it.'

'It's you. It's you.'

And it *was* her. It was the barmaid from The Bricklayer's Arms.

'Take it quickly, there's no time.'

'Take what? What?'

The beautiful barmaid thrust a golden package into Russell's hand. 'The programmer, keep down, don't let them see you, and, Russell . . .'

'What? What?'

'I love you,' she leaned across the counter and she kissed him. Full on the lips. Russell felt his toes begin to curl and his hair becoming straight.

'Oh,' said Russell, as she pulled away. 'I don't . . .'

'Understand? You will. And thank you, for everything.'

'I . . . er.'

Metallic clangs and crashes. She glanced back towards the way she had come, clicked something on her belt. Another white disc sprang up upon the far wall. 'Keep down,' and with that she ran towards the disc.

Russell watched her dash across the bar, leap at the disc on the wall, which swallowed her up. And she was gone.

'Oh,' said Russell once more, and then he turned his head, saw something rather fearful and took a dive for cover. From two dimensions into the third they came, clashing and clanking. They were like knights in dead black armour.

Two of them, both tall and wide, of terrible bulk, the floor shook to their footfalls. The helmets were spherical, featureless, without visors or eyeholes. The metal gauntlets had but the three fingers. These clasped enormous black guns of an advanced design. Little red lights ran up and down the barrels.

They came clanking to a standstill before the bar.

Morgan raised his head but Russell forced it down again, rammed a hand over his mouth.

Above, the mighty figures stood immobile as statues, and then their heads began to revolve. Whirring, clicking sounds, the heads turned. Round and round they went.

'The woman is not here,' said one, in a voice like a long-distance telephone call.

'Readjust the coordinates. Search mode. And delayed correct, two minutes.'

Lights flickered upon the carapace breast plates. The white spot grew once more upon the far wall.

Crashing and banging they ran towards it. Terrible creaks and groans of grating metal. Into the disc of light, then zap. Gone. Kaput. Vanished.

Russell peeped out once more. The walls of the bar were as before, no trace of anything remained. Morgan struggled up. 'What the bloody Hell . . . ?' he mumbled.

'I think we're in some kind of trouble,' Russell said.

'Trouble?'

'Trouble?' The voice was that of Luis Z the Spanish landlord. '*Trouble?* You bastards, what have you done to my pub?'

'It wasn't us.' Morgan took to backing away. Luis had his big peace-keeping stick in his hand. Russell took to backing away also.

'You bloody mad men! I step out for a moment and you smash my pub to pieces. You're dead. You're frigging dead.'

'Run,' Morgan said.

'Run,' agreed Russell.

Luis put up a spirited chase, but Morgan and Russell had youth to their account and they finally out-ran him down near the Butts Estate. Bent double in an alleyway, hands upon knees, they gasped and gagged for breath.

'What bloody happened?' Morgan managed. 'What went on back there?'

'I don't know.' Russell had a bit more breath left in him than Morgan. 'I just don't know.'

'Earthquakes,' croaked Morgan. 'And bright

lights and flashes and crashes and bangs and voices and—'

'I still don't know.'

'What did you see? Tell me what you saw.'

'I don't know, I—'

'A woman, I heard a woman.'

'A woman, yes.'

'You knew, Russell. Whatever it was, you knew it was going to happen.'

Russell nodded slowly. He *had* known something was about to happen. Though he hadn't known what and he didn't know how he'd known. So to speak.

'We're in deep shit,' puffed Morgan. 'That Luis will call the police for sure. We're wanted men. We could go to prison.'

'It wasn't our fault, we didn't do anything.'

'So *who* did, Russell?'

'I don't know. The walls sort of opened, she came out, then these things came out. Great black things in armour. I don't think they were people.'

'Will that stand up in court, do you suppose?'

'We've got to go back.'

'What?'

'Go back, try to explain, apologize, offer to make good.'

'*What?*'

'We must take the blame,' said Russell. 'I know we must. We'll say we were drunk and fighting. We'll tell him we'll pay for the damage.'

'Have you gone stark raving mad?'

'It's the best way. If he's called the police, I don't want them bashing down my mum's door at six in the morning.'

'But the bar's wrecked, it could be thousands of pounds.'

'We could lie,' said Russell.

'What did you say?'

'I said we could lie.'

'You don't know how to lie, Russell.'

'But *you* do, Morgan. You lie all the time.'

'That's not true, I never lie. It's Bobby Boy who tells all the lies, not me.'

'What about those mushrooms you say you've got growing in your shed, the ones that are the size of dustbin lids?'

'A slight exaggeration perhaps.'

'What about when you were late for work and you told Frank that terrorists had hijacked the bus?'

'Now that *was* true.'

'No it wasn't.'

'No, you're right.'

'So *you* should do the lying.'

'What am I going to say?'

'You'll say that armed men burst into the bar to raid the place and that we fought them off.'

'Oh,' said Morgan. 'Actually that's quite a good lie, isn't it?'

'Better than most of yours.'

'Paramilitaries,' said Morgan, warming to the

idea. 'With their faces blacked out, carrying General Electric mini-guns, and I fought them off single handed using certain martial arts techniques I learned from the lamas in Tibet.'

'Two big blokes in balaclava helmets,' said Russell. 'With coshes and we *both* waded in, *together.*'

'We could come out of this as heroes.' Morgan rubbed his hands together. 'Get in the newspapers and everything.'

'If we can stay out of court it will do for me.'

'Quite so.'

They trudged back. Trudging had become the order of the day really. Back they trudged.

There were no police cars outside The Ape of Thoth. All was very quiet. A young couple were just going in.

Russell and Morgan exchanged glances, steeled themselves, took deep breaths and entered the bar.

And then they just stared. They didn't speak. They didn't breathe. They just stared.

The bar was normal. All completely normal. No broken furniture. No smashed glasses, no shattered ashtrays. Chairs and tables just as they had been, the dartsboard on the wall, everything normal. Utterly, utterly normal.

Morgan let his breath out first. 'What the fu—'

'*You!*' Luis the landlord vaulted over the bar. '*How* did you . . . ? *What* did you . . . ?'

'What?' went Morgan.

'I come back and all is well. Nothing is broken. How did you do that? How . . . how?'

'I . . .' went Morgan.

'What are you talking about?' Russell asked.

'What?' went Morgan.

'What?' went Luis.

'What are you talking about?'

'This place, all smashed up, I chased you.'

'You never chased us,' Russell said. 'We've only just come in. This is the first time we've been in this evening.'

'What?' went Morgan.

'You bloody have, you bloody—'

'This man is clearly drunk,' said Russell. 'Come, Morgan, we will drink elsewhere. Good night to you, landlord.'

'What . . . what?'

Russell hustled Morgan from the bar.

Outside Morgan went 'What?' once more.

'Something's happened,' Russell said. 'Something big, somehow I knew the bar would be OK. Don't ask me how, but I knew it.'

'When did you know it?'

'Just before we went back in. Something big is happening, Morgan, and we're in it.'

'You can be in it, Russell, I don't want to be. I'm just an ordinary bloke. I don't want anything to do with this.'

'But you always said—'

'Don't worry about what I always said, I was

probably lying. I don't want any adventures, I want to go home for my tea.'

'You're in it, Morgan, whatever it is.'

'No, no, no. Hurricanes in the bar, things appearing and disappearing. Wreckage becoming unwrecked. This isn't my thing, I don't get involved in that sort of stuff.'

'That sort of stuff?' Russell made a thoughtful face. 'Like an adventure, do you mean? Like a real adventure?'

'There was nothing real about any of that.'

'She knew me. She knew my name, she called me Russell and she kissed me and she said, I love you.'

'I'm going home.'

'I'm not, I'm going to find out.'

'Look, call it quits. Whatever has happened, has now unhappened, maybe it was a black hole or something, but it's over. We got away with it. Let's go home.'

'It's not over. It's far from over. It's only just beginning.'

'Well, you do it on your own.'

'Morgan, come on.'

'No.' Morgan put up his hands. 'I don't want to know about it, I'm going home. Goodbye, Russell.'

'Goodbye, Morgan.'

Morgan didn't trudge this time, he stalked. Russell watched him as he shrank into the distance, presently to be lost in the shadow of the gasometer.

Russell stood a while. The sun was going down now beyond the great oaks on the Kew side of the Thames, shadows lengthened on the flowing waters. A heron circled in the rose-painted sky.

Russell reached into his poacher's pocket and brought out the golden package. 'We shall see,' he said, and, turning on his heel (for heroes always turn upon their heels and Russell might, just might, yet prove himself to be the stuff of which a hero is composed), he strode off (for heroes also stride), to seek whatever great things fate might hold in store for him.

Oh yes.

# CHAPTER 9

# BACK TO THE FÜHRER II

'It's her evening off,' sneered the landlord of The Bricklayer's Arms (the one who *was not* Neville). 'Some bloke was chatting her up at lunch-time, Perrier drinker. I think he's taken her to the pictures.'

'Are you sure?' asked Russell.

'Of course I'm bloody sure, he picked her up in his car half an hour ago. What's it got to do with you anyway?'

'Nothing. Do you serve food?'

'Ask me if we serve crabs.'

'Why?'

'Just ask me.'

'All right, do you serve crabs?'

'We serve anyone, sir.' The landlord laughed heartily. Russell didn't.

'That was a joke,' said the landlord.

'Most amusing,' said Russell. 'Could I have a sandwich?'

'A crocodile sandwich? And make it snappy, eh?'

'How about ham?'

'Don't know, never been there.' The landlord guffawed further.

'Is this some new innovation? You weren't laughing too much at lunch-time.'

'Things were iffy at lunch-time, they're sorted now.'

'I'm so pleased to hear it, a ham sandwich then, if I may.'

'Anything to drink? The best bitter's very good.'

'A Perrier water, please.'

'Poof,' the landlord served a bottle and a glass, took the money and shouted Russell's food order through the hatch to the kitchen.

Russell removed himself to a side table. The bar was filling, merry chit chat, raised voices, laughter. Russell took the golden package from his pocket and placed it on the table. What was in it, eh? She had said, 'the programmer'. What was that, a remote control for the telly? Something more than a remote control, surely? Should he open it now? Take a look?

'Ham sandwiches,' the landlord slapped the plate down on the table.

'That was quick,' said Russell.

'Fast food. So what's that you've got? Your birthday, is it?'

'A present for my mum,' said Russell, troubled by the ease with which the lie had left his lips. 'She's seventy tomorrow.'

The landlord looked Russell up and down. 'Enjoy your meal,' he said and slouched away.

'Oh yes,' he said, turning back, 'and I'll have a word with you later about hiring the room and the costumes and everything.'

'Oh good.'

The landlord went his wicked way.

Russell picked up a sandwich and thrust it into his mouth. And then he spat it out again. It was stale. Very stale. Russell sighed, his stomach rumbled. Russell picked up another sandwich and munched bitterly upon it.

Open up the package. That was for the best. Russell opened up the package. The paper was odd, almost like silk, almost like metal also, but somehow neither. Odd.

A slim black plastic carton presented itself. And a letter. Russell unfolded the letter and perused its contents.

*Dear Russell,*
*You won't know why you got this yet, but you will. If things are going right you should now be sitting in The Bricklayer's Arms eating a stale ham sandwich—*

Russell nearly choked on stale ham sandwich.

*If you're not, then we've both screwed up, but if you are, then finish your sandwich and take this to the address below. All will be explained.*
*Hopefully.*
*All my love,*
*Julie.*

Russell read the address below, it was a warehouse on the Brentford Dock at the bottom of Horseferry Lane.

Russell reached to open the box; as he did so he placed the letter face down on the table. Something was written on the back. Russell read this.

DON'T OPEN THE BOX, he read.

'Oh,' said Russell, not opening the box.

Night was on the go now. One of those balmy Brentford nights that poets often write about. Those nights that make you feel that everyone for miles around must be in bed and making love. You know the ones: Russell knew the ones.

The air was scented with jasmine and rare exotic fragrances wafted across the Thames from the gardens of Kew. The splendours of Brentford's architectural heritage caught moonlight on their slate rooftops and looked just-so. Just-so and more. The way they always have and, hopefully, they always will.

Russell breathed in the night air. It was a good old place, was Brentford, folk who didn't live there never understood. There *was* magic in the air. Perhaps there always had been magic in the air. Perhaps the tales he'd heard *were* true. Of Neville and Pooley and Omally and The Flying

Swan. On a night such as this you could feel that almost anything was possible.

And given what had happened so far . . .

Russell turned from the high street into Horse-ferry Lane. Sounds of merriment issued from The Shrunken Head. Papa Legba's Voodoo Jazz Cats, laying down that gris gris on the slap-head base, with Monty on accordion.

Russell passed the pub and entered the cobbled way that led past the weir and Cider Island, on towards the ruins of the old docks. By the light of the moon Russell re-read the address.

Hangar 18.

A sudden thought occurred to him. Why am I doing this? this thought went. Surely I am walking into some kind of trouble here (this was a second thought, which quickly joined the first). Surely I would be better tossing this package into the Thames and going home (third thought).

Russell looked up at that old devil moon. 'Something is happening,' he said softly, 'and I am part of it. I don't know what it is, but I am determined to find out.'

And so he walked on.

There were a number of buildings left at the old dock. Not many. Just the three, in fact. And two of those pretty gone to seed. The third looked rather spruce. Newly painted. The number 18 was writ mighty large up near the apex of the roof. Big sliding hangar-type doors.

Russell wondered just what sort of hangar this might have been; was now. Aircraft hangar? Could be. After all, it had been a plucky Brentonian who achieved the first man-powered flight*, although he'd been written out of history and the Wright brothers had got all the credit. Typical, that was. Americans always got the credit.

Not that Russell had anything against the Americans. Russell didn't have anything against anyone.

Russell was not that kind of a fellow.

It was quiet here. The occasional heron call. A salmon going plop. Something snuffling in a bush near by. But quiet overall.

Russell strode towards the big hangar-type sliding door. Should he knock? Was he expected?

*Might there be danger?*

That was a thought, wasn't it?

Best to be cautious.

Russell's stride became a scuttle. In a big sliding door there was a little hinged door, Russell gave the handle a try. It turned and the door clicked open. Russell drew a nervous breath. This was breaking and entering. Well, it wasn't *breaking*, but if he entered, it was *entering*. Was *entering* a crime? It might be entering with intent. Entering

---

* 1859, Charles 'Icarus' Doveston flew his Griffin 4, pedal-driven ornithopter, the plans may be seen in Brentford Library's permanent exhibition, 'WE DONE IT FIRST'.

with intent to *enter*. That couldn't be a crime, surely.*

Russell pushed the door before him and stepped into darkness. And a number of things happened very fast indeed. Russell sensed a movement. He heard the swish of something swinging down. He jumped to one side. There was a sharp metallic clang, closely followed by a cry of pain that wasn't Russell's. And a hand that wasn't Russell's found its way onto the face that *was* Russell's.

Russell gripped the wrist of this hand and gave it a violent twist. A second cry of pain, somewhat louder than the first, echoed all about the place and after this came many pleas for mercy.

'Where's the light switch?' Russell shouted.

'Up there somewhere, let me go. Leave off me. Oh. Ow. Help!'

Russell fumbled about in the darkness with his non-wrist-twisting hand and found the light switch.

Click went the light switch and on came all the lights.

'Oh, oh, oh,' went Russell's captive, and then, 'Oh shit, it's you.'

'And it's you,' said Russell, releasing his grip and viewing the figure at his feet. A chap of his own age, dressed all in black, long thin hair, a long thin face, a long thin body, long thin arms, and legs that were long and thin. He also had a long thin nose, with dark eyes, rather too close for comfort

* It could well be trespass.

at the top end, and a most dishonest-looking little mouth at the bottom. This was now contorted in pain.

'Bobby Boy, what are *you* doing here?'

'You almost broke my bloody wrist.'

'You attacked me with something.' Russell glanced around in search of that something. It lay near by. It was a long length of metal something. Piping, it was. 'You could have killed me with *that*!'

'You were breaking and entering.'

'Ah,' said Russell. 'This is not strictly true, I have considered this and—'

'Never mind that.' Bobby Boy struggled to his long thin feet and stood rubbing his long thin wrist. 'What are you doing here?'

'What are *you* doing here?'

'I asked first, and how did you manage to do that to me? I thought you were a man of peace.'

'I did ju-jitsu at a night-school course.'

'*You* did ju-jitsu?'

'It was a mistake, I signed on to do upholstery, but there was some clerical error and I didn't want to upset anyone by mentioning it.'

'You were being polite, as usual.'

'I suppose so,' said Russell.

'So what *are* you doing here?'

'I was given something to deliver. Something important, I think.'

'Who gave it to you?'

'The barmaid from The Bricklayer's Arms.'

'The one who can do the splits while standing on her head?'

'I think that's probably the same one.' Russell nodded gloomily.

'Why did she give it to you?'

'I don't know.'

'Well, didn't you ask her?'

'I didn't get a chance. Look, stop asking me all these questions.'

'Do you know what it is?'

'That's the last one I'll answer. It's a pro-grammer.'

The dishonest-looking mouth dropped open and the eyes that were too close for comfort grew quite wide. 'You've got the programmer? Let me see it, give it to me.'

'I'll let you see it,' said Russell, 'but I won't give it to you until you explain to me exactly what it does.'

'I can't do that.'

'Then you can't have it.'

'Oh come on, Russell, it's mine. I'll make it worth your while, I'll give you money.'

'I don't want money. I want . . . Holy God, what's *that*?'

Russell stared and pointed. Bobby Boy bobbed up and down before him, trying to obscure Russell's vision. 'It's nothing, don't worry about it. Just give me the programmer.'

'It *isn't* nothing,' said Russell, gently easing Bobby Boy aside. 'It's a . . . it's a . . .'

'It's a UFO,' sighed Bobby Boy. 'But it's *my* UFO.'

'You *built* it?'

'I . . . er, acquired it.'

'You stole it.'

'Technically speaking, yes.'

Russell took a few steps forward and stared up at the UFO. It wasn't really a UFO. Which is to say that it *was*, but also it *wasn't*. A UFO is an unidentified flying object and this object was clearly identifiable. It was clearly identifiable as the thing it was, which was, to say, a flying saucer. But then a flying saucer would qualify as a UFO. Many consider these to be one and the same. Russell was one of these.

'A flying saucer,' Russell whistled, and it *was* as James Campbell would say, 'the full Adamski'. About fifteen feet in diameter, standing upon the traditional tripod legs. The neat little dome at the top. Several portholes. An open hatch, a nifty extendible ladder (now extended).

This flying saucer varied from others which have been reported over the years, in the fact that it had certain markings on the side. Not cryptic symbols of a possibly Venusian nature, but symbols Russell recognized at once. And the recognition of them put the wind up him something awful.

'It's not *strictly* a flying saucer,' said Bobby Boy. 'It's a *Flügelrad*.'

'A German word,' whispered Russell. 'And those symbols are—'

'Swastikas, yes. They still have the power to put the wind up you, don't they?'

'Yes, they do.' Russell shook his head slowly. 'This is old, isn't it? All the nuts and bolts and stuff. I mean, it looks as though it was built years ago. And yet it looks brand new.'

'If I tell you all about how I got it, will you give me the programmer?' Bobby Boy had a reedy little voice. A real whiner, it was. If his appearance said, *tricky*, then so did his voice. Well, it didn't actually *say* 'tricky', but it *was. Tricky*, that is.

'If I consider that you've told me the truth,' said Russell.

'Tricky,' said Bobby Boy's mouth.

'Would you like to have a go at it?'

Bobby Boy's mouth made little smacking sounds. Tricky little smacking sounds. 'All right,' said he. 'I will tell you everything. Exactly how it happened. Shit, I've been dying to tell some-one, but I just couldn't. I didn't know who I could trust.'

'You can trust me,' said Russell.

'Yes,' agreed Bobby Boy. 'You *can* be trusted, Russell. So if I tell you, I want you to promise me you'll not tell anyone else.'

'Well . . .' said Russell.

'That's the deal. Hurry now, before I change my mind.'

Russell, who had felt sure that *he* had the upper hand, now felt that somehow he didn't. 'All right,' he said, 'I swear.'

'OK, come on into my office and sit down. This will take a bit of telling.'

'All right,' said Russell once more and followed the long thin fellow in black.

The office was suitably grim. Suitably grim for *what*, was anyone's guess. But suitably grim, it certainly was. There was a wretched desk, two terrible chairs, a carpet that didn't bear thinking about. And a great many film posters up on the walls. These were grim, being Fudgepacker productions. Russell spied these out at once.

'Those are from the Emporium,' he said. 'You nicked those.'

'I've saved them from mouldering away in that mausoleum. Movies are my life, Russell, you know that.'

'I know that you want to be a movie star, yes.'

'And I'm going to be. The biggest that ever there was, now you've brought the programmer. Oh yes indeed.'

Bobby Boy dropped onto one of the terrible chairs, which let out a terrible groan. Russell settled uncomfortably onto the other.

'Do you want a drink?' asked Bobby Boy.

'Yes, actually I do.'

Bobby Boy produced a bottle of Scotch and a pair of glasses from a desk drawer.

Russell viewed the label on the Scotch bottle. It was *Glen Boleskine*. The very expensive stuff that Mr Fudgepacker kept in his drinks cupboard for favoured clients. Russell raised an eyebrow.

'Look, Russell,' said Bobby Boy, 'there's no point in beating about the bush. I'm dishonest, I know it. Always have been and probably always will be. My father was dishonest and so was my grandfather before him. Actually my grandfather was an interesting man, did you know that he knew the exact moment he was going to die?'

'Get away?' said Russell, accepting a glass of stolen Scotch.

'Yes, the judge told him.'

'That isn't funny.'

'No, but it's true.'

Russell sipped the Scotch. He'd never tasted it before, although he'd always wanted to and he *did* have ready access to the drinks cupboard. It tasted very good.

'So,' said Bobby Boy, 'I will tell you the story, which you promise you will divulge to no-one and you will give me the programmer.'

'All right,' said Russell, tasting further Scotch.

'All right,' Bobby Boy took out a packet of cigarettes, removed one, placed it in his tricky mouth and lit up. Blowing smoke in Russell's direction, he began the telling of his tale.

'It was about a week ago—'

'Which day?' asked Russell.

'What do you mean, *which day*?'

'I mean,' said Russell, 'Which day *exactly*. I want the truth from the very beginning.'

'Thursday,' said Bobby Boy.

'Truly?'

'All right, it was Wednesday. It doesn't matter.'

'It does. Go on.'

'It was last Wednesday. I had the day off because I was sick.'

'I bet you weren't *really* sick.'

'All right, OK, I wasn't *really* sick. Look, do you want to hear this or not?'

'Go on,' Russell finished his glass of Scotch and reached out for a refill. Bobby Boy gave him a small one.

'It was last Wednesday and I was off work, skiving. Actually I'd gone to an audition. I *had*, truly. They were casting for a movie based on one of the Lazlo Woodbine thrillers. *Death Wore a Motorhead T-shirt*, adapted from the book *Death Wore a Green Tuxedo*. I was hoping to get the part of third-menacing-hood-in-alleyway. I didn't get it though. They said I didn't look tricky enough. Anyway I didn't get back until quite late and I was taking a short cut across the allotments, checking the sheds to make sure they were all locked up properly.'

Russell raised an eyebrow once more.

'They *were*, as it happens. When out of the blue, or the black really, as it was quite late at night, comes this god-awful racket. Like engines failing. I thought it must be a plane about to crash. And I remember thinking, that's handy, because I could help.'

Russell raised the other eyebrow.

'All right. Well it didn't sound like a big

aircraft. A light aircraft. Maybe carrying drugs or something. But it wasn't an aircraft. I looked all around and I couldn't see anything. Then out of the black, out of absolutely nowhere, in fact, that thing in the hangar. That *Flügelrad* materializes in the air about twenty feet in front of me and crashes right down onto the ground. I nearly shat myself, I can tell you. And I ran. I won't say I didn't. You'd have run. I ran for a bit and then I thought, *Roswell*. Alien autopsies. Video rights. What would a dead alien be worth? You'd have thought the same.'

Russell shook his head.

'No, you wouldn't have thought the same. But I thought it, so I crept back and hid and watched. And after a while the hatch opens and the ladder comes down and then out they come. Not aliens, like I was expecting, but Nazi soldiers. SS blokes, all the uniforms and everything, and they climb down and look around. Looking really baffled. And then there's all this shouting in German, like ranting. And I thought, I've heard that voice and then—'

'Adolf Hitler got out,' said Russell.

'Adolf Hitler got – What do you mean? How did you know *that*?'

'A lucky guess?'

'Hm. Well, it *was* him, Russell. It really was. Looking exactly the same as he did in the pictures.'

'I believe you,' said Russell. 'I *really* do.'

'Blimey,' said Bobby Boy. 'Well, it *was* him. And he gets out and climbs down the ladder and shouts at these SS blokes and they shrug and continue to look baffled. And one goes back in and gets a map or something. And they study this and then they all march off. And I watch them go and when they're well away into the distance, I creep over and have a shifty inside. Wait until you see it. It's all old radio valves and dials and turncocks and levers. So I'm inside and I'm wondering what to do. It seems as if this thing's crash landed and I think, well, should I pull out a few bits so it can't be mended and phone the newspapers and do a deal? I mean, well, this has to be news, doesn't it? So I'm tinkering about, wondering which bit to remove when I twiddle this dial and the next thing that happens is the ladder retracts, the hatch snaps shut and the whole thing shakes like crazy. And once again I have to hold onto my guts.'

Russell had finished his second stolen Scotch and he rattled his glass on the desk top. Bobby Boy poured another small measure into it.

'So I'm thinking, Get out before the frigging thing blows up. But then the rattling stops, the hatch opens again and the ladder goes down. So I rush out. And this is where it gets weird.'

'Oh, *this* is where it gets weird.'

'This is where it gets *really* weird. You see, it isn't night any more. Only a few minutes have passed inside the *Flügelrad* but outside it's daytime. And it isn't the *next* daytime either. Oh no. When I take a look outside, everything's different. The *Flügelrad*—'

'Why do you keep calling it that?'

'Because that's what it is. I found the instruction manual and notes and stuff. I got a German dictionary from the library.'

'They don't let you take out dictionaries, they're in the reference section.'

'I nicked one, all right? But I managed to do a translation. But that's later on, let me tell you what happened next. I get out and I'm not on the allotment any more. Well, I am. I am where the allotment used to be. Now it's a park. A nice park and all around it are these smart new houses. But they're futuristic houses. I'm in the future, Russell.'

Russell made the face that says, *Yeah, right!* without actually saying it.

'OK, I didn't know it *then*. The *Flügelrad* has landed in amongst a load of bushes and it's pretty well hidden. I'm standing up on the dome looking around, so I figure that as I'm here, wherever I am, I might as well have a look round. So I get out and take a walk. I cross the park and I go out into the street. And the first thing I see is The Bricklayer's Arms. It's hardly changed. Except for the name on it, now it's called The Flying Swan, and the road isn't the Ealing Road any more, now it's the something-strazzer or something.

'German name, right? I'm pretty shaken up by this, as you can understand, but I go walkabout.

And up where the Great West Road should be, there's this huge shopping centre. Huge. Oh yeah, Russell, and there's cars. Flying cars, I kid you not. Volkswagens they are. But sort of souped up and flying. Landing in car parks on top of the shopping centre.'

'What about people?' Russell asked.

'Yeah, there's people. They look pretty hot. Tall and blond, really well dressed. The women have these golden scaly dresses. The men have the futuristic uniforms, like *Star Trek*, but they've got swastikas on them. Freaky, right? Well, I'm pretty sure now that I must be in the future, but I know there's one way to find out – because they always do it in the movies – find a newspaper shop and check the date. Well, there's no newspaper shop, because there's no newspapers.'

'So how did you find out?'

'I'm coming to that. I'm all in my black, right, like I always am. Because it suits me so well, as you know.'

Russell nodded, although he didn't agree.

'Well, as I'm walking along the street, blokes keep saluting me, flapping their right palms up, like the short Nazi salute. So I keep saluting back, and I stop one bloke and I say excuse me, like. And he snaps to attention and looks really worried and I ask him the date.'

'You just asked him the date?'

'Yeah, well actually it was a pretty stupid thing

to do, but it was all so freaky and I couldn't think of anything else.'

'And he told you?'

'He like barked it out. "Twenty-third of May." What year? I ask. "2045," he says, and "Sir". "Very good," said I, and he salutes again and off he goes.'

'Ludicrous,' said Russell. 'That never happened to Reece in *The Terminator*.'

'That was just a movie, Russell.'

'Oh yes of course, and your experience was real life. My mistake.'

'Do you want some more Scotch?'

'Yes please.'

Bobby Boy poured another short measure. 'Well, he told me and he saluted and off he went. I went off to the shopping centre. The stuff in the shops seemed mostly as you'd expect. Clothes, things like that. Except in the gift shops there were all these posters and mugs and plates and things, all with Hitler on them. Whole shops that sold nothing else. I didn't go in any of those. But I came across this one shop that really interested me, it was like a Tandys, but it had some German name. It was an electrical shop, right, TVs, hi-fis. Shit, Russell, you should have seen the gear they had. Computer games like you wouldn't believe. Holographic stuff. Kids were in there playing them, sitting on little chairs, but they didn't have those silly virtual reality helmets on, they were right in the middle of the games they were playing, spaceships

121

whizzing past them, laser beams going everywhere. And that's when I saw him.'

'Saw who?'

'Elvis,' said Bobby Boy.

'Oh yes, right.'

'Elvis. And Marilyn Monroe and James Dean, oh and Marlene Dietrich. She was there.'

'Shopping?'

'Not shopping, Russell. Just sort of standing there, chatting.'

'I don't believe you,' said Russell.

'You will, because they weren't real. They were holograms.'

'Oh, I see, go on.' Russell took another sip of Scotch.

'Holograms, so I go into the shop and the bloke behind the counter salutes me and looks edgy. And I have a stroll about and check out these holograms. Movie stars, Russell, it's like I'm standing beside real movie stars. Like my life's ambition, right? And you can't see through them. And the shop bloke comes cringing up and asks if he can help me, so I said, "What's all this then?" And he explains that it's a new computer role-playing game, like a 3D Karaoke. It's called *Cyberstars*. You play a part in a famous movie alongside the stars and someone videos it for you. You're actually *in* the movie, do you understand?'

'Yes, I get the picture.' Russell tittered foolishly.

'You don't want to drink too much of that stuff, it's very strong.'

'I can take it,' said Russell, which was not strictly true. 'Go on, tell me the rest.'

'Right, so I say to this shop bloke, "Give us a go", and he says, "What movie do you want to be in, sir?" And I say, "What have you got?" And he flashes up lists on his computer terminal and I've never heard of any of these movies, they're all about The Glorious Fatherland and The Freedom of The State and stuff like that. And I say, "I don't know any of these", and then he gets really edgy and I say, "Can the Cyberstar holograms be programmed to, like, do anything, not play parts in a film, just do what you wanted them to do?"'

'Why would you ask that?'

'Because I've always wanted to shag Marilyn Monroe, Russell, that's why. Imagine that on video.'

'I can't and I don't want to.'

'You've no imagination.'

'I have, but it's not like yours.'

'Yeah, well. But the bloke says yes. And I'm thinking, If I could acquire one of these computers and get it back into my own time, imagine that.'

Russell tried to, but he couldn't quite.

'Millions of pounds,' said Bobby Boy. 'Make a movie starring all the golden greats, all the *dead* golden greats, and myself of course. Imagine *that.*'

Russell thought he could imagine that. Slightly.

'So I asked the bloke, "How much?" And he says, "Free to you, sir, of course." *Of course!*

123

I've gone to heaven, right? This bloke is going to give me the technology that can make me a world-famous movie star, if I can get it back home, of course, for *nothing*. For *free*! So I say, "Right, absolutely, thank you very much." And he packs me up a system and gives it to me. Then he says, "Please eyeball the screen." And I say, "*What?*" And he shows me this little screen on the counter and says, "Eyeball." So I give it a look in and make for the door. Then the bloody world goes mad. Well, madder. All those alarms go off and lights start flashing. So I run like a bastard. I run. I run out of the shopping centre and back up what was once the Ealing Road. And this black car drops out of the sky and these bloody great metal things, like robots, get out and they come after me. I do have to say this, Russell, and I wouldn't tell just anyone. I shit my pants.'

Russell burst into what can only be described as drunken laughter.

'Yeah, you can laugh, but if you'd ever seen these monsters.'

Russell stopped laughing. He *had* seen them, chasing after the beautiful gold-clad blonde at The Ape of Thoth. 'Go on,' he said.

'I ran. Like I say. Back to the *Flügelrad*. I lost the big black monsters in the park and I got back on board. But I didn't know what to do. I didn't know how you worked the thing. I didn't have the driver's manual.'

'Driver's manual,' Russell began to laugh again.

'Stop bloody laughing. You're pissed, you.'

'I'm not pissed. Go on, tell me what happened next. I'm loving all this. Well, *some* of all this.'

'I only wanted to escape. At that moment I didn't care whether it was forwards or backwards. Any time would do. So I started pushing buttons and pulling levers and then there was all this banging on the hull. I pissed myself.'

Russell curled double. 'I bet it didn't half smell in there then.'

'You're not kidding. But I got it going. Somehow I got it going and I got it going into reverse. I know you're going to say, "That's handy." Well it was, I can tell you. And I ended up back here. Right back where I started off from. Except, and this is the good bit, the good bit that got the bloody *Flügelrad* here, into *this* hangar. I got back a day earlier than I set out.'

'That would be the Tuesday,' said Russell.

'That's right,' said Bobby Boy.

'That's wrong,' said Russell.

'No it bloody isn't.'

'Yes it bloody is.'

'Isn't.'

'Is.'

'Is not.'

'It *is*,' said Russell, 'because you were at work on Tuesday.'

'I know,' said Bobby Boy. 'I saw me. I peeped through the window and actually saw me.'

'This is all lies,' said Russell. 'Although . . .'

125

'I did worry about that,' said Bobby Boy. 'Because there were two of me then. And I thought how can that work? Will there always be two of me now?'

'And are there?' Russell reached for the bottle. Bobby Boy drew it beyond his reach.

'No, the other one caught up, you see.'

'I don't think that would work.'

'Who cares what *you* think?'

'Good point.' Russell creased up again.

'I got back before Hitler and his henchmen had arrived, so I had time, you see. Time on *my* side. So I covered the *Flügelrad* up with branches and corrugated iron and stuff and I went off and borrowed Leo Felix's pick up.'

'You nicked it.'

'I didn't nick it, as it happens. He's a mate, he lent it to me.'

'And you hoisted up the *Flügelrad* and brought it here?'

'That's what I did.'

'Well,' said Russell, 'I don't know what to say really.'

'You could say, "What a hero you are, Bobby Boy."'

'I could,' said Russell. 'But I'm not going to. So what happened next, or is that the end?'

'No, it's not quite the end. Having got the old *Flügelrad* here and having had a shower and changed my trousers, I set about rigging up the Cyberstar equipment.'

'Er, just one thing,' said Russell. 'You brought the *Flügelrad* here. But who owns this hangar, anyway?'

'I do.'

'*You* do?'

'My dad gave it to me for my eighteenth birthday, it was going to be my own film studio.'

'Oh yeah,' said Russell. 'Your dad owns the brewery, doesn't he? But I thought you and he—'

'Had a bit of a falling out. Yes, he's cut me out of his will and everything. I don't want to talk about that.'

'Sorry I mentioned it. Go on about the Cyberstar equipment.'

'Yeah, well, I unpacked it and set it up and plugged it in and read the instructions and then . . .'

'Then?'

'Then I find that the bloody programmer is missing. It's not in the box. I can't get the thing to work.'

'That's tough,' said Russell. 'After all you'd been through, so dishonestly and everything.'

'Up yours, Russell. So I thought, Well, there's nothing for it, I'll just have to zap forward to 2045 again and acquire a programmer.'

'So you won't need the one I've got then.'

'Oh yes I will, because I can't get the *Flügelrad* to work any more. I think it's out of fuel or whatever. I was going to have another crack at it tonight, then you showed up.'

'And you tried to stave my head in with a length of piping.'

'Yeah, well, you could have been anyone, you could have been—'

'I could have been Hitler, or one of his henchmen.'

'You're damn right. But all's ended well. Give me the programmer please, Russell.' Bobby Boy stuck out his hand.

Russell moved beyond its range and gave his nose a bit of a scratch. It was a tad numb, was that nose. 'I don't know,' he said slowly.

'What do you mean, you don't know? I've told you the story and you agreed to give me the programmer. What is there to know?'

'Quite a bit, as it happens. Like the circumstances by which I came by this.'

'You're pissed, Russell.'

'Just a bit, just a bit. But how I came by the programmer, that was very strange. There had to be a reason why it was given to *me* personally. I'm involved in this, or I'm *going* to be involved in this.'

Bobby Boy nodded his long thin head. 'I'll tell you what, Russell, *don't* give it to me.'

'What?' asked Russell.

'Just *lend* it to me. You keep possession of it, right? It's *yours*, right? But you just give me a lend of it.'

'I suppose that couldn't do any harm.' Russell rattled his glass and Bobby Boy hastened to refill it. To the top.

'So, we have a deal. We'll be partners if you want. Like Merchant and Ivory, or Metro, Goldwyn and Mayer, or, er . . .'

'Pearl and Dean?' Russell suggested. 'Russell and Bob, we could call ourselves.'

'Or, Bob and Russell.'

'I like Russell and Bob best.'

'Look it doesn't bloody matter, Russell. There'll be millions of pounds knocking about for both of us. I'll draw up a contract.'

'*I'll* draw up a contract.'

'We'll both draw up a contract together. Now, if you will kindly *lend* me your programmer, I'll show you something you'll never forget.'

Russell knocked back his glass of Scotch, fell off his chair and said, 'Can I use your toilet first?'

# CHAPTER 10

# MONEY MAKES THE WORLD
# GO AROUND. TAKE 1

It certainly *was* something Russell would never forget. And not just the one something, loads of separate somethings. Bobby Boy set up the Cyberstar equipment, took the programmer and fiddled about with it. It was a bit like one of those radio-control things, with a joy stick and switches to work the arms and legs of the holograms and a throat mic, so that when you spoke, what you said came out of the hologram's mouth in *their* voice. It was truly amazing. And the holograms were truly amazing. They looked so damn real. Bobby Boy had a video camera on a stand and they took it in turns to act alongside the golden greats of Hollywood. Bobby Boy squared up against Sylvester Stallone (in his Rocky persona) and knocked him out in a single round. Russell danced with Ginger Rogers. They did excerpts from everything from *The Fall of the House of Usher* to *The Sound of Music*. Songs from the shows and laughter echoed around Hangar 18 and tape after tape went in and out of the camcorder.

It was five in the morning when Russell staggered

home to collapse onto his bed. It was three in the afternoon when he woke up.

And he did not feel at all well. Russell looked at his bedside clock and a strangulated cry escaped his parched lips.

Late for work. He was late for work! He'd never been late for work in his life. He'd let the side down, let his work mates down, this was terrible. *Terrible!*

Russell dragged his legs from the bed and put his head in his hands. He'd really screwed up here. How irresponsible. He'd have to apologize to everyone. Perhaps he should take Mr Fudgepacker a bottle of his favourite Scotch, after all . . .

Russell groaned. He'd spent the night drinking stolen Scotch, mucking about with stolen technology, recording it all on what was just bound to be a stolen camcorder. He was a bona fide criminal. Terrible. *Terrible!*

The room went in and out of focus. Somehow more terrible, were all those unanswered questions. What *was* going to happen? How did it involve the barmaid from The Bricklayer's Arms? How had she been in the future, and where was she now? Was she safe? Had those clanking things caught up with her? And what about Hitler? That human fiend was abroad on the streets of Brentford. And streets of Brentford that would one day be given German names, in a future run by the Nazis. Terrible hardly seemed a strong enough word. If Russell could have come up with a stronger one, he would have.

'I have to get to work.' Russell tried to rise, but sank back onto his bed. 'Oh God. What have I done?'

Fallen from a state of grace in a big, big way. That was what.

With much groaning and moaning and many a sideways stagger, Russell left his bedroom, then his house and bumbled off towards Fudgepacker's.

The day was another sunny one. Brentford, as usual, was breaking all the records when it came to hot summers. Across the river, the rain poured down on Kew and in the distance, a heavy fog lay over Chiswick. You couldn't see Hounslow from where Russell was bumbling along, but it was odds on that snow was falling there.

Russell pushed upon the big church door and found that it would not open. Russell pushed again. No go.

'What's going on?' Russell asked himself.

There was a note nailed to the big church door. It wasn't the one Martin Luther had nailed up several centuries before. That one was inside in a showcase. This was a new note. It was written in Frank's handwriting. It read:

CLOSED FOR BUSINESS.
IN CASE OF EMERGENCY
PLEASE CONTACT FRANK AT
THE BRICKLAYER'S ARMS

'What?' went Russell. 'What is all this?'

It was a shame that he hadn't been told, what with him having just walked by The Bricklayer's Arms, and everything.

Russell tried to turn upon his heel, but he couldn't quite manage it this time, so he sort of stumbled in a circle, then set to trudging.

Sounds of much merriment came from The Bricklayer's Arms. Russell pushed upon the door and it opened without a fuss. As he lurched inside a big cheer went up.

'Eh?' went Russell.

'For he's a jolly good fellow,' sang a crowd of merrymakers. Russell viewed these with his blood-shot eyes. As they went in and out of focus he could make out Bobby Boy and Morgan and Frank and old Ernest, and a few production buyers he hadn't seen for a while. *And* the blonde barmaid. Julie, wasn't it?

Russell went 'eh?' once more as old Ernest came hobbling over.

'You are a genius, my boy,' said old Ernest, feebly patting Russell on the back. 'And when I say genius, I know what I'm talking about. There's inspired and there's genius, inspired is all well and good, but genius is genius. And I should know, I—'

'What is going on?' Russell asked.

Old Ernest turned to the crowd, who raised glasses to Russell. 'He asks what's going on, the

133

boy who's saved the company. The genius. Have a drink, have a drink. Champagne, Julie my darling, more champagne.'

Ernest patted Russell towards the bar.

'I am perplexed,' Russell said.

Bobby Boy grinned at him. 'Such modesty.'

'What?'

'I told them everything,' said Bobby Boy. 'About *your* invention.'

'My what?'

'Your invention. Your *holographic* invention, the Cyberstar system, that *you* invented. The one you demonstrated to me last night.'

'*Me?*'

Bobby Boy made the face that says, 'Go along with this, I'll explain everything later,' without actually saying it.

'Oh,' said Russell. '*That* invention.'

'*That* invention, yes. And how we discussed its applications and who we should get to direct this movie that is going to be the biggest blockbusting movie ever made. Apart from the sequel, of course. And how *you* suggested Mr Fudgepacker as the director.'

'Oh,' said Russell. And it was a low 'Oh,' a kind of low groaning kind of an 'Oh'. He hadn't suggested any such thing. Although he did recall going on at Bobby Boy about how he wanted to help out Mr Fudgepacker.

'So we're all celebrating.'

'Yes,' said Russell. 'So you are.'

134

'And I *really* want to thank you,' said the blonde beauty behind the bar.

'*You* do?' Russell tried to focus his eyes upon her and succeeded with next to no effort at all.

'Giving me a lead role, I've always wanted to be in the movies.'

Russell glanced towards Bobby Boy, who raised his eyebrows and his glass. 'Cheers,' said Bobby Boy.

'Do you want some champagne, Russell?' asked the barmaid.

'No,' said Russell. 'Just a Perrier water. And a sandwich.'

'Coming right up.' The beautiful barmaid gave Russell such a smile that he began to tingle all over. Most pleasantly.

Bobby Boy stuck his tricky little mouth close by Russell's ear. 'Don't thank me now,' he said.

'So,' smiled Frank, giving Russell a pat on the back. 'Prop man, brilliant.'

'Prop man?' Russell asked.

'Thank you very much,' said Frank. 'Making me a prop man again. It will be just like the old days at Pinewood. These holograms of yours, do they smoke? Because I'd really like to light Marilyn Monroe's cigarette.'

'I'm sure that could be arranged.'

'You're a gent,' said Morgan, patting Russell on the parts that Frank wasn't patting. The 'back' parts, nothing more personal. 'Promotion.'

'Promotion?'

135

'Well, I'm in charge of the Emporium now, manager. Now Frank's going to be the prop man for the movie.'

'Oh, yes, right.'

'Perrier and sandwiches, Russell.' Julie placed a glass in Russell's hand and pushed a splendid plate of sandwiches towards him. 'If there's anything else you want, all you have to do is whistle. Whistle, eh? Like thingy in that film.'

'*To Have and Have Not*,' said Frank. 'Lauren Bacall, I hailed a cab for her once.'

'Sure you didn't *drive* it?' asked old Ernest. 'You talk like a bleeding cabbie.'

Russell sipped at his Perrier water. 'Hang about,' he said suddenly. 'Mr Fudgepacker is directing, Morgan is running the company, Frank is prop man, Bobby Boy is—'

'Starring,' said Bobby Boy. 'What else?'

'What else, right. So what am *I* doing in all this?'

'You're producing,' said Bobby Boy. 'You're the producer.'

'Oh,' said Russell. 'The producer. That's really important, isn't it?'

'About as important as it can be.'

'Apart from the director,' said Ernest. 'But then the director could never direct if the producer didn't produce.'

'Well,' said Russell. 'That is pretty good and important, isn't it?'

'You're right,' said Ernest. 'You're so right. You genius.'

Glasses were raised once more and another verse of 'For He's a Jolly Good Fellow' was sung. It was the same verse as the first verse. As 'For He's a Jolly Good Fellow' only has the one verse. And the chorus, of course, which is 'And so say all of us'.

'Thank you,' said Russell. 'Thank you all very much.'

'No, thank *you*,' said the 'all of us'.

'Er, Bobby Boy?' said Russell, sipping Perrier and munching on a sandwich that contained *fresh* ham. 'What *exactly* does a producer do?'

'He raises the money to make the picture.'

'Oh,' said Russell. 'That's what he does.'

'That's what he does.'

'And how does he do *that? Exactly?*'

'He finds backers to invest in the picture. Sort of buy shares. They get a percentage of the take afterwards. Should be an absolute piece of cake, considering what *we* have to offer. What about last night, eh? You and Elvis, eh? What a duet.'

'Oh yes, I'd forgotten about Elvis.'

'So that's what you do. You're a hero, Russell.' Bobby Boy now spoke in a confidential tone, which is to say, a whisper. 'I've let *you* take all the credit. Well, I couldn't tell them the truth, could I? They'd never have believed it, but this way it will work, I showed Ernest the videos and he went for it. It'll save his company and everyone's jobs. And we'll get rich in the process. You *are* a hero.'

'A hero.' Russell grinned. 'Thanks a lot. A hero, well. My goodness.'

'There you go,' said Bobby Boy. 'You deserve it, you've got it.'

'Thanks a *big* lot.'

'No problem.'

'Right. Here, Bobby Boy. One thing. As producer it is all *my* responsibility, right? I mean the movie can't be made unless *I* get the money, right?'

'Right.'

'So how much money do *I* need to raise?'

Bobby Boy stroked his long thin chin. 'About forty million pounds should cover it,' he said.

The crowd sort of parted as Russell fell down. But they gathered about him and they looked all concerned. They looked *very* concerned, after all, he *was* the producer.

'Are you all right, Russell?' they went. 'Speak to us, are you all right?'

# CHAPTER 11

# MONEY MAKES THE WORLD GO AROUND. TAKE 2

Russell's bank manager eyed him through the long-distance section of his bi-focals. 'Forty million pounds, you say?' said he.

'Give or take,' said Russell. 'We haven't worked out all the details yet.'

'I see.' The bank manager took up a sheet of paper, which is called in the trade, a 'statement', and ran his eyes up and down it. 'You have one thousand one hundred and one pounds and one penny in your account,' said he. 'Quite a memorable sort of sum really.'

'My life savings,' said Russell. 'To buy my mum a stair lift. I've almost enough.'

'And according to the records, you've never had an overdraft.'

'I wouldn't dream of such a thing.'

'Dream of such a thing, no, I suppose you wouldn't.'

'Not me,' said Russell.

'Not you, no. But . . .' The bank manager made 'ahem' noises. 'You wish me to advance you a loan of forty million pounds?'

139

'We've tried elsewhere. My associate, Bobby Boy, called Hollywood. He tried to speak to Mr Spielberg. But Mr Spielberg didn't phone back. And Walt Disney's dead, apparently. Although "Walt Disney" continues to produce films. I don't quite understand that.'

'I don't think you quite understand about finance at all, do you?'

'Not a lot,' said Russell. 'But you *have* seen the videos. You can surely see the potential.'

'Ah, the videos, yes. The ones with you beating Arnold Schwarzenegger at the arm wrestling contest.'

'That was a good one, wasn't it?'

'Very inspired, yes. You seemed a bit—'

'Drunk,' said Russell. 'Yes I was drunk, I admit it. But you'd have been drunk, if you'd been there, realized the potential and everything.'

'I don't drink,' said the bank manager. 'I am Plymouth Brethren. We do *not* drink. Neither do we loan out forty million pounds to drunkards.'

'Wasn't Aleister Crowley Plymouth Brethren?' asked Russell.

'Get out of my bank,' said the bank manager. 'And don't come back.'

'What about the loan?'

'We don't swear either,' said the bank manager, 'but in your case I am prepared to make an exception.'

'Well thank you for your time,' said Russell. 'I'll be going now.'

★   ★   ★

Russell trudged a bit more. Along the streets of Brentford. Nobody was *really* going to lend him forty million pounds. That was ludicrous. In fact, everything about this was ludicrous. Forty million pounds! Movie making! Holograms and time travellers! Ludicrous. It was like some plot from a really daft book. Like one of those Pooley and Omally yarns. Not real life at all. Nonsense.

Nonsense? Russell ceased his trudging upon a street corner. What *was* all this? What had he got himself involved in? It had all started out with his quest to locate The Flying Swan, to see whether Neville and Pooley and Omally really existed. And now *he, Russell*, Mr Ordinary, Mr Common Sense, had got involved in something as ludicrous as the things Pooley and Omally had supposedly got themselves involved in, in some mythical Brentford past.

Was it something about this place? About this town?

Russell sighed. It was something. But people were now relying on him. Old Ernest. Everyone at Fudgepacker's. Jobs were at stake. The company would go under if he didn't pull this off, it was *his* responsibility. And the technology *was* true. It *did* work. You really could make a movie with it. And one that would sell big time.

The forty million was a problem though.

Forty million!

'Forty million,' said Russell. 'Hang about, we

don't need forty million. We don't need any millions at all. All we need is a camera and some lights. We're not paying anything for the stars, they're holograms. Bobby Boy and Julie can act and get paid later. Everyone can get paid later, out of the profits. A camera and some lights, that's all we need. We can do the show right here. Bobby Boy has the studio, Ernest has the props.' Of course they didn't actually have a script. But they could work *that* out. *Forty million pounds!* That was just Bobby Boy trying to line his pockets.

'We can do this,' said Russell. 'This we can do.'

Russell returned to Fudgepacker's Emporium with a spring in his step. Bobby Boy was up in old Ernest's office. They were drinking the expensive Scotch.

'Wot-ho!' said Ernest, upon Russell's entry. 'Do you have the scratch?'

'Not as such,' said Russell.

'Well, you want to hurry on up. Bobby Boy and I are almost finished on the script.'

'You are?'

'We are. And this is a killer. Blood and guts and sex and splatter. But with a strong social comment, or content, or something.'

'And lots of bits to make your eyes water,' said Bobby Boy. 'As in weep. At the pathos.'

'I can't raise the money,' said Russell. 'No-one will lend *me* forty million. It's too much. The bank manager was really rude, he told me to, well, he wasn't interested.'

'Then we're all doomed,' said Ernest Fudge-packer. 'The company goes down like the *Titanic*. Everyone is ruined. Shame and misery. How will you ever be able to live with yourself? I know I couldn't.'

'We don't need the money,' said Russell.

'We don't?' said Ernest. 'That's a very silly thing to say. And I should know, I say some very silly things myself.'

'We don't need the money,' Russell reiterated. (Reiterated, I ask you!) 'If we borrow forty million, then we have to pay back forty million, plus a percentage. If we *don't* borrow anything at all, then we don't have anything at all to pay back. *All* the profits are ours.'

'I *do* like the sound of *that*,' said Ernest. 'But how do you make a movie with no finance?'

'Well, we'll need *some* finance, just enough to pay for a camera and film and some lights.'

'No problem,' said Ernest. 'I know chaps in the trade, I could hire all that.'

'And the only actors will be Bobby Boy here and Julie, the only actors we have to *pay*.'

'This really isn't the way movies are made,' said Ernest. 'But this *is* going to be a very special movie. Let me make a couple of phone calls.'

'Hold on there!' cried Bobby Boy. '*I'm* in this! And *I'm* going to be starring alongside the Hollywood greats. I want paying and I want paying big time. Proper Hollywood fees, I won't work for less than five million. That's not a lot to ask.'

Ernest scratched at his old head, raising flecks of scalp that drifted all about the little office, sort of dangled in the air, most unpleasantly. 'I can appreciate that,' he said. 'A labourer is worthy of his hire, and things of a likewise nature. But that's not down to me, of course, I'm *only* the director. That's down to Russell. And it's Russell's technology we're using and Russell *is* the producer.'

Bobby Boy glared daggers at Russell. Big daggers, they were, and sharp with it.

Russell didn't glare any back. He did grin at Ernest though. Ernest had really changed. He wasn't rambling any more. He was focused. *Dead* focused. Russell really felt for the old fellow. He felt that he would *not*, under any circumstances, let him down.

And he saw Ernest wink a big magnified eye.

'I *am* the producer,' said Russell. 'So the finances *are* my responsibility.'

'Of course if you're not happy, Bobby Boy,' said Ernest, 'I suppose you could quit. Walk off the set, as it were. We could possibly get in a replacement. Perhaps Russell here might care to star as well as produce.'

'Well—' said Russell.

'Only joking,' said Bobby Boy. 'Of course Russell is in charge, the financial responsibilities are all his. What he says goes.'

'Well put,' said Ernest. 'I'll get on the phone then.'

And he did. He phoned this fellow and the next, struck this deal and the next and when this, that and the next deal had been struck, he put down the telephone and smiled up at Russell. 'We're rocking and rolling,' he said. 'I can hire us a camera, panavision of course, absolute below-the-line discount, get us lights and get us film. We can shoot the whole thing right here, on location, in Brentford and in Bobby Boy's studio.'

'Brilliant,' said Russell. 'I knew we could do it.'

'We certainly can. All I'll need is a cheque.'

'A cheque?' said Russell.

'A cheque from you. Well, *I* don't have any money, do I? And *you* are the producer, taking full financial responsibilities.'

Bobby Boy grinned evilly.

Russell made that groaning 'Oh' sound once more. 'How much?' he asked.

'One thousand, one hundred and one pounds, and one penny,' said Ernest. 'Quite a memorable sum. Really.'

# CHAPTER 12

# MORE OF THAT BOX 23 BUSINESS

And so it came to pass that Russell's mother didn't get her stair lift. She didn't get it, but she didn't mind. She didn't mind because she had no idea that Russell intended to buy her one and even if she had known, she still wouldn't have minded.

She was dead nice, was Russell's mum. Much of Russell's niceness came from her side of the family. So she wouldn't have minded. And not only because she was nice, but also because she lived in a bungalow.

Of course Russell's one thousand, one hundred and one pounds and fifty pence (no longer such a memorable sum as it had earned a bit of interest) was *not* going to finance the making of an entire movie. Russell would have to come up with a lot more than that. But being Russell and being nice and being a hard worker (and everything), he *would* come up with it. But not at this precise moment.

At this precise moment I would like to relate to you a tale told to me by a close friend of mine. He told me this tale in response to me telling him the one my Uncle John told to me, about the man who wasn't really a man at all.

The reason for the telling of this tale is that it plays a large part in what will shortly occur to Russell. And even if it didn't, it's a real raging stonker of a story.

My close friend's name is Mr Sean O'Reilly and I know what you're going to say, 'Oh yeah right, Bob. *Sean O'Reilly!*' But he *is* a real person and it *is* his real name and being a Sean O'Reilly *is not* without its problems.

For instance, a couple of weeks back he was having a night out in Brighton. The final bell had gone and no more orders were being taken at the bar. Sean, for whom the night was yet young, set off in search of a club with more civilized licensing hours, where music played and ladies of negotiable affections might be found. And he came across the Shamrock Club.

Now being of Irish descent, and being a Mr Sean O'Reilly, he reasoned that a welcome would lie within for him and proceeded to engage in friendly chit chat with the bouncer (or 'door-supervisor' as he preferred to be called). This able-bodied fellow agreed to waive the usual formalities, accept a five pound gratuity for so doing and sign Sean in as a member.

'Phwat is yer nam?' enquired the door-supervisor.

'My name is Sean O'Reilly,' said Sean O'Reilly, and was promptly booted from the premises on the grounds that he was 'taking the piss'.

147

It's not much of a story, I know. But it's a true one and the trouble with true ones is that they never usually amount to very much. The one Sean told me, however, in response to the one I told him, is a different kettle of carp altogether. It is a strange and sinister story and again the warning is issued to those of a nervous disposition, those wimpy individuals who get squeamish about watching a snuff movie or a live execution (hard to believe, I know), that now would be the time to flick on forward to the next chapter.

Right, well now we've got rid of that lot, on with the gory stuff.

At the time Sean heard all the gory stuff of which this tale is composed, he was sitting in the casualty department at Brighton General. Sean had been working as a roofer, and, as anyone who has ever worked as a roofer will tell you, roofers periodically fall off roofs. It's a sort of perk of the job. Sean had been working on a garage roof and Sean had fallen off and sprained his ankle.

Now, as those who have never worked on, or fallen off roofs, but *have* sat waiting in a casualty department will tell you, about fifty per cent of the other folk sitting there have got sprained ankles. This is not because they are all roofers, you understand, it is because most injuries occur to your extremities. Your hands and feet. A nurse once told this to me, as I sat waiting to have *my* sprained ankle looked at. (I hadn't fallen off a roof, but I'd tripped up in one of the potholes that no-one wants to take responsibility for, in the-lane-that-dare-not-speak-its-name, where I live.)

'It's hands and feet mostly,' she told me. 'And hands and feet are *low priority*, so you'll just have to wait.' Adding, 'Would you care for a copy of *Hello!* magazine to read? It's the one with James Herbert in it.'

Sean *did not* have to wait to have *his* sprained ankle looked at. Because Sean had been tipped off by a friend of his who was a male nurse about how to get seen at once in a casualty department, even if you only have a sprained ankle. Sean passed this tip on to me, and I, in turn, pass it on to you.

The tip is SCREAM!

Scream as loudly as you can and scream continuously. Doctors and nurses can't abide screaming in their waiting-rooms, it upsets them and it makes the other patients uneasy. That's the tip, but keep it to yourself.

So Sean had screamed like a maniac and Sean had been wheeled away to a cubicle and given an injection of something quite nice. And while he lay there, awaiting the results of the X-rays, he overheard a conversation going on in the next cubicle between an old man and a priest. And the substance of this conversation is the substance of Sean's tale, which has a later bearing on Russell.

And what Sean overheard was this.

The old man was groaning a lot and Sean recognized The Last Rites being read. Then the old man spoke.

149

'I must tell you, father,' said the old man. 'Tell it all to you.'

'As you wish, my son.'

'It all began for me some years ago. I was living up North at the time, in the town of H—'

'The town of H—?'

'As in Hamster.'

'Oh, that one, go on then.'

'I was chief wick-dipper at the candle works, a position of considerable responsibility and prestige. Many doors were open to me then, even some with the closed-sign up. But fate being fickle and man ever weak to desires of the flesh, I fell in with a bad crowd and engaged in acts of drunkenness and debauchery.'

'Would you care to enlarge upon these, my son?'

'No, father, I would not.'

'A pity, but go on.'

'My employer was a goodly man who greatly feared God and was rarely to be seen without his hat on. He was the very soul of forgiveness, but even he, for all his God-fearing ways and the wearing of his hat, could not find it in his Christian heart to pardon my wickedness.'

'Was this fellow a Protestant?'

'That he was, father.'

'Shameful, go on with your story.'

'After the episode with the pig he—'

'A pig, did you say?'

'And a modified power tool.'

150

'Was that a Black and Decker?'

'No, just a pig on this occasion.'

'Sure it happens to the best of us, go on.'

'I was stripped of my trappings, my badge of office torn from my bosom, my woggle trampled underfoot.'

'And all for a pig and a modified power tool?'

'Father, would you let me just tell my story? I'm dying here.'

'Go on then, I won't interrupt.'

'Thank you. I was cast out, expelled from The Guild of Candlemakers, a social pariah. Ostracized, a proscribed person. Boycotted, black-balled—'

'*Blackballed?* But I thought you said—'

'Father, will you shut the fuck up?'

'I'm sorry, my son. Go on now, just tell me what happened.'

'I was an outcast, all doors that had previously been open to me were now closed. Even the closed ones were closed. I walked the streets as a man alone, none would offer me ingress.'

'Not even the pig?'

'*Father!*'

'Sorry, go on.'

'I was alone. Alone and unwanted. I would sit for days at a time in the library, poring over the papers in the hope that I might find some gainful employment, no matter how humble. But so foul was the stigma attached to my person that all turned their backs upon me. I was low, father, so low that I even considered returning to the occupation I'd had before I entered candlemaking.'

'And what occupation was that? If you'll forgive me asking.'

'Priest,' said the old man.

'Right,' said the priest.

'But it never came to that, although now I wish that it had. Rather would I have thrown away the last vestiges of my dignity and rejoined the priesthood than—'

'Don't lay it on too thick,' said the priest. 'You might be a dying man, but you'll still get a smack in the gob.'

'I saw this advert, father. In the paper. It said, SELL YOUR SPINE AND LIVE FOR EVER.'

'Would that not be a misprint? Would it not be sell your *soul*?'

'It was SELL YOUR SPINE. There was a telephone number, I rang that number and there was a recorded message. It said that a seminar was to be held that very evening at a particular address and to be there by eight o'clock.'

'And so you went along?'

'Yes, I went along. I don't know why I went along, but I did. Madness. Sell your spine? How could such a thing be? But I went along, oh fool that I was.'

'Should I just be quiet now and let you do all the telling?' asked the priest. 'Build up the atmosphere, and everything.'

'That would be for the best. As I said, I went

along. The seminar was being held in this little chapel affair that was once an Anabaptist hall. It was very run down and all boarded up. The door looked as if it had been forced open and a generator was running the lights. Old school chairs stood in bleak rows, there was a small dais where the altar had been. On the chairs sat a dozen or so folk who were strangers to me, upon the dais stood a tall man dressed in black. He welcomed me upon my entrance and bade me sit down near to the front. And then he spoke. Of many things he spoke, of the wonders of modern medicine and great leaps forward made in the fields of science. He was an evangelist, he said, come to spread the word of a new beginning, that each of us could have a new beginning, cast away our old selves and begin again.

'He had been sent among us, he said, by an American foundation that had made a major breakthrough. It was now possible to extend a person's lifespan. Not for ever, he did admit that, because, as he said, there is no telling exactly how long for ever might be. But he could guarantee at least five hundred years. And how could he guarantee this? Because the special units, constructed to replace the spines that were to be removed, were built to last at least this long.

'He explained that the ageing process was all to do with the spine. Certain genes and proteins manufactured within the spinal column, certain natural poisons, made you grow old. Total

153

spine replacement freed you from ever growing old.

'He talked and he talked and although I did not understand all that he said, there was something in the way he talked, something compelling that made me trust him. And when he had finished I found myself clapping. But I was clapping all alone. The other folk had gone, I'd never heard them go, but they were gone, there was only myself and the man in black.

'He asked me whether I would like to live for another five hundred years and I said yes. I said yes and praise the lord. Yes, father, you may well cross yourself. I said yes and praise the lord and I said, show me, show me.'

'And he showed you?' The priest spoke slowly.

'He led me into a little back room, sat me down upon a chair and then he took off his clothes. In front of me, right there. He removed his jacket and his shirt and then he turned around. And I saw the buttons, father. I saw them.'

'The buttons?'

'On his skin. On his back. The skin, you see, had been cut, from his wrists to the nape of his neck and from there right down the middle of his back. And the skin was turned back and hemmed, as would be the material of a garment and there were buttonholes with buttons through them.'

The priest caught his breath. 'You saw this?'

'I saw it. He was inside a suit of his own skin. Do you see?'

'I see.'

'Do you *want* to see?'

'Want to see?'

'See them, father. See those buttons. See them on *my* back?'

'No . . . I . . . my son, no.'

The old man coughed and the priest mumbled words of Latin.

'I saw his back, father. He explained to me how it was done. How they made a cast of you, of your body and they constructed this perfect replica of you which you climbed into through the back. I don't know, father. Is it my skin on the outside? How much of me is still me? But I saw it and he told me how it was done, how you climbed inside yourself and they removed your spine and buttoned you up and you would live for five hundred years.' The old man coughed hideously. 'You make decisions, father. All through your life, you make decisions, wrong decisions. You can't rewind to the past and remake those decisions, set your life off in a new direction. No-one can do that. I made the wrong decision and now I must die for it.'

The priest spoke prayers as the old man rambled on.

'Why would I have wanted to live for five hundred years? I was out of work. Did I want five hundred years of unemployment? But I was greedy for life. For more life. I said yes, do it to me, give me more life.

155

'I stayed all night with him. I let him make casts of my body. I stood naked before this man whom I'd never seen before. He took photographs of me and samples of my hair and when it was all done, he told me to come back the next evening, that all would be ready then.

'I didn't sleep that day, I was sleeping rough anyway. I just walked around the town, this town that hated me so much. And I thought, Look at these people, they may have jobs, they may be rich, but they will all die, die soon. Not me. I'll outlive the lot of them. I will cheat death. I'll go on into the future. Dance on their graves.'

The priest let out a small sigh.

'And so I went back the next night. The man in black, I didn't even know his name, he took me again into that room and he showed me. He showed me the new me. It was a perfect me, taller, better built, younger-looking, more handsome. It stood there and it was an empty shell. I hadn't eaten, I felt sick and light-headed and he showed me the back, my back. And there, at the back, were these little doors, hinged doors, of polished wood. On the arms and the legs, like a suit of armour, but of polished wood, beautifully made, brass hinges and little catches, the skin closed over these, you see, once you were inside. But I don't know how that worked, I didn't understand. And they'd built it so fast. It was a work of art. Sort of like ship-building, polished wood, little bits of rigging—'

The old man broke down once more into a fit of coughing.

The priest wanted to call for a nurse, but the old man stopped him.

'He said it was built to last. Built to out-last. To continue. Then he told me to take off my clothes and climb in. Step into the future.

'I knew this was wrong, father. I knew it. You can't cheat death. You have only your own time. But I made that wrong decision, I tore off my clothes and climbed into the back of this new self. I put my head up inside its head, like a mask, you see, put my arms inside the arms, my hands into the hands, like gloves, legs inside the legs. And then he shut the little doors at the back, snapped them shut and clicked the catches. And there was this terrible pulling, this shrinking as that new skin shrank around me, embracing me, clinging to me.

'My neck tightened, this awful compression and he said, "I must take your spine now. The exchange must be made." I struggled, but he took hold of me and he had this instrument, like a pump, polished brass, very old-looking and he put it against the small of my back and he—'

'*Nurse!*' called the priest.

'No!' cried the old man. 'No, let me speak, let me finish. What he did to me. The pain. I woke up in a doss house and when I woke up I screamed. And I looked around and I laughed then, and I thought, oh no, it was a dream. A nightmare, drunk

157

probably, oh how I laughed. But then, but then, as I sat up on that wretched bed, I knew it had all been true and I felt at my neck and I could feel the flap and the button and I knew that that other self was now *inside me*, I wasn't inside *it*. The backs of my arms, hard under the skin, like wood and my legs, my back, rigid and I was numb. I couldn't smell anything, even there in that stinking doss house, not a thing and I no longer had a sense of taste. I got up and I was like a robot, an automaton, I was not a person any more, like a doll, not a person.

'I walked about and I looked at people, but they weren't like people any more, they seemed like animals, or some remote species. But it wasn't *them*, it was *me*. I wasn't one of *them*. I was something different. And now they meant nothing to me. I was remote from them, aloof. I couldn't feel them any more. Emotionally, I couldn't feel them emotionally. I had *no* feelings. No love, no hate. Nothing, just a great emptiness inside.'

There was a moment of silence and then the priest said, 'I am afraid, my son. You have made me afraid.'

'I am afraid, father. Afraid of what I have done.'

'Will you tell me more?'

'I will tell you all. I knew that I was afraid then. But I could not feel it. I knew that I was angry, very angry, but I couldn't feel it. I couldn't remember how those things felt. But I knew one thing and that was that I could not go through five hundred years of this. Of this emptiness and solitude. This apart-ness. I wanted my self back, wretched thing that it was, but it *was* me.

'I returned to that chapel to seek out the man who had taken my spine. But he was gone, the chapel was all boarded over, the door chained shut. I did not know where he might have gone to, I couldn't know where. But I knew I had to find him, to reclaim my self. And so I searched. I walked, father. I walked across England. And I didn't need to eat – I felt no hunger – or sleep – I never felt tired. I walked and walked from town to town until the shoes wore off my feet and then I begged for more. I searched through the pages of every local newspaper.

I walked, father, for fifty years I walked.'

The priest caught his breath. 'For fifty years?' he whispered.

'For fifty years. But I found him. I finally found him, right here, right here in Brighton. Another small advert in the local paper, another chapel just like the first. And there he was, up upon the dais. Same man, same suit, exactly the same. He hadn't aged by a day. I kept to the rear of the hall, in the shadows and I watched and I listened. It was all the very same. And I watched his audience. The same audience, father, the same people, even after fifty years I recognized them all, sitting there, straight-backed.

'He spoke, a newer speech now, of micro-technology and silicone chips, but he was selling the same thing. The five hundred years. And as he spoke the other folk drifted out, leaving only me, hiding at the back and one lone downtrodden-looking man at the front, and after he had spoken he led this man away.

'I crept after them. I had a gun and I could feel no fear. I stood at the door of another little back room, listening. I knew he would be removing his shirt. I had waited so long for this, but I was like a sleepwalker, so distant. I turned the handle and pushed open the door. He stood there, half naked. I shouted at him, raised my gun, the young man saw the gun and he ran away. He was safe, he would be spared my torment.

'The man in black slipped on his shirt, he was cool, I knew that he could feel nothing. Or *what* did I know? He did this to other people, yet *he* knew what it was like. I had many questions. Fifty years of questions.

'"So," said he. "This is most unexpected."

'"Give me back my spine," I told him. "Give me back my self."

'And he laughed. Laughed in my face. "After fifty years?" he said. "It is gone. It is dust."

'My hand that held the gun now shook. Of course it was dust. Of course after all this time. After all these years.

'"But you go on," he said. "You go on into the future. Look at you, still young, still fit."

'"No!" I cried. "No. I will not be like this. Not what you have made me. I will kill myself, but first

160

I will kill you. You will do to no more folk what you have done to me."

'He shook his head. He smiled. "You fail to grasp any of this," he said. "I am just one, there are many like me. Like *us*. Our number grows daily. Soon, soon now, *all* will be as we are. You will achieve nothing by killing me."

'"Why?" I asked him. "Why do you do this?"

'"A new order of life," he said. "A new stage in development. A world freed of emotion, without sickness or hatred."

'"Without love," I said and he laughed again.

'"Put aside your gun," he said, "and I will show you why this must be and then you will understand."

'I put aside my gun. I *would* kill him, I knew this. And I would kill myself. But I had to know, to understand.

'"Follow me," he waved his hand and led me from the room. Along a dirty corridor we went and down a flight of steps towards the boiler house below. Here he switched on a light and I saw heaps of ancient baggage, old portmanteaus, Gladstone bags. "All mine," he said, and opening a musty case he took out an ancient daguerreotype in a silver frame. He held it up to me and I looked at the portraiture. A gaunt young man in early Victorian garb.

'"It is you," I said.

'He inclined his head. "I was the first. I opened up the way for Him and He gave this life to me."

'"For *Him*?" I asked.

'"I am His guardian, until all are converted. It is conversion, you see, real conversion."

'"Who is this person?"

'"Oh, He's not a person." The man in black stepped back from me. There was an old red velvet curtain strung across a corner of the room, he took hold of it and flung it aside. And I saw Him. I saw the thing. It sat there on a sort of throne, hideously grinning. It was like a monstrous insect. Bright red, a complicated face with a black V for a mouth and glossy slanting eyes. And this face, it seemed to be composed of other things, of people and moving images, moving, everything moving. Shifting from one form to another. I cannot explain exactly what I saw, but I knew that it was wrong. That it was wrong and it was evil. That it shouldn't be here. That it was not allowed to be here. He had brought it here, this tall gaunt man, he was its guardian. All he was and all he did was for the service of this creature.

'"Meet your maker," said the man in black. "Meet your God."

'"No!" I fumbled for my gun, but I no longer had it, the man in black had somehow stolen it from me. I wanted to attack this thing. I felt no fear, you see. I couldn't fear. But the sight of this thing was such that I *knew*, simply knew, that I must destroy it. I raised my hands to strike it down, but the gaunt man held me back.

'"You must kneel," he cried, "kneel before your God."

'I fought, but he forced me before it. It glared down at me and it spoke. The voice was like a thousand voices. Like a stadium chant. "You wanted more time," it said. "But I have *your* time, your *real* time. The time you had to come. And now I will have all your time. You have seen me and so I must have *all* of your time."

'And it opened its horrible mouth. Wide, huge and it sucked in. And I knew it was sucking me in. Sucking in my time. All the time I'd already had, all my *life*. That's what it did, you see, father. From the spines. It had my real future time and now it was sucking in my past. It was taking all the time I'd had before. The time of my childhood, my youth. It was taking all that. And it wasn't fair, father. It wasn't fair.'

'It wasn't fair, my son.' The priest was weeping now. 'It isn't fair.'

'It took my time, it took *all* my time.'

The pub had gone rather quiet. As Sean had been telling this tale to me more and more folk had been gathering around to listen. And they were listening intently, as if somehow they knew the truth of this tale. Or had heard something similar. Or knew of someone who had told such a tale to someone else.

'Is that it?' I asked Sean, when finally I found my voice.

163

'Not quite,' Sean took a pull upon the pint of beer that had grown quite warm, while the listeners' hearts had chilled. 'The priest was weeping, crying like a child and he ran out of the cubicle. He ran right past me, he looked terrified. And I sat there, I could hear the old man wheezing, he was dying. He had told his awful tale and now he was dying. He had lost all his time and now he was going to die alone. Utterly alone.

'I sat there and I thought, I can't let this old man die like that, it's so wrong. Someone should be there with him, to hold his hand. *I* should be there with him. *I* heard his tale too.

'So I got down from my bed and I limped around to his cubicle. My ankle didn't hurt because of the injection, but even if it had hurt, I wouldn't have cared. I pushed back the curtain and I went inside. He was lying there on the bed and he smelled really bad. The smell of death. I smelled that on my Gran when I was a child. The man was about to die.

'He was all covered up, except for his head and his face looked old. Like *really* old. Like a hundred years old. It made me afraid just to look at him. I pulled down the cover so I could get at his hand, he was pretty much out of it by then, he probably didn't even know I was there. But I pulled down the blanket and I took hold of his hand.

'But it wasn't a man's hand. It was a child's hand. A little child and when I pulled the blanket right back I could see his body. It was a baby's body. This old man's head on top of a baby's body.

164

And as I took hold of the hand, this little hand, it was shrinking. Shrinking and shrinking. His time had been stolen, you see, his previous time, his past time. The thing had stolen it all from him and he was going back and back until he wouldn't exist at all, would never exist at all. I tried to hold the hand, but I couldn't. It just got smaller and smaller. All of him, smaller and smaller, his head was the size of a grape and I saw the eyes look up at me and the mouth move. And he spoke.'

'And what did he say?' I asked Sean.

'He said, "help me, help me," and then he just vanished.'

# CHAPTER 13

# ACCIDENTAL MOVEMENTS
# OF THE GODS

Three months have passed since Russell parted with his life's savings, thus depriving his poor mother of the stair-lift for her bungalow. Three months that have seen great activity in Hangar 18. Russell, who had never actually watched a movie being made, would have loved to have stood quietly by and done so. But he did not.

Russell's days of standing quietly by were gone for ever. Russell had to find more money. *Much* more money.

And he'd done just that. Because, as has been said (to the point of teeth-grating tedium), Russell was a hard worker and when he was given a job to do, he did it. And he did it to the best of his abilities. And so if he was producer, then he *would* produce.

Armed with a carrier-bag full of videos (the ones he and Bobby Boy had made) he'd set off 'up town', which is to say 'towards the West End', which is to say, London. And there he'd made appointments, shown his videos and eaten many lunches. And being what is known as 'an innocent abroad', he had signed a number of rapidly drawn-up contracts and been 'done up like a kipper', which is to say, 'taken to the cleaners', which is to say, swindled.

It became clear to Russell at an early stage, that the backers (or 'Angels' as they preferred to be called), were far more interested in acquiring a share of the Cyberstar technology than Mr Fudgepacker's movie. And *that* wasn't Russell's to sell.

But he sold it anyway. Many times over. Reasoning, that if the movie was the great success he was sure it would be, he could just pay everybody back what they'd lent and a bit of a cash bonus on top and all would be happy.

Oh dear.

So he had raised a considerable sum. More than sufficient to finance all the great activity in Hangar 18 that he would have loved to have watched, but could not.

They kept him at it from morning till midnight. Mr Fudgepacker shot the movie during the day, while Russell was out doing the business, then he locked away all the test videos and technology and what-nots in his big safe before Russell got back to spend the evening trying to figure out the accounts. It just wasn't fair.

And so now, at the end of a particularly tiring day, Russell sat all alone in Bobby Boy's suitably grim office, that was now Russell's suitably grim office, with his head in his hands, in a state of stress.

A state of stress and one of worry.

Russell worried about everything. He worried (not without good cause) about all the deals he'd made, but that was the least of his worries.

Russell worried a lot about the *Flügelrad*. For one thing, where was it now? Bobby Boy had shifted it out of Hangar 18 before anyone else got a look at it. But he wouldn't tell Russell where he'd shifted it to. All he said was that it was in a very safe place and that Russell should remember he was sworn to secrecy about it.

'It doesn't matter,' Bobby Boy told him. 'It is no longer important.'

But it did matter and it *was* important. That thing had brought Adolf Hitler into the present day. And where was Adolf now? Lurking somewhere close at hand? Plotting and planning? Committing unspeakable acts? It didn't bear thinking about. But Russell thought about it all the time.

And what about the future? That Nazi future Bobby Boy claimed to have seen? And what about the beautiful Julie? She had somehow come back from that future to give Russell the programmer, kiss him and tell him she loved him. How had *that* come about? She'd vanished with two evil clanking things in pursuit. Things that had followed her from the future. And neither she nor the clanking things were travelling in *Flügelrads*. What did *that* mean?

Was time travel commonplace in the future? Did folk from the future come back and tamper with the past?

Russell raised his head from his hands and gave it a dismal shake. And what about the movie? If it was made using technology stolen from the future and was a great success, then copies of it would exist in the future. Therefore someone in the future would be able to trace where and when the movie was originally made and dispatch a couple of evil clankers to reclaim the technology and therefore stop it being made. But of course if they did that and the movie didn't get made, then copies of it could not exist in the future, so someone wouldn't be able to trace where and when it was made and send back the clankers. But what if—

'Aaaaaaaaagh!' Russell reached into the desk drawer and brought out a bottle of Glen Boleskine. He was drinking now on a regular basis and it really wasn't good for him. But all of this was all too much and what made it worse was that Russell was the only one doing any worrying about it.

Old Ernest wasn't worried. He was back behind the camera reliving his golden days. And Bobby Boy wasn't worried, he'd passed all the responsibility on to Russell and he was fulfilling his dream to become a movie star. And Frank wasn't worried. And Julie wasn't worried. And Morgan probably didn't even know how to worry. Only Russell worried. And it wasn't fair.

It just wasn't fair.

Russell tasted Scotch and glared at the papers on his desk. Piles of them and many the fault of Frank. Frank just loved paperwork and now he was a prop man again he could give his love full head (so to speak). Frank was currently employed by *Fudgepacker Films* as well as *Fudgepacker's Emporium*. Which put him in the marvellous position of being able to send paperwork to himself. Every time something hired from the Emporium got broken on the film set, the Emporium charged the film company. The film company then borrowed back its own money, bought a replacement item, leased it to the Emporium which then rehired it to the film company. Frank had never been happier.

Russell pushed Frank's paperwork aside and glared at some of Mr Fudgepacker's. The ancient film maker had told Russell this very day that the shooting was now all but over, so they would soon be into 'post production' and post production would require even more money. Could Russell have a word with the Emporium, who Mr Fudgepacker felt were overcharging his film company for breakages on the set?

Ludicrous. And all in the cause of a movie that Russell had not seen one single minute of. And *he* was the producer.

'It just isn't fair.' Russell made the sulkiest of faces. 'I'm sure everyone's been working very hard, but it's me who does all the worrying and takes all the responsibility. They might have shown me some of it.'

Russell huffed and puffed and glared through the partition window to the studio floor beyond. Bare now, but for a few tables and director's chairs and the video monitor on its stand.

Russell's glare moved back into the office and returned to an area where it spent a good deal of its time these recent evenings: the area filled by Mr Fudgepacker's safe. Mr Fudgepacker's mighty *INVINCIBLE*, brought over from the Emporium and lowered through the roof by crane (at great cost, Russell recalled). Several tons of worthy steel containing . . .

Russell glared at the safe. Only Mr Fudgepacker knew the combination. Only he and nobody else.

Well . . .

This was not altogether true. Russell did a bit of thoughtful lip-chewing as he poured himself another Scotch. There was one other person who knew the combination. And that person was he, Russell.

He'd discovered it quite by accident many months ago. It had been lunch-time and there'd been no-one around and so Russell thought that now would be a good time to do a bit of cleaning. Have a go at Mr Fudgepacker's safe, the old boy would like that. But Mr Fudgepacker hadn't liked that. He'd returned unexpectedly to find Russell worrying away at one of the big brass bosses and he'd thrown a real wobbly. Russell had thought he was going to snuff it. Baffled by Mr F's over-reaction, Russell had returned later with a magnifying glass to examine the big brass boss. And yes, there they were, a little row of scratched-on numbers. And it didn't take the brain of an Einstein to work out what they were.

Of course, Russell would not have dreamed of opening the safe. That would have been a terrible thing to do. Russell felt guilty about the whole thing for ages.

But he didn't feel quite so guilty now.

It wouldn't hurt if he took a look at one or two of the test videos, would it? Just run them through the monitor and then put them back. What harm could that do?

Russell's brow became a knitted brow. To open the safe might be a crime in itself. Breaking and entering, without the breaking. Or the entering. But it could be trespass and it was definitely a breach of trust. But then he did have a *right* to see the movie. He was responsible for the movie. And what if? And this was a big, what if? A 'what if?' that also worried Russell and worried him greatly. What if the movie was a load of old rubbish? All ultra violence and hard-core pornography? A movie that would never be given a certificate by the censors?

It could well be. Fudgepacker loved his gore and with Bobby Boy having a hand in the script and the starring role, Marilyn Monroe would be sure to be getting her kit off.

And what about Julie?

'I'll kill him,' said Russell. 'If he's persuaded Julie to . . . I'll kill him. I will.'

Russell glared once more at the mighty *INVINCIBLE*. And then he reached into his desk drawer and brought out his magnifying glass. He looked at it and he made a guilty face. He could not pretend he hadn't been planning this.

'Oh sod it,' said Russell. 'It can't hurt. I'm doing the right thing. I know I am.' And with that said, Russell got up from his desk, went over to the safe, examined the numbers on the brass boss, twiddled the combination lock and swung open the beefy metal door.

And there it all was. The precious Cyberstar equipment. The rented camera. Cans of exposed footage. Stacks of video cassettes in neat white numbered boxes. Russell did shifty over-the-shoulder glances. But there was no-one about, he was all alone in Hangar 18. He'd locked himself in.

'Right,' said Russell, pulling out a stack of videos.

On the studio floor Russell settled himself in for a private viewing. He plugged in the monitor, slotted the first video, poured himself another Scotch, took up the remote controller and parked his bottom on Mr Fudgepacker's personal chair.

'Right,' said Russell once more. 'Roll them old cameras. Let there be movie.'

Russell sat there and pressed 'play'.

The monitor screen popped with static and then

a clapperboard appeared. On this were scrawled the words NOSTRADAMUS ATE MY HAMSTER. Act one. Scene one. Take one.

Russell hmmphed. 'I don't think much of that for a title,' he said.

'You know, I don't think much of this for a title,' said the voice of Bobby Boy.

'Just clap the bloody clapperboard,' said the voice of Mr Fudgepacker. Clap went the clapperboard.

Act one, scene one, was the interior of a public house. A gentleman in a white shirt and dicky bow stood behind the bar counter. His surroundings were in colour, but he was in black and white.

'Oh,' said Russell, 'it's David Niven. I like David Niven, but why is he in black and white?'

This question was echoed by the voice of Mr Fudgepacker. Although he phrased it in a manner which included the use of words such as 'bloody' and 'bastard'.

The screen blacked and there were raised voices off. Then the clapperboard returned with the words 'take two' written on it. Now Charlton Heston stood behind the bar, he was in full colour. And a toga.

The screen blacked again and the voices off were raised to greater heights. Russell shook his head and took another taste of Scotch. The clapperboard returned once more. It was time for 'take three'.

Tony Curtis replaced Charlton Heston. Tony wore a smart evening suit. He smiled towards the camera, raised his right hand in a curious fashion and then strode, ghost-like through the bar counter.

'Cut!' shouted Mr Fudgepacker. 'What the fuck are you doing?'

'It's tricky,' Bobby Boy's voice had a certain edge to it. 'He's a hologram. He can't lift up the counter flap. We'll have to rig some strings, or something.'

Russell gave his head another shake and fast-forwarded. By 'take eighteen' Bobby Boy had managed to steer Tony from behind the counter and nearly halfway across the bar floor. Tony was carrying a Christmas tree fairy. Or rather, Tony was *not* carrying it. The fairy was dangling on a length of fishing line and it was rarely to be found in the same place as Tony's outstretched hand.

'Oh dear,' said Russell, 'it's not very convincing, is it? But fair dos, I can see how difficult it is. They've certainly been working hard.'

Russell fast-forwarded once more. After many unsuccessful attempts, Mr Curtis finally managed to hang the fairy on the top of a Christmas tree. And then the tape ran out.

'That would be about ten seconds in the can,' said Russell, who had picked up all kinds of movie-speak. 'Not much for a full day's shooting. Perhaps I'll go straight on to tape number five.'

Russell went straight on to tape number five and now it was party time in the pub. And quite a Cyberstar-studded occasion it was.

Humphrey Bogart was there and Lauren Bacall

and Orson Welles and Ramon Navarro, and even Rondo Hatton, who was one of Russell's very favourites. But they weren't doing very much. In fact, they weren't doing anything at all. They were just standing there like statues, with dangling glasses going in and out of their hands.

'Ah,' said Russell. 'I see the problem here. The machine can project their images, but there's only one programmer, so you can only work one at a time. Pity.'

Bobby Boy made his first on-screen appearance. Dressed in his usual black, he walked carefully and awkwardly between the holograms. 'A pint of Large please, Neville,' he told Tony Curtis and then, 'You'll have to work him, Ernie. Waggle the joy stick.'

'You can't talk to me while you're acting, you bloody fool. *Cut!*'

Russell did further head shaking. 'Oh dear, oh dear,' he sighed. And then he said, 'Hang about,' and he fast-forwarded the tape.

'I'm the Johnny G Band, sir,' said Elvis Presley.

'What?' went Russell, as tape number five ran out.

Russell rushed back to the safe and returned with an armful of video cassettes. Out of the monitor came number five and in went number ten.

'It's the Ark of the Covenant,' said Norman Wisdom. 'I dug it up the other week on my allotment.'

'*What?*' Russell put on the freeze-frame. Norman's

176

now legendary grin lit up the screen. It didn't light up Russell.

'That's the story Morgan told me,' he mumbled. 'About Pooley and Omally and The Flying Swan. The story that started all this off. But they can't film *that*. Surely that came out of a book. We don't hold the copyright; we'll get sued for it. Oh dear, oh dear.'

Russell ejected tape number ten and slotted in tape number fifteen. An outside shot this time. A little yard.

'Location footage,' said Russell. 'I thought they were going to shoot it all here in the hangar.'

Someone crept across the little yard. It was Bobby Boy and it had to be said, Bobby Boy could *not* act. He moved like something out of a Hal Roach silent comedy, knees going high, shoulders hunched. He turned to face the camera and put his finger to his lips.

'Cut,' said Russell, but Mr Fudgepacker didn't.

Bobby Boy crept across the little yard to a clap-board shed with an open window and ducked down beneath it. Russell looked on, that shed and that window seemed rather familiar.

The camera tracked forward, passed the croaching ham actor and panned up towards the open window. Sounds of ranting came from that window. Ranting in German.

'Oh no!' gasped Russell. But it was 'Oh yes!' Through the window moved the camera, like that really clever bit in *Citizen Kane* and there, seated at a table, with two SS types standing before him was—

'Alec bloody Guinness,' whispered Russell. 'And he's playing—'

'Herr Führer,' went Anton Diffring*, one of the SS types.

'Bloody Hell!' Russell thumbed the fast-forward and sent Bobby Boy scurrying through The Bricklayer's Arms and off up the Ealing Road 'What's going on here? He's playing *me*. Why is he playing *me*? Morgan! Morgan must have told them what I told *him*. But why put it in a movie? This doesn't make any sense.'

Russell ejected the tape and put it carefully to one side. He would be having stern words to say about this. No-one had asked his permission to do this. It was invasion of privacy, or something. He could sue over this. Sue the producer of the picture.

'Hm,' went Russell, who could see a bit of a flaw in that.

'Right then.' Russell rooted through further cassettes. Two were in black boxes. 23A and 23B. Russell slotted 23A into the monitor.

Black and white this time. A street scene set in the nineteen fifties. It looked very authentic.

'Old stock footage?' Russell asked. 'Oh no, here he comes again.'

This time Bobby Boy was dressed as a policeman.

* Well, he always used to be when I was a lad.

178

He was camping it up with exaggerated knee bends and thumbs in top pockets.

'Well, at least he's not playing me this time. So what's all this about?' Russell fast-forwarded, stopping here and there to see what was on the go. Sid James was in this one, and Charles Hawtrey and Kenneth Williams. But this wasn't a remake of *Carry on Constable*, anything but.

Russell viewed a final scene. It was set in a police station. A man was being held down on a table by a number of soldiers. The cast of *Cockleshell Heroes*, the great David Lodge amongst them.

But what were they doing? They were tearing at the man. They were pulling him to pieces.

Russell slammed the off button and rammed a knuckle into his mouth. 'A snuff movie,' he gagged. 'They've made a snuff movie. Oh dear God, no.'

Russell tore tape 23A from the monitor, held it a moment in his hand and then threw it down in horror and disgust. This was bad. This was very bad. What did they think they were up to? What else had they done? Russell steeled himself with further Scotch and took to pacing up and down. There were loads more tapes. He'd have to view them all. He didn't want to, but he knew he'd have to.

Russell made fists. 'Right,' he said.

In went a tape at random. Russell settled back nervously in Mr Fudgepacker's chair.

Colour again and more location stuff, filmed this time in one of those super-duper shopping malls.

179

Very flash and ultra modern. Russell didn't recognize the place, or the extras – handsome young men with blond hair, wearing black uniforms and fabulous women in gold-scaled dresses. They walked about, looking in the windows and talking amongst themselves. They were *not* Cyberstars. But there was something odd about them. The way they moved, very stiff and straight-backed, almost as if they wore suits of armour under their clothes. Strange that.

Russell shrugged and looked on.

Out of a shop doorway came Bobby Boy. And Julie was with him. And she was wearing that dress, that golden dress. The one she'd worn when she appeared to Russell in The Ape of Thoth.

Russell sat up and took notice.

'They'll kill you,' said Julie. 'If you stay here in the future, you'll die.'

'I can't leave yet,' said Bobby Boy. 'Not with *Him* here. Not if there's a chance to destroy *Him*.'

'I won't go back alone. I won't.'

'You must. Take the programmer. Go back to the date I told you and the time. I'll be in the pub with Morgan. Give me the programmer there. Leave the rest to me.'

'But the you-back-then won't know what's going to happen. The you-back-then won't know how to stop it.'

'I'm not an idiot,' said Bobby Boy. 'I'll figure it out. I'll make them do the right thing and stop all this from ever happening. Trust me, I can do it.'

'Bloody hell,' said Russell.

'I love you,' said Julie, taking the thin man in her arms and kissing him passionately.

'Tell that to the me-back-then. Now hurry, go on, we don't have time. There *is* no time.'

Julie kissed him again and then she touched something on her belt and vanished. Terrible clanking sounds echoed in the shopping mall, Bobby Boy turned and stared and then he ran. And then the picture on the screen slewed to one side as the tape got snarled up in the monitor.

'Oh shit! Oh shit!' cried Russell, leaping from the chair. 'Don't do that, I have to see what happens.'

Russell fought the cassette from the monitor. The tape was chewed to pieces, Russell tried to wind it in, but it broke. 'Oh no, oh dear.' Russell snatched up another cassette and rammed it into the monitor. 'Work,' he pleaded. 'Just work.'

The screen lit up to another interior. It was Fudgepacker's Emporium. Russell recalled Frank's paperwork for this scene, the hire of half the props in the place, plus the rental for location. It ran to many hundreds of pages. But that really wasn't important now. It hadn't been important then, actually, as Russell had binned the lot.

The camera's eye took in the aisles and iron walkways, moving slowly and lingering here upon a nail-studded Congolese power figure and there upon a mummified mermaid. Then on.

181

Two figures were approaching. One was the inevitable Bobby Boy. The other was Peter Cushing. Peter wore thick-lensed horn-rimmed glasses. He was evidently playing the part of Mr Fudgepacker.

'Do not look directly upon Him,' said Peter Cushing. 'And never, never into His eyes. Just keep your head bowed and kneel when I tell you.'

'How long?' asked Bobby Boy. 'How long has He been with you?'

'For many years. I am His guardian. All this, all this in the Emporium is His. Time captured, you see, in the taxidermy, in the religious relics and the pickled parts. That is how He likes it. How it must be.'

'Now what is all *this* about?' Russell asked.

'Will He know me?' asked Bobby Boy. 'Will He know why I'm here? What I want?'

'He knows all. He knows that you want more time. More time to correct the mistake you made. The mistake that changed the future.'

Russell put his hands to his face. 'What did I do? Or what didn't I do? This is bad. This is really bad. And who is this *He*?'

The figures on screen approached a small Gothic door at the end of the aisle.

'There's no door there,' said Russell. 'How did they do that?'

Bobby Boy pressed open the door and the two men passed through the narrow opening.

182

The camera followed them down a flight of steps and into a boiler room.

'And there's no boiler room,' said Russell. 'Or at least I don't think there's one.'

'This way,' Peter led Bobby Boy between piles of ancient luggage, old portmanteaus, Gladstone bags, towards a curtained-off corner of the room.

'Part the curtain,' said Peter, 'and avert your gaze.'

Bobby Boy drew the curtain aside.

Russell looked on.

Something moved in the semi-darkness, an indistinct form.

Russell squinted at the screen.

Something lifted itself into the light.

Russell gaped in horror.

The terrible thing sat upon a throne-like chair, its grinning insect face a vivid red. A face that moved and swam with many forms. The black maw of a mouth turned upwards in a V-shaped leer. The fathomless eyes blinked open.

'Aaaaaaaaaagh!' screamed Russell, falling backwards off the chair.

The face gazed out from the screen. Tiny naked human figures writhed upon its skin, drifting in and out of focus.

Russell scrambled up and stared. 'Holy God,' he whispered.

The eyes bulged from the screen. '*I* am your God,' cried the one voice which was many. 'Kneel before your God and I will give you more time.'

'No,' went Russell. 'No no no.' He snatched up the remote control and pressed the eject button. The cassette slid out from beneath the screen. But the face stared on.

'No,' went Russell, pushing the 'off' button.

'Yes,' went the dreadful voice, and the leering face stared on.

'Oh my God.' Russell snatched at the cable, wrapped his fingers around it and tore the plug from the wall socket.

'You have deviated,' boomed the voice, and the eyes that bulged from the screen stared into Russell's. 'You have deviated from the script. You must be rewritten.'

'You can go to Hell.' Russell took the monitor in both hands raised it high above his head and dashed it down to the floor.

Sparks and crackles.

Silence.

Bobby Boy's voice broke that silence. 'You shouldn't have done that, Russell,' it said.

Russell swung around to gawp at the long thin fellow. He stood beside the sliding door of the hangar. Mr Fudgepacker was with him.

'Very expensive SFX,' said the old boy. 'That will have to come out of your wages.'

'What wages? I mean, my God, what have you two done? What was that creature? What is this movie? Why is it about me? Why . . . ?'

Bobby Boy shrugged his high narrow shoulders. 'So many questions. And you really shouldn't be asking them. You're the star player in all this. You started it. But you have to follow your script. You've deviated from the plot. You weren't supposed to do this.'

'We could write it in,' said Mr Fudgepacker, scratching at his baldy head and sending little flecks of skin about the place. 'It might make an interesting sequence.'

'No,' the thin man shook his head. 'I think we should just write Russell out. As of now.'

'What?' went Russell. 'What are you talking about?'

Bobby Boy sidled over. 'You don't get it anyway,' he sneered. 'But then, you were never supposed to.'

Russell had a good old shake on. He reached for the Scotch bottle.

'And drinking my booze.' Mr Fudgepacker threw up his wrinkled hands. 'That's definitely not in the script. I'd never have put *that* in the script.'

'What script?' asked Russell. 'The script of this abomination? I don't want to be in your script.'

'But you're already in it. You've watched the videos. You've seen what you do, what you're going to do.'

'You're mad,' said Russell. 'This is all insane.'

'Sit down,' said Bobby Boy.

'Stuff you.'

'Quite out of character,' said Mr Fudgepacker.

'Sit down, Russell,' said Bobby Boy.

185

Russell sat down. And then he jumped up again.

'Sit down and I'll tell you what you want to know.'

Russell sat down again.

Bobby Boy took the Scotch bottle from his hand. He hoisted himself onto a table and dangled his long thin legs*. 'Are you sitting comfortably?' he asked.

'No.'

'Well never mind,' Bobby Boy put the Scotch bottle to his tricky little mouth and took a big swig.

'Oi,' croaked Mr Fudgepacker. 'My booze.'

'Shut it old man.'

'Well, really.'

'Tell me, Russell,' said Bobby Boy, wiping his slender chin, 'what do you remember?'

'About what?'

'About your childhood, say.'

'Mind your own business.'

'Come on now. What school did you go to?'

'Huh?' said Russell.

'Come on, tell me. I'll give you a nip of this Scotch if you tell me.'

'I can take the bottle from you whenever I want.'

Bobby Boy produced a gun from his coat pocket. 'I'll bet you can't,' he said.

* It was a very *high* table.

'Come off it.' Russell put up his hands.

'Tell me which school you went to.'

'I . . .' Russell thought about this. 'I . . .'

'Slipped your mind?'

'I . . .'

'Tell me your earliest memory, then.'

Russell knotted his fists.

'Careful.'

'All right. My earliest memory, all right. It's . . . it's . . .' Russell screwed up his face. 'It's . . .'

'Come on, spit it out.'

Russell spat it out. 'It's Morgan,' he said. 'Morgan telling me about The Flying Swan.'

'And nothing before that?'

Russell scratched at his head of hair. Before that? There had to have been something before that. But what had it been?

'No?' asked Bobby Boy. 'Lost your memory?'

'I'm drunk,' said Russell. 'I don't feel very well.'

'There's nothing before it, Russell. You didn't exist before that. You were called into being, Russell. So that you could fulfil a particular role, play a certain part. And you were playing it well, before you started to deviate. Opening the safe? An honest fellow like you, quite out of character.'

'I am *not* a bloody character,' said Russell. 'What are you implying? That I'm just a made-up character in a book?'

'Character in a book?' Bobby Boy laughed his grating laugh. 'Now that really *is* absurd. No,

Russell. But you're not a real person. You're a construct. A bit of this person, a bit of that.'

'Crap,' said Russell. 'And so what does that make you?'

'Oh, I know what I am. I'm a tricky lying villain. And Mr Fudgepacker here is a clapped-out old pornographer.'

'How dare you!' gasped the old one. 'I am a maker of Art House movies.'

'A clapped-out pornographer who has sold his soul to—'

'Don't say His name.' Mr Fudgepacker began to totter. Russell leapt up and guided him into his chair.

'Thank you, Russell,' said Mr Fudgepacker. 'You're such a nice young man.'

'Well, you'd know,' said Bobby Boy. 'You made him up.'

'Bollocks,' said Russell.

'Just tell him, Bobby Boy.' Mr Fudgepacker scratched at a bubo on his wrist. 'I want to get home and rub some pig fat on my scrofula.'

'OK. Russell, you have been brought into existence to achieve a great end: to aid the changing of the world. You see everyone's confused. What am I here for? What does it all mean? Have you ever asked yourself those questions?'

'No,' said Russell. 'I don't think I have.'

'We wrote it out,' said Mr F. 'It was very slow and it didn't say anything new.'

'Accidental movements of the gods,' said Bobby

188

Boy. 'Everything that goes on on Earth. We dance to the tunes the gods don't even know they're playing.'

'Strangely enough, I don't understand a word of that.'

'People aren't important,' said Bobby Boy. 'Not singly. It's what they do *en masse* that matters, the direction mankind goes in as a whole. Mankind is really a vast multi-cellular organism, spread across the face of the planet. Or like billions of tiny silicone chips that when all wired together would form this single planetary brain. That's the way forward, you see. That's the ultimate purpose of it all.'

'Well,' said Russell, 'at last I've met the man who has the answer to the meaning of life. This is a privilege.'

'Are you taking the piss?'

'No, I thought you were giving it away.'

'In the beginning the way was clear. All men spoke the same language. All the little chips were wired together. Remember the story of the Tower of Babel?'

Russell wondered whether he did.

'You do,' said Mr Fudgepacker. 'You've got Christianity programmed into you.'

'Oh, I'm so glad.'

'All spoke the same language and so they could function as a mass mind. But the gods weren't too chuffed with that, so they knocked down the tower, which was really this huge transmitting

189

device to communicate with other worlds, and they scrambled the language. Mankind has been fighting amongst itself ever since.'

'Very interesting,' said Russell. 'So just where do *I* fit into all this?'

'Your job was to raise the money for the movie.'

'There isn't going to be any movie,' said Russell. 'I'm going to put a stop to the movie. The movie is evil. You've done something evil and I'm going to stop it.'

'You can't stop it now. The movie will be shown and all who see it will be converted. It's not the plot of the movie that matters, Russell, it's what's *in* the movie.'

'And what's that going to be?'

'Have you ever heard of subliminal cuts?'

'I've heard of them, but that's like Satanic back masking. It's rubbish. It doesn't work.'

'Ours will work. But then ours came straight from the horse's mouth, as it were. Or rather, straight from the mouth of God.'

'That thing?' said Russell. 'That thing on the screen?'

'You shouldn't call your God a thing, Russell.'

'That's no God of mine.'

'It's the only one you've got. The others are gone, long gone. They tired of playing games with man. Once in a while they think of us in passing and their accidental thoughts, their accidental movements of thought, cause waves on the planet. Religious fervour. Holy wars. But they play no active part. All but one of them, that is. He likes the place. He sticks around. He has *the time* for us.'

'No,' said Russell. 'You don't know what you're saying. That thing's the devil. You shouldn't worship that.'

'There's no devil, only rival gods.'

'You're barking mad. I'll stop all this.'

'Enough,' said Mr Fudgepacker. 'Quite enough. All who see the movie will be converted. A new order of life, Russell. A new order of being, freed from all worry. You should appreciate that. To be free of all worry and care, all hatred, all doubt. Free to merge into the whole. A new future, Russell. Sadly you will not be here to see it.'

'Because we're writing you out,' said Bobby Boy.

'Oh no you're not.' Russell launched himself at the thin man on the table. But the thin man ducked aside and he hit Russell hard on the top of the head. And then things went very dark for Russell.

# CHAPTER 14

# THAT LUDICROUS 'IT WAS ALL JUST A TERRIBLE DREAM' BIT THEY ALWAYS HAVE

Russell awoke with a groan and a shudder. He jerked up and blinked all about the place. The place was his office (suitably grim). He'd been sleeping in his chair.

Sleeping?

Russell yawned and stretched and then the memories came rushing back like bad beer from a banjoed belly.

'Oh my God!' went Russell, as this phrase seemed to find favour with him at the present. 'Oh my good God.'

He floundered about and tried to get up, but his knees were all wobbly. On the desk before him was the bottle of Glen Boleskine. Without so much as a second thought, Russell took a mighty swig from it.

And then coughed his guts up all over the floor.

'Oh my God.' Russell's eyes went blink again, all about the place again. The safe door was closed. Sunshine streamed in through the skylight. Russell turned his blinking to his wristwatch. It was just after three and that would be three in the afternoon.

The office door swung open. 'Ah, you've broken surface, have you?' Bobby Boy breezed in with a grin.

'Get away from me.' Russell snatched up the whisky bottle and swung to his feet.

'What's all this?' asked the thin one. 'Are you all right, Russell?'

'Are you kidding?' Russell displayed his spare hand. He'd made a useful-looking fist out of it. 'I'll stop you. I've seen the tapes. You've made a big mistake not killing me when you had the chance.'

Bobby Boy made tiny smacking sounds with his tricky little mouth. 'I don't think you're very well, Russell. Mr Fudgepacker said I should let you sleep. You've been over-working, you've not been yourself.'

Bobby Boy spied the mess on the floor. 'Thought I knew that smell,' he said. 'That's pretty disgusting, isn't it?'

'You're finished,' Russell brandished the bottle. 'Finished.'

'Come on,' said Bobby Boy. 'We've a big surprise for you.'

'Yeah, I'll bet you have.'

'There's something we want you to see.'

'Some . . . thing?' Russell's eyes widened and his face, which was pale, although it hadn't been mentioned that it was pale, although given the circumstances you would naturally assume it to be pale, which it fact it was, grew paler. Phew!

'That thing is out there,' croaked he of the pale face. 'That terrible thing.'

'That's no way to speak about Frank.'

Russell waggled the bottle, spilling Scotch down his trousers. 'I won't let you show it. I'll destroy the movie.'

'What? You don't like it before you've even seen it?'

'Oh, I've seen it all right. You know I've seen it.'

'You have not.'

'I have too.'

'Have not.'

'Have too.'

'Not.'

'Too.'

'        '

'        '

(Well, there's not much else you can do with that, is there?)

'Russell, you can't have seen the movie. We've been keeping it as a special surprise for you.'

'Back off.' Russell menaced with the bottle. Bobby Boy backed off in an obliging manner.

Russell pulled open the desk drawer and sought his magnifying glass. It wasn't there. 'Fair enough,' said Russell, 'it's daylight. I'll be able to see the numbers.'

'What numbers?'

'You know what numbers. The combination numbers.'

'Yeah, right.' Bobby Boy shook his long thin head.

Russell backed over to the safe and keeping Bobby Boy at arm's length, he sought the little numbers. He squinted at the big brass boss.

And then he squinted again.

And, yes, you all know what's coming.

'There's no numbers,' gasped Russell.

'There's no combination lock,' said Bobby Boy.

Russell stared at the safe door. 'Bloody Hell,' said he.

The safe did *not* have a combination lock. It had a big keyhole.

'But . . .' went Russell. 'But . . . but . . .' Because, you have to confess that if this happened to you, you'd be quite flummoxed.

'I don't know what you were on last night,' said Bobby Boy, 'but if I were you, I'd give it a miss in the future.'

'Yeah yeah, well you'd know all about the future, wouldn't you? Having been there, and everything.'

'*Me?* Been to the future? What are you talking about, Russell?'

'I'm talking about the Cyberstar program. The one you stole.'

'The Cyber-what?'

'The hologram film stars. There's no point in denying them. The movie's full of them.'

'There's nothing like that in our movie,' said Bobby Boy. And it did have to be said that he looked and sounded most genuine, even though, of course, he *was* a professional liar. 'Mr Fudgepacker isn't much of a one for modern technology. He's a pretty basic fellow.'

'You bastards!' Russell had a serious shake on. 'You can't trick me. No, hang about, I get it.'

'What do you get?'

'There's always a bit like this, isn't there? Where something devastating happens to the hero and then he wakes up and it was all a dream. Or it *wasn't* a dream, but the villain is making it seem as if it's a dream. It's a right hacked-out cliché, that is.'

'Tell it to Hollywood.'

'It's a trick. That isn't the same safe. You switched it while I was unconscious. You knocked me out.' Russell felt at the top of his head. It did *not* have a bump on it. 'Oh,' said Russell.

'People are waiting for you,' said Bobby Boy. 'This is all very childish.'

'Yes!' Russell shook his fist. 'My childhood. What about my childhood?'

'What about it?'

'Well, I can't remember it.'

'Can't you?'

'I . . .' Russell thought about his childhood. He *could* remember it. He could remember lots and lots and lots of it. 'I *can* remember it,' he said slowly.

'Well, bully for you, Russell. Now, are you going to come out and get your big surprise, or not? There's food. Although most of it's been eaten now. There's a few ham sandwiches left.'

Russell nodded his head. 'Yes,' said he. 'All right.'

'After you then.'

'No, after *you*.'

'What a weirdo you are,' and Bobby Boy led the way.

As Russell emerged from his office a great cheer went up and 'For He's a Jolly Good Fellow' was sung at full blast with much gusto.

Russell blinked anew.

There was bunting hanging here, there and all about the place. There was a table, with the remnants of a mighty spread upon it. There were chairs set out in rows before a viewing screen. And there was quite a crowd of people.

Mr Fudgepacker was there. And Morgan was there. And Julie was there. And Frank was there (with a bit of paperwork he wanted Russell to take a look at). And several local publicans were there. And several production buyers were there (ones who hadn't come into the Emporium to hire anything in months, but always have that knack of turning up when there's a free drink). And Russell's mum was there. And even Russell's sister, who Russell was quite sure lived in Australia. Even she was there. And a few other folk also.

And they were all cheering and singing 'For he's

197

a jolly good fellow', although they'd got to the 'and so say all of us,' bit by now.

'What's going on?' Russell viewed them with suspicion. He was still not utterly convinced.

'It's all for you,' said Bobby Boy, reaching over to give Russell's back a pat, but then thinking twice about doing so. 'After all, if you hadn't had that win on the National Lottery and put it all into the movie to help Mr Fudgepacker out and save the Emporium, none of this would have been possible.'

'You're very thorough,' muttered Russell, beneath his breath. 'You haven't missed a trick.'

'What was that?'

'Oh, nothing.'

'Well, come and have a sandwich and watch the movie.'

'Hip hip hoorah!' went all present, with the exception of Russell, who was looking from one to the other of them and worrying. Oh yes he was worrying all right, and he was in a state of stress. And he was thinking many thoughts.

And one of the many thoughts that he was thinking was . . .

What if I'm dreaming *this*?

Although considerably confused, he still felt certain that he hadn't dreamed the rest. So if that was the case, then he had to be dreaming *this*.

And if he *was* dreaming this, then no-one could do any harm to him, and if he *knew* he was dreaming, he could do pretty much anything he wanted.

'OK,' said Russell, 'fine. Thank you very much everyone. You're all very kind. I'll have some of that champagne, if I might. Ah, Julie, you're looking well. Perhaps after the movie you'd like to come back to my place for some sex.'

Julie's mouth dropped open.

'Oral sex is fine by me,' said Russell. 'That's a date then.'

The crowd parted before him and Russell made his way to the table. Glances were exchanged, shoulders shrugged.

'He's been over-working,' said Mr Fudgepacker.

'Hey, Fudgy.' Russell gave the old boy a jovial pat that sent him reeling. 'How's it hanging, you old spawn of Satan?'

Murmer murmer murmer, went the crowd.

'Over-working.' Mr F struggled to stay upright. 'He's not normally like this, as we who know and love him know. This is quite out of character.'

Russell winked at Ernest and whispered close by his ear. 'I'll give you "character", you old bastard. Just show the movie.'

'Yes, yes.' Ernest eased his way past Russell. 'Take a seat, dear boy. Down at the front.'

'With you and the man in black behind me, I don't think so.'

'Anywhere you like, then.'

'At the back.'

'As you please. Well, seats everyone. Bobby Boy, get the lights switch on the projector and come and sit down the front with me.'

199

The crowd, looking somewhat bewildered, bundled for the best seats. Russell's mum wrung her hands and shook her snowy head. The sister Russell was sure lived in Australia said, 'Typical.' But whether this was directed against the bewildered bundlers or against Russell must remain uncertain.

When the bundling had finished and everyone was settled into their seats, the lights went down and the screen lit up.

A RUSSELL NICE* PRODUCTION
in association with
FUDGEPACKER INTERNATIONAL
BIO PICS
presents . . .

'*NOSTRADAMUS ATE MY HAMSTER*,' said Russell.

A SHOWER OF GOLD

'Eh?' said Russell. 'A shower of *what*?'

'Ssssh!' went Russell's mum.

'Typical,' said his sister.

Russell sat back, sipped champagne and stared on as the movie unfolded before him.

Bobby Boy played the part of a blind watchmaker's apprentice. The time was the present and the place

* So *that's* his name.

200

was Brentford. The watchmaker's business was going bust and a wicked developer was doing all he could to acquire the premises, demolish them and build some great corporate enterprise on the site.

Julie played the developer's PA, a high-powered woman with a troubled conscience. In fact, everyone in the picture seemed to have a troubled conscience. The watchmaker harboured some terrible secret from his past. His apprentice, while on the surface pretending to support the old man, was in fact scheming to sell him out. The developer was in love with Julie, but he had done something awful concerning the brother she didn't know she had. And Julie, through a chance encounter, had fallen in love with Bobby Boy, neither of them knowing who the other one was. There was enough in the way of stress to bring joy to any Hollywood producer's heart, and the plot, superbly crafted, led eventually to a denouement so apposite and touching that there wasn't a dry eye left in the house.

And certainly not one in Russell's head.

Russell sat there and blubbed into his champagne. The movie was a masterpiece. There was nothing trite or schmaltzy about it. The direction was impeccable. There was excitement, there was intrigue. There was *not* a Cyberstar to be seen in it.

The cast was entirely composed of local folk. And all were wonderfully professional. Bobby Boy out-Hanked Tom Hanks and the sallow creep who ran The Bricklayer's Arms all but stole the show with a compelling performance as a crippled footballer trying to rebuild his life after the tragic death of his wife.

It was a film for all the family. And not The Manson Family, as had been the case with Mr Fudgepacker's previous efforts. There was no sex here and no violence. There was humour, there was joy. There was love and there was hope.

It was very Heaven.

Russell blew his nose on his shirt sleeve. He could already see the reviews.

*Sensational. A film you'll want to see again and again. Simply sensational.*

**The Times**

*I don't have to actually watch a picture to know whether it's good or bad, and I haven't watched this one. But I love it. Marvellous.*

**Barry Norman**

*Ernest Fudgepacker is one of the rare guys who can always make me cry.*

**Terry Pratchett®**

And so on and so forth.

When the end credits had all rolled away and the lights went back on, folk rose from their seats and set up a thunderous applause, with the occasional break for eye-dabbing and sniffing.

Ernest struggled unsteadily to his feet and limped to the screen. He raised his wrinkly hands to the audience. 'I think a round of applause should go to the man who made it all possible. The man who has worked harder than any of us. For Russell. Take a bow, my boy.'

Russell flapped a hand and grew a little rosy at the cheeks. But to cries of 'speech, speech' and 'well done that man', he got up from his seat and took a little bow.

'It's quite something, isn't it?' said Morgan. 'Almost had me sniffling. Almost.'

'They were all so good.' Russell scratched at his head. 'All those amateur actors, they were brilliant.'

'Old Ernie knows how to get a performance out of people.'

'It's a work of genius.'

'You made it happen, Russell.'

Russell shook the head he'd been scratching. 'This has got to be a dream.'

'Then it's a bloody good one.'

Mr Fudgepacker came hobbling up. 'You liked it, Russell? You think you can sell it for us?'

'Oh yes!' Russell's head now bobbed up and down. 'I'll call Eric Nelluss,* he's the man to handle this.'

* The biggest independent film producer and distributor in the western world. Try to remember his name, because he turns up in the last chapter.

'That's my boy,' said Mr F.

'Mr Fudgepacker.'

'Yes, Russell?'

'I'm sorry about, you know, me being rude and everything.'

'Forget it, my boy. You've been over-working. We'll all help you now.'

'Great. Just great.'

'As soon as the movie's finished, we'll all give you a hand with the marketing.'

'Finished?' Russell asked. 'But it is finished, surely?'

'You have to be kidding, lad. That's only about half of it. There's all the other bits to go in. The important bits. The meaningful bits.'

Russell's heart departed through the soles of his feet. The *important* bits? The *meaningful* bits? Not . . . ? Russell's top lip began to quiver. 'Not *those* bits?' he managed. 'Not the stuff about *me*? Not that *thing*? Oh no, not *that*.'

Ernie shook his ancient head. 'Whatever are you on about, Russell? There aren't any bits about you. And there's no *thing*. Whatever the *thing* is. These are other scenes that flesh out the performances.'

'But not about *me*? And not about a *thing*?'

'No, Russell.'

'Phew,' went Russell. 'Well, I don't know how you can improve on perfection and the movie was as near to perfect as anything I've ever seen.'

'Not a bit of it. It will be a lot better when it gets the rest in.'

'Well,' Russell gave his head another shake, 'I'll be prepared to be amazed then.'

'You will.' Old Ernie smiled a mouthload of sunken gums. 'You just wait until you see the gang bang at the bikers' barbecue and the shoot-out with the General Electric mini-gun and the bit where the cannibal cult breaks into the convent and the amazing slow-motion sequence when the escaped psychopath takes this hedge-clipper and puts it right up this . . .

# CHAPTER 15

# MORE HORROR FROM BOX 23

The party moved on into evening, gathering mass and momentum. More folk that Russell didn't know arrived together with a further delivery of champagne that Russell had to sign for. Music played and people took to dancing, drunkenness and bad behaviour, as is the accepted social norm at any decent bash.

Russell slipped outside and tried his hand at flying. Well, he'd always been able to fly in his dreams and if this was a dream . . .

But he couldn't get off the ground and after a quarter of an hour of bunny-hopping foolishly around the car park, Russell slipped back inside again. It seemed as if this wasn't a dream but he still had his doubts about the rest.

There was just too much to it. Too much detail. The *Flügelrad* and the Cyberstars and the horrible red-faced insect thing. He didn't have a mind like that. He could never have dreamed such awful stuff.

Russell poured himself champagne and watched the revellers revel. They seemed to be enjoying themselves. Were they all in on it? All part of the great conspiracy? The great Satanic conspiracy? Russell downed champagne and poured some more and stood aside and wondered.

'Why so sad?' asked Julie, the barmaid-cum-movie star.

Russell turned to face the beautiful woman. 'Oh,' said he. 'Ah.'

'Yes?'

Russell made the face of shame. 'I'm very sorry,' he said. 'About, you know, what I said to you earlier.'

'I forgive you, Russell. But I'd rather you'd said it to me in private.'

'Oh,' said Russell, once again. 'Oh. Really?'

Julie smiled her wonderful smile. 'And after you've had a bath. You smell rather—'

'Yes.' Russell took a step back. 'I was sick earlier in the day. I'm sorry.'

'You look a bit drunk now.'

'Yes, I'm sorry about that too. I'm really sorry.'

'You're such a sweet man, Russell.'

'Thank you and I really am truly sorry.'

'Just forget it.'

'Yes.' Russell smiled back at the beautiful woman. Now *she* was a dream. A real dream. And she *did* seem to like him. A relationship wouldn't be out of the question. Russell felt sure that she couldn't be up to anything sinister. She might well have seen something though. The Cyberstar machine. She might have seen that.

'So why are you so sad?'

'I'm confused,' said Russell. 'I wonder, could I ask you a question?'

'Anything you like.'

'Well, when you were making the movie, did you use any weird equipment?'

*Smack!* went Julie's hand on Russell's face.

'What did I say?' Russell watched her storm off into the crowd, 'What did I say?'

'That's a pretty crap technique you have there,' said Bobby Boy, sidling up. 'Not a patch on my own. But then we actors have a certain charisma, especially with the starlets. Anyway, that's my bit of tail, so keep your eyes off it.'

'Why you—' Russell raised a fist, but Morgan caught his wrist from behind.

'Don't let him wind you up, Russell,' said Morgan. 'Come and have a chat with us.'

Russell glared Bobby Boy eyeball to eyeball. There was much macho posture-work and you could almost taste the testosterone.

Russell let himself be led away.

'He's not worth it,' said Morgan, as this was the done thing to say in such circumstances.

Frank stood talking with a couple of half-cut production buyers, the two young men joined them.

'All right, Russell?' asked Frank. And then, sniff sniff sniff. 'It's vomit again, isn't it?'

Russell sighed.

'Now, let me see if I can identify it correctly. It was Garvey's Best Bitter last time, if I recall. Hm, let's sniff. It's Scotch. It's a malt. It's a five-year-old. It's Glen Boleskine. Am I right, or am I right?'

Russell nodded helplessly.

'Frank certainly knows his vomit,' said Morgan.

'It's a knack,' said Frank. 'You see a lot of vomit in the film game. I remember one time I was drinking with Rock Hudson in his hotel room. We'd had a few, well, I'd had more than him and I chucked on the carpet. But he was a real gent, cleaned it all up and when I passed out he tucked me up in his own bed. I woke up the next day with a right hangover and I don't know what I must have sat on the night before, but my bum wasn't half sore.'

Looks were exchanged all around. Frank and Morgan hastily changed the subject. 'That movie was a real stonker,' he said. 'Er, I mean, it was really good, wasn't it?'

'And it will stay that way too,' said Russell. 'I'm not going to let Mr Fudgepacker ruin it by putting in all that gore and guts.'

'Shame,' said Morgan. 'I was looking forward to seeing the bit where the psycho gets the hedge-trimmer and sticks it right up—'

'Absolutely *not*!' Russell waved a wobbly hand about. 'But tell me this, Morgan. Did you actually watch any of the movie being shot?'

'Can't say that I did. I was looking after the Emporium.'

'What about you, Frank?'

'Too much paperwork. Which reminds me—'

'So it was all down to Bobby Boy and Mr Fudgepacker?'

'And Julie,' said Morgan. 'Is that woman a babe, or what? Why did she whack you, Russell?'

'I don't wish to discuss it. But all those other people in the movie. Apart from the landlord of The Bricklayer's, I don't know any of them personally, do you?'

Frank and Morgan shook their heads. 'Local colour,' said Frank. 'Local characters. Fudgepacker knows how to get a performance out of people. Do you want a top-up, I reckon we're in for an all-nighter here.'

'No thanks.' Russell put his glass aside. 'I don't want any more. I've had too much already. I'm going home to have a good shower and get a good night's sleep. Things might make more sense to me in the morning. Has anybody seen my mum?'

'I think she left hours ago,' said Morgan, 'with your sister.'

'Ah yes,' said Russell. 'My sister.'

Russell breathed goodbyes over Mr Fudgepacker.

'You take all tomorrow off,' the old one told him. 'Clear your head. You've done a splendid job and we're all proud of you.'

'Thank you,' said Russell. 'Thank you very much.'

'And change your clothes. I like a bad smell as much as the next man. More actually. But you have to draw the line somewhere. No offence meant.'

'None taken, I assure you.'

'Goodbye to you.'

'Goodbye.'

And Russell waved goodbyes about the place and left.

Russell bumbled along the little riverside path that led by Cider Island and the weir. It was another of those perfect Brentford nights that poets like to write about. And had there been one present, and had he brought his Biro and notebook with him, he would probably have penned something of this nature.

> The waters of the Thames flowed on
> Towards the distant sea.
> With moonlight moving on the waves
> Like ribboned mercury.

> And Russell breathed the fragrant air
> And viewed the stars on high
> And trod alone his path for home
> In deep serenity*.

> And all was peace and all was held
> As in a looking glass
> And Russell stepped in doggy-do
> And slipped upon his . . .†

'Ohh! Ow! Bloody Hell!' Russell struggled to his

* Poetic licence.

† Cheap laugh.

feet and hopped about, a-sniffing. 'God,' groaned Russell. 'Dog shit too. Whiskey and vomit and dog shit. I stink like an open sewer. It's not fair. It's just not fair.'

Russell rammed a hand over his mouth. He was quite sure he'd spoken those fateful words before. The previous evening. And they'd led him to all kinds of horrors. Or *had* they? He still didn't know for sure.

'It's all too much.' Russell shuffled his feet in the grass and bumbled on his way.

The stars shone down, the moonlight mooned and the Thames went quietly on its way.

After numerous abortive attempts and much in the way of beneath-the-breath swearing, Russell finally got the key into the lock and the front door open. He tip-toed into the house and closed the door as quietly as he could, the lights were all off. His mum was probably fast asleep. And what about his sister? Where was she? Not in *his* bed, he hoped.

Russell looked in at the front room. A bit of borrowed moonlight showed his sister snoring on the sofa.★

Russell swayed back into the hall and stumbled upstairs. Then, recalling that he was in a bungalow, he stumbled down the stairs again (which promptly vanished). Taking a shower now was out of the question, he'd wake his mum up. Russell thought

★Try saying that with something big in your mouth.

he'd best make do with a bit of in-the-dark face-splashing at the kitchen sink. This he achieved with remarkable dexterity and now wearing on his shirt front much of the floating contents of the cat's bowl which had been soaking in the dishwater, he wiped his face on what he thought to be the tea towel, but wasn't, and stumbled off to his bedroom.

Fully clothed and wretched he collapsed onto his bed and fell into a troubled sleep.

The moon moved on across the sky.
The Brentford night went slowly by.

In the front room the mantel clock on the feature fire place struck three. Westminster chimes it had. You don't hear those much any more. Except in Westminster, of course. But there was a time, not too long ago to escape fond memory, when most folk had a mantel clock with Westminster chimes. One of those 1940s jobbies, shaped like a hump-backed bridge, with two big keyholes in the face and the big key that fitted them tucked underneath, where the kids were forbidden to touch it. And it always had one corner with bits of folded-up Woodbine packet packed under it, to keep the thing level so it kept perfect time. And it was always folded-up Woodbine packet. Because in those days, before the invention of lung cancer, everybody smoked Woodbine: film stars, footballers, even the queen. Mind you, she wasn't the queen then, she was the queen mum.

Well, what I mean is, she *was* the queen, but she was also the queen mum. I mean, she's the queen mum now, but she was the queen then. Yes, that's it. But she was a mum then, of course, mum of the queen. Not that the queen was the queen *then*. Her mum was.

Well, one of them was anyway and whoever it was used to smoke Woodbine. Or it might have been Player's. Or maybe she smoked a pipe.

But, be that as it may, the mantel clock with the Westminster chimes struck three and a dark van pulled up outside the bungalow of Russell and his mum. And as the chimes died away, Russell's sister stirred from the sofa, slipped into the hall and opened the front door.

Four furtive figures climbed from the van, drew up the shutter at the back and manhandled something indistinct and bulky into the uncertain light of the street.

Struggling beneath its weight, they laboured up the garden path and through the doorway, then along the hall towards Russell's bedroom.

Russell's sister went before them. She quietly turned the handle on Russell's door and pushed it open.

Russell moved in his sleep, grunted uneasily and let go what can only be described as a fart. In the darkness, Russell's sister fanned her nose, whispered the word 'typical' and took her leave.

There was sudden movement, there was sound

214

and there was a big bright light. And Russell was cannoned into consciousness.

'What?' he went, then 'mmmmph!' as a hand clamped across his face. He tried to struggle and to strike out, but other hands held down his wrists and others still, his ankles. Russell strained and twisted, but they held him fast.

Russell's eyes went blink blink blink in the brightness. And had he been able to speak he could have named his attackers without difficulty. Bobby Boy was one, another Frank, and Morgan was another. And in the doorway, standing by a great dark shrouded something, was one more, and this was Mr Fudgepacker.

He was smiling, most unpleasantly.

'Gmmph mmph mm mmphmmph's' went Russell, which meant 'get off, you bastards'. And 'grmmmph mmmph mm mmckers!' which meant something along the same lines, but with a bit more emphasis.

'Let him breathe, Bobby Boy,' said Mr Fudgepacker.

The thin man lifted his hand from Russell's mouth. Russell tried to take a bite at it, but missed.

'Naughty,' said Bobby Boy.

'Let me go,' spat Russell.

Mr Fudgepacker waggled a frail fore-finger in Russell's direction. It looked a bit like a Twiglet, Russell wondered just what he might have been doing with it. 'Now now now,' said

Mr Fudgepacker. 'I want you to be very quiet, Russell. If you make a noise you might wake up your mother. And if that happens, we will have to deal with her.'

'*Deal with her?*' Russell whispered this.

'As in, cut her throat!' said Mr F. 'I've got the hedge-trimmer out in the van.'

'Shall I bring in the camcorder?' asked Bobby Boy.

'No no no. Russell's going to be very quiet. Aren't you, Russell?'

Russell nodded.

'Shame,' said Morgan. 'I *do* want to see the bit with the hedge-trimmer.'

'Maybe later. But we have much to do now.'

Russell struggled a bit more. 'Let go of me, you bastards,' he whispered.

'That's the spirit.' Mr Fudgepacker waggled his Twiglet again. 'But they won't let you go. They only do what *I* tell them to do.'

Russell twisted his neck from side to side. He stared up at Frank. At Morgan. 'Morgan,' he said, 'you're my friend. Why are you doing this?'

'It's for your own good, Russell. For the common good.'

'What?'

'You'll thank us for it afterwards. Well, you probably won't actually thank us. But it's all for the best.'

'Definitely for the best,' agreed Frank.

'Get off me,' Russell whispered. 'Let me go.'

Mr Fudgepacker sighed, shuffled over and sat down on the foot of Russell's bed. 'It's a great pity you didn't stick to your script,' he said. 'None of this would have been necessary, if only you'd stuck to your script. And we did give you a second chance, today. All you had to do was believe that the rest had been a dream. We went to so much trouble, changing the safe, dressing your head wound. But you weren't convinced, were you?'

'No,' said Russell. 'But I might be prepared to give it another go.'

'I don't think so.'

'What are you going to do?' Russell asked.

'Convert you, my boy. Convert you.'

'I don't want to be converted. I'm happy as I am.'

'Happy?' Mr Fudgepacker wheezed a little laugh. 'What is *happy*? No-one's really happy. They just bumble along from one crisis to another, hoping that things will all work out next week, or next month, or next year. But they never do. And even if they did, what then?'

'What then?' Russell asked.

'Well, you die then, don't you?'

'That's the way it is,' Russell said.

'But not the way it has to be. You can have more, you see. More much more. More life, more time. You just have to forfeit a few bits of baggage. Emotional baggage. Then you get it all.'

'I really don't want it, whatever it is.'

'That's a shame. Because you're going to get it anyway. Take his clothes off, lads.'

'What?' whispered Russell. 'No.'

Mr Fudgepacker sniffed, then rooted in his nose with his Twiglet finger. Something gory came out on his nail, Mr Fudgepacker popped it into his mouth and sucked. 'It's *yes*, I'm afraid, Russell. And not without good cause anyway. I do declare you've added dog shit and cat food to your aromatic wardrobe since I saw you last.'

Russell took to further silent struggling, but it was three against one and he was just the one. It was Bobby Boy who pulled down Russell's boxer shorts.

'Blimey, Russell,' said the thin man. 'Mother Nature didn't sell you short, did she?'

Russell was too mortified to answer.

'Errol Flynn used to have a tadger like that,' said Frank. 'He showed it to me once, in the bog at Pinewood. Used to call it his Crimson Pirate.'

'That was Douglas Fairbanks,' said Mr Fudgepacker.

'Could have been, I couldn't see properly from the angle I was at.'

'You sick bastard.' Russell spat at Frank. Real spit this time. Mr Fudgepacker brought his Twiglet once more into play. 'Remember your mum,' was his advice.

'Please let me go. Please stop this. Please.'

'It won't take very long and it's better if you

218

don't struggle too much. Let's have him up on his feet, lads.'

Russell was dragged into the vertical plane, which is to say, upright. And he was held very firmly in that position.

Mr Fudgepacker struggled to his feet and limped over to the large covered something that stood by the bedroom door. 'Your new life awaits,' he declared. 'We measured you up for it last night while you slept.'

'What? What?'

With a flourish Mr Fudgepacker whipped away the covering and Russell found himself staring at . . .

Himself.

And it *was* him. A tall naked him. But a better-looking him. A better-proportioned, better-formed and idealized version of him. And it stood there, as if regarding Russell through its blank eye sockets. Like a noble corpse, or a shell, or a skin.

'Get him into it,' ordered Mr Fudgepacker. 'Get him into the back.'

Russell fought and kicked and jerked from side to side, but they held him fast and they dragged him around to the back of his other self. To the back with its little doors on the arms and legs and the polished bolts and catches and hinges. And the hollow inside, with the strap and the rigging, the miniature ship's rigging, with the tiny ropes and pulleys.

'Into the back, lads. Into the back.'

Russell dug in his heels, but they pushed him and pushed him and pushed him in.

'It won't take long, Russell.'

Russell turned frightened eyes towards the old man. He held a strange device, something Victorian, of burnished brass.

'Once your spine is out you'll have no more fears, Russell. No more worries, no more stress.'

'No.' Russell fought like a madman, but in vain. They forced him inside, into that thing that was himself. That mockery. And his head snapped up inside its head and his hands slipped inside its hands and his feet were inside its feet. And his neck stiffened and the brass instrument pressed upon the base of his spine and penetrated into his flesh.

# CHAPTER 16

# THE REICH STUFF

ussell awoke with a scream, fully clothed
on his bed.
'Oh my God!' Russell felt at himself and
blinked his eyes in the darkness. Downstairs the
clock on the mantelpiece struck three with its
Westminster chimes.

It had all been a terrible dream.*

The hall light snapped on and Russell's mum
stuck her head round the door. 'Are you all right,
dear?' enquired the sweet old thing. 'Did you have
a bad dream?'

'Yes.' Russell drew deep breaths. 'Yes, I did. But
I'm fine now. Sorry I woke you up, go back to bed.'

'Would you like a cup of cocoa?'

'No, it's OK.'

'Well, you get a good night's sleep. You work
too hard.'

'Yes, thank you, Mum. Goodnight.'

'Goodnight.'

'Typical,' said the voice of Russell's sister from
the hall.

---

* But I had you going that time, didn't I?

Russell clutched at his heart. Those were palpitations and that had been the mother of all nightmares. That was truly gruesome.

'Someone is messing around with my head,' mumbled Russell. 'God, that was frightening.' He swung his legs over the side of the bed. He still had his shoes on. One of them smelled rather strongly.

Russell took a deep breath, then kicked off his offending shoe and nudged it under the bed with his heel.

What was that dream all about? Conversion? Mr Fudgepacker had spoken all about conversion the previous night. Him and Bobby Boy. Was that the conversion? And what about that brass instrument? And what about taking his spine? Russell shivered. He needed a drink. No, he didn't need a drink. The last thing he needed was a drink. He felt fiercely sober now and that was how he intended to remain.

Russell squeezed at his arms. He was still himself. He wasn't inside something else. 'Enough is enough.' Russell pushed himself to his feet. 'I am going to get this sorted out. And I'm going to do it now. But I'm *not* going to do it smelling like this.'

Russell went to the bathroom and took a shower. He was sorry if it kept his mum awake, but it had to be done. Russell returned to his bedroom, dried himself off and dressed in a clean set of clothes: sweatshirt, jeans, clean socks and trainers. He took his other waxed jacket with the poacher's pockets (the one that he wore for best) from the wardrobe and put that on. And then he looked up at the wardrobe and thought very deeply.

'All right,' he said. 'It has to be done.'

Russell took a chair, put it next to the wardrobe and climbed onto it. From on top of the wardrobe he took down a shoebox and placed this upon his bed. Laying the lid aside, he revealed something wrapped in an oil cloth. That something was a Second World War service revolver. Russell folded back the oil cloth and looked down at it.

It had been his father's gun. His father had given it to Russell on his eighteenth birthday. Russell had taken one look at the gun and pleaded that it be taken at once to the police station and handed in. But his father had said no.

'Keep it safe on top of the wardrobe. One day you might need it. One day.'

Russell took up the gun and held it between both hands. This, he concluded, was *that* one day.

Russell slipped from his house and made off up the road. He walked briskly and rehearsed beneath his breath the friendly hello he would offer to any patrolling beat policeman whose path he might happen to cross.

Down Horseferry Lane went Russell, his trainer soles silent on the cobbles, along the short-cut past the weir and Cider Island and into the car park at the back of Hangar 18.

And here Russell stopped very short in his tracks.

There was still a large number of cars here: Frank's mini, Morgan's Morgan, several four-wheel drives belonging to the production buyers. But there was one other vehicle which caught Russell's particular interest. It stood there in the middle of the car park looking quite out of place.

That vehicle was the *Flügelrad*.

Russell let a little whistle escape from his lips. Now here was a piece of evidence, if ever he needed one.

Gun in slightly trembling hand, Russell crept up close, keeping to the shadows, the hatch was open and the extendible ladder down. A soft blue light welled from within the cockpit. Russell took a step or two up the ladder and peeped in. Empty. Russell looked this way and the other, then shinned up and in.

Russell hadn't been inside the *Flügelrad* before. On the night he'd first seen it he'd spent all his time playing with the Cyberstar machine. But it was just as Bobby Boy had said: old fashioned, all dials and stop-cocks and big glass radio valve things. A bit like a cross between the interior of a Second World War tank and Captain Nemo's *Nautilus*. And this craft could travel through time? Russell glanced all around. Bobby Boy had mentioned a loose valve, or some such. Russell spied a large and likely looking one. Large and likely enough looking to be essential to the running of the *Flügelrad*.

Russell carefully removed it from its socket and slipped it into his poacher's pocket.

'Put it back,' said a voice with a German accent.

Russell turned swiftly. One of the tall young SS types was framed in the open hatch. He was pointing a gun.

Russell pointed his.

'Drop your weapon,' said the German.

'Drop yours,' Russell said.

'But I asked first.'

'Drop yours anyway.'

'I'll shoot you,' said the German.

Russell clutched at his jacket, holding the big glass valve close to his chest. 'Then you'll smash this. And your Führer wouldn't like that.'

'My Führer?'

'Listen,' said Russell, 'I'm on your side. Mr Fudgepacker sent me out here to see that everything was safe.'

'Ah,' said the German.

'Heil Hitler,' said Russell, raising his free hand in the Nazi salute.

'Heil Hitler.' The German raised his hand too. But he raised the one with the gun in it. Russell hit him very hard in the face.

The German fell backwards from the ladder and hit the ground with a terrible bone-crunching thump.

'Oh dear.' Russell hastened down the ladder to attend to the unconscious figure. 'Are you all right?' he asked, and then, 'What am I saying? Stuff you.' And with that he marched across the car park towards Hangar 18.

225

Merry sounds issued from within. The celebrations were far from over. Russell crept around to the big sliding door and pushed open the little hinged one.

There was a whole lot of shaking going on. Russell cast a wary eye about the place. Morgan was there and Bobby Boy was there and Frank was there and Julie was there. And many of the others he'd seen earlier. But there had been a few late arrivals at the Fudgepacker Ball. There was old Charlton Heston in his toga. And David Niven in his black and white. And the cast of *Cockleshell Heroes*, including the great David Lodge. The late arrivals weren't dancing though, they were just sort of standing around.

Russell nodded. Better and better. So where was Mr Fudgepacker?

Russell squinted beyond the dancing drinkers and the standing Cyberstars towards the office. In there, perhaps?

Russell eased his way into the hangar and closed the door behind him. Keeping his back against the wall and himself very much to the shadows, he edged towards the office. No-one was looking in his direction, they were all having far too good a time. Bobby Boy had the programmer, and, yes, there in the middle of the dancers, Marilyn Monroe was getting her kit off.

Russell reached the office unobserved. He ducked down beside the partition window, then stuck his head up to take a peep in.

226

And then he ducked right down.

'It's that man again,' whispered Russell.

And it was, seated across the desk from Mr Fudgepacker on one of the unspeakable chairs, with a glass of *Glen Boleskine* clutched in a chubby hand, was the evil sod himself.

Mr Adolf Hitler, it was he.

And he looked in the very peak of good health.

Russell dithered (and wouldn't anyone?). What to do for the best? Creep away and phone the police?

'Hello, yes, I've got Adolf Hitler cornered in an old aircraft hangar on Brentford dock, and I've got his time machine too. Could you send over a couple of constables? Thank you.' Russell weighed up the pros and cons. All cons, he concluded. He would have to go it alone. Go in there like a hero would, and do the right thing.

Now Russell, like all right-thinking individuals, was a great fan of the science fiction movie. And being so, there was, of course, one particular line he'd always wanted to shout at someone.

No, it was *not* 'I'll be back'.

And so, taking a very big breath, he kicked open the office door and with gun held tight between both hands and pointed at the Führer's face, he shouted it out.

'Lead or a dive you're coming with me. I mean . . .'

'What is this?' Hitler spoke with a thick Cockney

accent. 'Who let this Yankee* in here?'

'I'm not a Yankee.' Russell held the gun as steadily as he could. 'Dead or alive you're coming with me.'

'Don't be absurd.' Mr Fudgepacker flapped his fragile hands about. 'I'll have this oaf removed at once, my Führer. Russell, put down that toy pistol at once.'

'It's not a toy.' Russell squeezed the trigger and a round parted the Führer's hair.

'Oh my God.' Russell gawped at the gun and at the Führer. 'I'm so sorry. I had the safety catch off. Are you all right?'

'You stupid Russian†.' The Führer clutched at his head.

'I'll call a doctor,' said Russell. 'No, what am I saying again? Stuff you. Put your hands up, I'm making a citizen's arrest.'

'Russell!' said Mr Fudgepacker, sternly. 'Look behind you, Russell.'

'You don't think I'm going to fall for that old trick?' Russell took a quick peep over his shoulder, and then he said, 'Oh dear.'

The noise of the gunshot had rather put paid to the partying. The sound system had been switched off. Many eyes were now turned upon him. Many faces were wearing angry expressions.

'I've got a gun.' Russell flashed it in their

---

* Nazi rhyming slang. Yankee food parcel: arsehole.

† We did this one earlier.

direction. 'Well, you probably guessed that, hearing it go off and everything. But I'm not afraid to use it. I just used it then, didn't I? And I'll use it again, I will.'

The crowd looked rather unimpressed. Unimpressed, but surly, the way crowds can look when they're composed of people who've had too much to drink and are suddenly bothered by some fool who wants to break up the party.

'I'm arresting this man,' Russell continued. 'He's an escaped war criminal and I'm taking him to prison.'

The crowd replied with a sinister growl that Russell found discouraging. But he was still prepared to put a brave face on it. 'Don't try to stop me,' was the phrase he chose to use.

'Growl' and now, 'snarl,' went the crowd.

'Russell,' said Mr Fudgepacker, 'put that gun down at once.'

'No I won't.' Russell took stock of the two men in the office.

'And *you* put your hands up,' he told Adolf Hitler. 'I won't tell you again.'

The Führer's hands shot into the air, no hero he with a gun pointing in his direction.

'You've let me down, Russell,' said Mr Fudgepacker.

'*Me* let *you* down?' Russell waved his gun, which had the führer flinching. 'You wicked old man. I respected you. I worked hard for you.'

'And you will again. Now put down that gun and let's talk about things.'

'Oh no no. No more talking. This man, Hitler, him, he's coming with me. I don't want to shoot him, but I will if I must. I'd probably get a medal from the Queen, if I did. Or maybe a presentation clock with Westminster chimes.'

'It's too late for that,' said Mr Fudgepacker.

'Too late for what?'

'Too late to start some running gag about Westminster chimes.'

'Yes, you're probably right. But he's still coming with me. This is the end, Mr Fudgepacker. It's all over now, the movie, everything.'

'You're overwrought, Russell, sit down and have a drink.'

'No. I don't want a—'

'*Russell, look out!*' Julie screamed the words.

Russell turned his head and met the eyes of Bobby Boy. The thin man leapt at him, gun in hand and then things seemed to move in slow-motion, the way they often do when something really awful happens. The thin man's gun came up to Russell's face, but Russell swept his wrist aside and brought his own gun into violent contact with his attacker's stomach. Still carried by the force of his own momentum, Bobby Boy plunged past Russell, into the office and struck his head on the mighty *Invincible*. As he fell backwards his gun went off and the bullet ricocheted from the safe and caught him square in the left kneecap.

Russell looked on in horror as the thin man

writhed on the office floor, blood pumping from his trouser leg.

'Call an ambulance,' Russell turned back upon the crowd. 'There's been an accident. Call an ambulance.'

Nobody moved.

'Come on,' shouted Russell, 'hurry up. I'll apply a tourniquet.'

Nobody moved once more.

'Well come on, do *something*.'

The people of the crowd did *something*. They threw back their heads and howled. It was a horrible sound, cruel, atavistic. If fair put the wind up Russell.

'Stop it!' he shouted. 'Stop it!'

But they didn't.

'Russell, quickly, come.' Julie's hand was on his arm. She tugged at Russell's sleeve.

'Yes, I will . . . I . . .'

Someone hurled a glass. It shattered above the office door, showering splinters down on Russell. Then a bottle too. The crowd advanced.

Russell fired a shot into the ceiling. The crowd held back a moment. Russell ran and so did Julie. Across the hangar floor they went and the howling crowd swept after them.

Russell tore open the little hinged door in the big sliding one and pushed Julie through the opening. He followed at the hurry-up, slammed shut the door and rammed the bolt home. You couldn't open *that* from the inside.

Russell gathered wits and breath. From within the hangar came horrible howls and the sounds of fists drumming on the big sliding door.

'Thank you,' Russell gasped. 'Thank you for warning me. We'll have to get to a phone, call an ambulance ourselves.'

'Are you kidding?'

'He could bleed to death.'

'He won't.'

'But—'

'We have to get away, Russell. They'll kill us. Both of us.'

'All right, do you have a car?'

'No, do you?'

'No, I don't have one. I wouldn't have asked you, if I had one.'

'You *should* get one, Russell. Something fast. A bright green sports car.'

'Well, I've always fancied a Volvo, they're very safe. Cage of steel and everything.'

'Volvos are driven by men who wear pyjamas,' said Julie, which Russell tried to picture.

'Waxed jackets surely,' he said. 'What's that sound?'

'What sound?'

'*That* sound.'

*That* sound was a sort of grating grinding sound. The sort of sound that a big sliding door makes as it's being slid along.

'Run,' said Russell.

'Where?' Julie asked.

'With me, I have an idea.' Russell took her by the hand and they ran, round to the car park at the back of Hangar 18. Russell pulled the big glass valve from his poacher's pocket. 'We can use *this*,' he said.

Julie stopped short and gawped at it. 'You dirty bastard,' she said. 'Is that all men ever think about?'

'What?' Russell stared at Julie and then at the valve. 'Oh no, it's not a . . . You thought it was a . . . No, it's a . . .' Sounds of loud howling reached their ears. 'This way, quickly.'

Russell dragged her to the *Flügelrad*. 'Get inside, come on.'

'I don't think so.'

'There's no time.' Russell pushed her up the ladder. The SS chap was starting to stir, Russell kicked him in the head. 'I'm sorry,' he said, as he followed Julie into the cockpit.

The howlers were now pouring into the car park. And yes, they *did* see Russell.

Inside the *Flügelrad*, Russell fought the valve back into its socket and worried at the controls. 'Now, how exactly does this thing work?' he wondered.

'Hurry, Russell, hurry.'

A bottle shattered against the hull. Russell bashed at the control panel.

Julie screamed.

Russell turned. Morgan's face leered in at the hatch, eyes round, mouth contorted. Russell leapt up and punched Morgan right in the nose. Amidst further howling from the mob, Morgan rapidly vanished from view. Fists now rained upon the *Flügelrad*.

'One of these must close the hatch,' Russell flicked switches, pressed buttons, pulled levers. The *Flügelrad* shook. But not from Russell's handiwork.

'They'll turn it over. Out of the way, Russell. Let me do it.' Julie pushed Russell aside, jumped into the pilot's seat and pushed several buttons. The extendible ladder retracted and the hatch snapped shut.

'Lucky guess,' said Russell. 'Now, let's see if I can—'

'No.' Julie's hands moved over the control panel, adjusting this, tweaking that, powering up the other. A vibration ran through the craft and a dull hum that grew to a high-pitched whine. Then there was a great rushing sound and after that, nothing but silence.

And much of this silence came from Russell.

# CHAPTER 17

# MY STEPMOTHER IS AN ARIAN

Julie worked at the controls, making adjustments, doing this and that. At length she sat back in the pilot's seat and smiled up at Russell. 'We're on our way,' she said.

'And dare I ask, to where?'

'To the future, of course.'

'Of course.' Russell scratched at his chin. It needed a shave. 'Would you care to tell me just what's going on?'

Julie tossed back her beautiful hair. 'All right,' she said. 'I'll tell you everything. Some of it you already know, but not all. I wonder where I should start.'

Russell said nothing.

'Aren't you supposed to say "at the beginning"?'

'No.' Russell shook his head. 'Everyone always says that. You start wherever you want.'

'All right. I'll start with the *Flügelrad*. I'll bet you'd like to know how I'm able to fly it.'

'The thought had crossed my mind.'

'Well, it's simple. I know how to, because my father built it.'

'Your father?'

'My stepfather actually, I was adopted. My stepfather is Mr Fudgepacker.'

'Oh,' said Russell.

'Except Ernest Fudgepacker is not his real name. His real name is Viktor Schauberger. He was an aeronautical engineer working for the Third Reich. Adolf Hitler is a friend of the family, you could say.'

'They certainly seemed very chummy.'

'The *Flügelrads* were constructed at the very end of the Second World War. Built under other-world guidance.'

'Other-world? Like, from outer space?'

'More like inner space, but let me explain. Two crafts were completed. One was to take Hitler forward one hundred years. The other was to take a number of military advisors back in time to readvise the German military on where the campaigns had gone wrong before they did, so Germany would win the war.'

'Which it didn't.'

'Because the other *Flügelrad* malfunctioned. Hitler went off into the future, expecting to step out in glory into a world dominated by the Nazis, but when he got there, it wasn't.'

'But Bobby Boy said it *was*, or *is*.'

'I'm coming to that. Hitler found that the future was *not* dominated by the Nazis, so he decided to go back in time and find out *why*. But he didn't want to risk going back as far as the Second World

236

War, so he stopped off here, in the nineteen nineties. He wanted to seek out his old friend Viktor Schauberger and find out what had gone wrong. The craft landed on the allotments and that's when Bobby Boy saw it.'

'And Bobby Boy got into it and went into the future.'

'And stole the Cyberstar equipment.'

'But Bobby Boy said it was a *Nazi* future.'

'And so it was when he got there.'

'Now hang about,' said Russell. 'This is all a bit of a coincidence, isn't it? I can buy Fudgepacker being Schauberger, but Bobby Boy being the one who finds the *Flügelrad*, and just happens to work for Fudgepacker.'

'Well he would, Russell. Bobby Boy is my stepbrother. He's Mr Fudgepacker's son.'

'I thought he was the son of the local brewery owner.'

'Mr Fudgepacker *is* the local brewery owner.'

'What?'

'Mr Fudgepacker owns half of Brentford. Bought with Nazi gold. Hitler knew he'd be here if he was still alive. Fudgepacker was planning to change his identity and move here after the war if the Germans lost. Hitler knew all about it. He set it up.'

'This is getting wilder by the moment. So Bobby Boy knew what the *Flügelrad* was when he saw it.'

'Exactly, and he couldn't resist getting inside and having a go. He flew into the future and nicked the Cyberstar equipment. He didn't half get a hiding from the old man when he got back.'

'I thought he got back before he left.'

'He lied about that.'

'Then he probably lied about the Nazi future as well.'

'No, he was telling the truth about that.'

'I'm confused,' said Russell.

'I'm trying to make it as simple as I can. Hitler's henchmen, the two SS guards, located Mr Fudgepacker. He arranged for me to hide Hitler in the shed behind The Bricklayer's Arms. Where *you* saw him. Bobby Boy turned up just after you'd gone. And he told his story about being in a Nazi future. Now Mr Fudgepacker put two and two together. The future had *not* been Nazi when Hitler got there, but it *had* when Bobby Boy got there. Why was that?'

'Good question,' said Russell. 'Why *was* that?'

'Because Bobby Boy had stolen the Cyberstar equipment and brought it back to the nineteen nineties.'

'I still don't get it.'

'Mr Fudgepacker told you about the movie. The movie to be made with the equipment. The movie that would change the world. Change the future.'

'Oh,' said Russell. 'I see. The stolen equipment from the future would be used to change the future. But surely that can't be done.'

'Why not?'

'Because it's plagiarism. They used the same idea in *Terminator 2*.'

'Whatever made you say that?'

'I just thought I'd get it in before anyone else did.'

'Fair enough.'

'So what you're saying, is that by going into the future and stealing the equipment that would change the future, the future Bobby Boy went into what was a future that had already been changed, by him having stolen the equipment and used it in the then-past, which is our present?'

'Exactly. It's all so simple when you put it like that.'

'So the movie *will* change the future.'

'With *His* help, it will.'

'This is the *He* I saw on the video, the red-faced insect thing?'

'It was *He* who guided the construction of the *Flügelrad*. The rise of Nazi Germany in the twentieth century offered the first real opportunity for a single man to rule the entire world.'

'Mr Hitler.'

'And if he'd won, it would have happened. Hitler is just a puppet of this creature. It feeds off people, feeds off their time. It swallows up their time, takes their feelings, their emotions. It intends to put something into the movie. Something subliminal, or active in some way that will control the minds of all who watch it. And everyone will want to watch it, they'll have never seen anything like it before.'

'Good God,' said Russell.

'*Bad* God,' said Julie.

'But is it a god? Or is it from outer space, or inner space, or what?'

'I don't know exactly what it is. Mr Fudgepacker knows. He's its guardian. At times it is moved to other places and others guard it. But it always returns to the Emporium. I've known of it since I was a child.'

'So aren't you afraid?'

'Very afraid. That's why I went along with everything. The making of the movie. Everything.'

'Yes, what about the movie? The one I saw on the videos wasn't the same one I saw the next day at the screening.'

'It was. You just didn't think it was. You saw what they wanted you to see. You were hypnotized while you slept. When they dressed your head and changed the safe.'

'They've made a right fool out of me, haven't they? But I'll have the last laugh. I won't market their evil movie. I'll stop it ever getting shown.'

'I don't know if you can. You see, after you left the party Hitler turned up in the *Flügelrad*. He'd come back from the future. The Nazi future he controls. He'd come back to congratulate Mr Fudgepacker on the success of the movie. It does get shown, Russell, with, or without your help. And it does change the world.'

'Then we've got to stop it. Somehow.'

'Oh yes, we have. It's all so evil. I couldn't be a part of it any longer.'

'So that's why you shouted out when Bobby Boy attacked me.'

'You're the one person I knew I could trust. The one person prepared to stand up to them. You're the one person I really care about, Russell.'

Julie's mouth was there to kiss. So Russell kissed it.

The *Flügelrad* flew on into the future.

Explicit things occurred within, which had only previously occurred there on one occasion. And that was in 1955, when a certain Miss Turton of 16 Mafeking Avenue, Brentford, who got a mention at the beginning of Chapter 6, had her brief encounter of the third kind.

The explicit things now, however, occurred with a great deal more gusto and mutual appreciation. Russell gave of his all unstintingly and Julie, for her part, responded in a manner that only an ex-contortionist go-go dancing sex aid demonstrator truly can.

Lucky old Russell.

Then *BANG!* went the *Flügelrad*.

'Did the earth move for you too?' Julie asked.

'Yes,' said Russell. 'Ouch.'

There was a curious vibration. Things seemed to go out of focus. Everything double, then merging into one again.

'Is it supposed to do that?' Russell rubbed at his eyes.

'Don't ask me, I've never flown the thing before.'

'That's comforting.'

'But I think it means we've arrived at whenever we've arrived at.'

'And so's that.'

Julie began to put on her clothes. 'Come on,' she said. 'Let's get out.'

'Aw, must we just yet?'

'I think we must.'

The ladder extended and the hatch snapped open. Russell stuck his head out and sniffed at the air. Did it smell like home? Well, it smelled of flowers. Spring flowers. Russell climbed up onto the dome and took a look around. The *Flügelrad* had landed in bushes, in the middle of a pleasant park. In the distance rose wondrous buildings of a futuristic nature. Closer, old housing, faintly familiar.

'I think we've landed in exactly the same place Bobby Boy landed.' Russell joined Julie back in the cockpit. 'Let's go for a walk and see what's what.'

'Do you think it will be safe?'

'Not for one minute. But let's do it anyway.'

Russell helped her down the ladder. The *Flügelrad* was pretty well hidden by the bushes and there was no-one about. It couldn't hurt to leave it there and take a quick look around.

Of course it couldn't.

'It's supposed to be all uniforms and golden dresses here.' Russell examined his appearance. Scruffy, he concluded. Julie looked marvellous. She was still wearing the short black evening number. The one that should have had more than a mention earlier.

'We could try and steal some clothes,' Julie said.

'Oh no. We're not stealing anything. We'll go and have a look around, size up the situation. But we won't get involved in anything.'

'Fair enough.'

They strolled across the park. Julie held Russell by the hand, which made Russell feel proud. Soon they reached the something-strasser.

'Look,' Russell pointed. 'It's The Bricklayer's Arms. And Bobby Boy told the truth. It has been renamed The Flying Swan.'

'I wonder why.'

Russell shrugged. 'I'm sure it will be explained eventually.'

And on they walked.

Folk passed them on the something-strasser, young folk, tall and handsome. But Russell didn't like the way they moved. So stiffly, so unnaturally. They did not so much as glance at Russell, but they did look twice at Julie.

Ahead, where The Great West Road had once been, they found the mammoth shopping mall. All high glass and chrome, with the souped-up Volkswagens flying around it and landing upon upper platforms.

'Shall we take a look at the shops, Russell?'

'Why not.'

Through the glass revolving doors and into a

massive entrance hall. Russell spied out the golden letters that crowned a silver arch, leading to a grand arcade of shops.

## THE SCHAUBERGER MEMORIAL MALL

Russell shook his head and they walked on.

And all the shops were there, the ones Bobby Boy had spoken of. The clothes shops and the gift shops and the Adolf Hitler souvenir shops. And the Tandys with the German name.

'That's the shop,' said Russell. 'The one he stole the Cyberstar equipment from.'

'Russell, look.' Julie pointed through the window. Inside children were playing upon the holographic video games. Famous film stars, Cyberstar projections, stood as if in conversation.

And beyond them, standing at the counter . . .

'It's Bobby Boy.' Russell stared. 'He's here, now. How can he be here, now?'

As they watched him, Bobby Boy turned from the counter, a parcel in his hands, and began to walk towards the door.

'He's coming this way.' Russell hustled Julie into a shop doorway.

'Why are we hiding from *him*?'

'Good question.' Russell made to step out and accost the thin man, but at that moment alarms sounded and lights began to flash.

'Best keep a low profile,' said Russell withdrawing once more into hiding.

Bobby Boy passed within feet of them, a frightened look on his long thin face. He took a couple of faltering steps and then broke into a run.

And then came the sounds of a terrible clanking. As Russell and Julie looked on, the two horrendous iron robots went by at the trot in pursuit of Bobby Boy.

'Let's hope they catch him,' said Russell. 'But I don't understand how—'

'Look.' Julie pointed. Men in black uniforms with swastika arm bands came marching down the mall. They marched into the electrical shop and approached the chap behind the counter.

'Come on,' said Russell. 'We're innocent bystanders. Let's go in and see what's on the go.'

Inside the shop, an officer type, with Heinrich Himmler glasses and a bad attitude, was interviewing the counter chap. Russell mingled close to catch an earful.

'He walked into the shop,' said the counter chap, wringing his hands and cringing as he spoke. 'He wore the black. Naturally I assumed he was a party member. And he looked at the Cyberstar system and he wanted to know whether the holograms could be made to do anything he wanted. Things not in the movies they're programmed to re-enact. And so I said, yes of course, sir, and so he said he would take one. But when he eyeballed the screen for retina and iris identification, the alarms went off. He is unregistered. How can this be?'

245

'This cannot be,' shouted the Himmler person. 'Unless—'

'Unless, capitan of security?'

'Unless this is the fellow mentioned in the document. The one we have been expecting. How was this fellow? Was he tall, very thin, with a tricky little mouth?'

'Got him in one,' whispered Russell.

'You have him in one, my capitan.'

'Then all is well. You are not to blame, citizen, carry on with your business, the cost of the system will be taken from your wages.'

'You're too kind, my capitan.'

'Yes, I am the nice one.'

Russell glanced down at the counter. There all on its own stood the programmer.

'The thief will be apprehended. All is well.'

'Thank you, my capitan. Oh and one thing, my capitan.'

'What is it?'

'Well, sir, in his haste he left without the programmer. The system is useless without it. I have it here. Oh, I *don't* have it here.'

Outside in the mall, Julie said, 'You stole it, Russell, I saw you.'

'Yep,' Russell patted at the pocket which had had so much use lately. 'And I'm keeping it. We can stop all this right now. If Bobby Boy never gets the programmer, he can't work the Cyberstar equipment. And if he can't work that, they can't make the movie.'

They walked back along the mall.

'I hope you're right,' said Julie.

'And why wouldn't I be?'

'Well, there's something bothering me.'

'And that's what?'

'Well, we both agree on what we just saw, don't we?'

'We just saw Bobby Boy steal the equipment. We must have arrived here only moments after he did, when he made the journey from the allotments.'

'That's what's bothering me.'

'Go on.'

'Well, Bobby Boy came here in the *Flügelrad*, didn't he?'

'Yes.'

'And we came here in the *Flügelrad*, didn't we?'

'Yes again.'

'And you think that we landed in exactly the same place he did.'

'Yes again, again.'

'But I didn't see another *Flügelrad* parked nearby, did you?'

'Ah,' said Russell. 'No I didn't.'

'So how would you account for that?'

The worried look returned once more to Russell's face. 'I don't know,' he said. 'I think we'd better get back to the park.'

They didn't run, they didn't want to draw attention to themselves. But they walked very fast and they were soon back at the little park behind the something-strasser.

They were just in time to see several black VW flying cars lift off and sweep away into the sky.

'Are you thinking what I'm thinking?' Julie asked.

'I'm afraid that I probably am.'

They searched the bushes and all about the place. They crossed and they recrossed their tracks. But all they found were three neat depressions in the soil. The marks of tripod legs.

The *Flügelrad* was nowhere to be seen and they were now trapped in the future.

# CHAPTER 18

# STRICTLY BAR-ROOM

They sat on one of the benches in the pleasant park. It had a little brass plaque on the back. *Donated to the Schauberger Memorial Park by the Nostradamus Ate My Hamster Appreciation Society.*

'The way I see it,' Russell said, 'we landed only moments after Bobby Boy landed and we landed in exactly the same place. And I mean *exactly*. To the inch. And there couldn't be two *Flügelrads*, that were the same *Flügelrad* anyway, occupying the same space, so ours sort of merged with his. The two became one. It probably obeys some basic law of physics. Remember when we landed and everything went out of focus, then went back together again? That must have been it.'

'And so Bobby Boy leapt into his *Flügelrad*, which was also our *Flügelrad*, and escaped back into the past.'

'Yes, but *I* have the programmer.' Russell gave his pocket a pat. 'Oh damn.'

'Oh damn, what?'

'I don't have my dad's gun any more. I must have left it in the *Flügelrad*.'

'You're not really a "gun" person, Russell.'

'No, I'm most definitely not.' Russell got up from the bench and stretched his arms. 'I could really do with a drink. What say we take a look in at The Flying Swan?'

'Do you think that's wise?'

'What's the worst that can happen?'

They left the park and walked hand in hand along the something-strasser.

'Do you have any money?' Julie asked.

'Not a penny,' said Russell.

And they reached The Flying Swan.

'After you,' Russell said, pushing open the door.

'You are such a gentleman, thank you.' And inside they went.

Russell glanced all about the place. This was *not* the interior of The Bricklayer's Arms. Nothing like. Here was a far more splendid affair. An alehouse with dignity. Etched-glass partitions, long polished mahogany counter with brass foot rail (and spittoon?). Mottled dartsboard over near the Gents. An elderly piano. Six Britannia pub tables. And that certain light. That pub light, all long shafts with drifting golden motes, catching the burnished silver tips of the eight tall enamel beer pulls to a nicety.

Russell breathed it all in. It felt *right*.

There were folk all about. Casting darts, discoursing at the bar, quaffing ale and smiling. They looked *right*. No stiffness of the limbs, no vacant eyes. Real they seemed, and right.

Behind the bar the barman stood, for such is where he does. Tall and angular, slightly scholar-stooped, pale of complexion with a slick-back Brylcreme job about the head. He wore a dicky bow and crisp white shirt and he looked nothing at all like David Niven. He looked noble, though.

'Good-afternoon, madam, sir,' the barman said as they approached him.

Russell looked up at the battered Guinness clock above the bar. It *was* afternoon. It was one o'clock. It was lunch-time. Russell's stomach rumbled. He was hungry. He was penniless.

How best to approach this problem?

'First drinks are on the house,' said the barman. 'Always are to new patrons. And do help yourself to sandwiches. There's a plate on the counter there. Ham they are and very fresh.'

'Right,' said Russell. 'Thank you very much. What will you have, Julie?'

'A Perrier water please.'

'And for you, sir?'

Russell looked at Julie.

'Have anything you want,' she said.

Russell cast his eye along the row of gleaming pump handles. The barman poured Perrier and added ice and a slice. He placed it on the counter before Julie and then followed the direction of Russell's gaze.

'We have eight real ales on pump,' he said, and a tone of pride entered his voice. 'A selection which exceeds Jack Lane's by four and the New Inn by three. You'll find it hard to out-rival The Swan in this regard.'

'Which would you personally recommend?' Russell asked.

'Large,' said the barman. 'Without hesitation.'

'Then a pint of Large it will be.' Russell watched the barman pull the pint. He had seen beer pulled before, but somehow not like this. There was something in the way this fellow did it, that elevated the thing into an artform. It was hard to say quite how, but it was there. The angle of the glass? The speed of the pull? Something. Everything.

The barman presented Russell with the perfect pint.

Russell sipped the perfect pint.

'This is the perfect pint,' he said.

The barman inclined his noble head. 'I am pleased that you find it so. Might I ask you, sir, are you Mr Russell Nice?'

Russell coughed into the perfect pint, sending some of the finest froth up his nose.

'Sorry to startle you, sir. But there are two gentlemen over there, though I hesitate to use the word gentlemen, two *fellows*, who said that you might drop in, and if you did then I was to steer you in their direction.'

Russell steered his eyes in the fellows' direction and thought worried thoughts. Secret police? Time cops? Terminators, perhaps.

'You've nothing to fear,' said the barman. 'They're quite harmless. Shiftless, but harmless.'

Russell viewed the two fellows. Two young fellows, quaffing ale at a table by the window. One had an Irish set to his features. The other did not. But it was hard to tell which one.

The one it wasn't waggled his fingers in greeting.

'What do you think?' Russell asked Julie.

'I think *you* should make the decisions.'

'Right.'

They approached the two fellows and as they did so, the two fellows rose and moved out chairs. And then extended hands for shaking.

'Good day,' said the one with the Irish set. 'My name is John Omally and this is my friend and companion, James the-next-round's-on-me Pooley.'

'The-next-round's-on-me?' asked Pooley.

'That's very civil of you, Jim.'

'Omally? Pooley?' Russell looked from one of them to the other and then back again, as the hand-shaking got underway. John shook Russell's hand and Jim shook Julie's then Jim shook John's hand and Julie shook Russell's, and an old boy who was passing by and didn't want to miss out on anything, shook all their hands, and started everything off again.

Throughout all this, Russell's mouth was opening and closing and phrases such as, 'you're them,' and 'you're those two,' and 'Pooley and Omally, it's you,' kept coming from it.

'Sit down, sit down,' said John Omally, helping

253

Julie onto a chair, whilst once again shaking her hand.

'You too,' Jim told Russell. 'I'd help you, but as you can see . . .'

Russell stared at Pooley, who was now shaking himself by the hand.

'Stop that, Jim,' John told him. 'It's impossible.'

'Sorry,' and Pooley sat down.

And when all were seated, the barman came over and placed a plate of ham sandwiches on the table.

'Cheers, Neville,' said Omally.

'Neville?' Russell looked up at the chap in the dicky bow. 'Neville the part-time barman?'

Neville winked his good eye and returned to the bar.

'I'm confused,' said Russell. 'I'm very confused.'

Omally grinned. 'And you have every right to be. But tell me, sir, is this the pre-showdown pint you're taking, or the post-showdown one?'

'I don't think that's helped,' said Pooley.

'Have you bested the villain?' Omally asked. 'Or have you yet to best him?'

'I've yet to best him,' Russell said. 'But what are you two doing here? How is this . . . ? I mean, you're real, and this place . . . I don't understand.'

Jim raised his glass. 'We generally take a pint or two at lunch-times,' he said.

254

'That isn't what I meant.'

Omally took a sup from his pint and dabbed a knuckle at his lips. 'I think, Jim, that what your man is asking, is, why are we here.'

'I've often asked myself that question,' said Jim. 'But I rarely get any sense for a reply.'

'Allow me to explain,' said John Omally. 'Now correct me if I'm wrong, but the last anyone heard of us, we were being atomised and sucked into space. And all on a Christmas Eve in some unrecorded year.'

Russell nodded.

'God rest ye merry gentlemen and then good-night.'

Russell nodded again.

'Crash bang wallop. A bit of a shock for all concerned.'

'I did ask what happened next,' said Russell. 'But Morgan said that nothing did.'

'Well, he would say that, wouldn't he?'

'He did,' said Russell. 'I was there when he said it.'

Omally took a further sup and drained his glass. He handed it to Mr James the-next-round's-on-me Pooley. 'Would it surprise you to know,' Omally asked, 'that it was all part of a diabolical plot, hatched by a fiendish entity with a red insect face?'

'Probably not,' said Russell.

'I'm heartened to hear it. You see, Jim and I have, in episodes past, been called upon to protect

255

Brentford from all manner of beastliness. We rise to the occasion, although Jim here always makes a fuss about it, but we get the job done. In the natural scheme of things we would be doing it now. But your man with the insect face is not part of the natural scheme of things and he doesn't play by the rules. He put us right out of the picture.'

'But he couldn't put Brentford out of the picture,' said Jim, tucking Omally's empty glass under the table and taking a sip from his own. 'When horror bowls a googly in Brentford, someone will always step into the crease and knock it for six.'

'Most lyrically put, Jim. And a clean glass would be fine, the same again if you will.'

Jim Pooley left the table.

'Now, let me get a grip of this,' said Russell. 'Obviously you're real, I can see you're real, and what you're saying is, that this creature flung you and The Flying Swan and everything into the future to stop you interfering with its plans.'

'In a word, correct. We were literally erased from the plot.'

'But if Morgan had never told me the story, I would never have got involved.'

'The story had to be told in order to put us out of the picture. Fate decreed that it would be told to you and that you would assume the role of hero and get the job done on our behalf.'

'But I haven't got the job done.'

'But you will.'

'And how can you be so certain?'

256

'Because we've seen the end of the movie. On the pub TV, we know how it ends.'

'*You* saw the movie?' Russell jerked back in his chair. 'Then you've been converted. You're one of *them*.'

'The movie did all its converting back in the Nineties. *We* weren't there in the Nineties, *we* didn't get converted.'

'I'm going to stop that movie,' said Russell. 'If I can.'

'Oh you *can* and you will. But you see the movie is really a metaphor. All of this is a metaphor. Once you've figured out the metaphor, everything becomes clear.'

Russell downed his perfect pint. 'Well, one thing becomes immediately clear, if you've seen the movie, you know how it ends. Kindly tell me what I do and I'll get right off now and do it.'

'That can't be done, I'm afraid. I've watched the movie four times. Each time it has a different ending. But why not ask the lovely lady here. She was *in* the movie.'

'Julie?' said Russell.

'You've seen all the bits I was in,' said Julie. 'I don't know how it ends.'

'I remain totally confused,' said Russell.

Pooley returned with two pints of Large. 'Have you told him your story yet, John?' he asked.

'I was about to.' Omally accepted his pint. 'As Jim's in the chair, would you care for another drink?'

257

'Julie?' Russell asked.

'A large gin and tonic, please.'

'And I'll have the same again,' said Russell. 'Thank you very much.'

Pooley returned, unsmiling, to the bar.

'Have you ever heard the story of the stone soup?' Omally asked. 'It's an old Irish tale. Told to me by an old Irishman.'

'No,' said Russell. 'Do you think it's going to help me?'

'Without a doubt. The metaphor is the same. Grasp it and you grasp everything.'

'Then please tell your tale.'

'Very well,' Omally said. 'The setting is old Ireland, in medieval times. A ragged traveller is trudging over a bleak, lonely moor. Night is approaching and he is hungry and tired. Ahead in the distance he spies a castle. He plods towards it and reaches the door as the sky blackens over and the rain begins to fall.

'The traveller knocks and at length the door opens on the safety chain and the face of the castle cook looks out.

'"Wotcha want?" asks the cook.

'"Shelter for the night," says the traveller.

'"Sling yer 'ook," says the cook. "There's no place for you 'ere."

'"Would you turn away a fellow man on such a night as this?"

'"Soon as look at 'im," says the cook. "Now be on your way."

'"I will gladly pay for a night's lodgings," says the traveller.

'"Oh yes?" says the cook. "You're a beggar man for certain, and how will you pay?"

'"I have magic," says the traveller.

'"What of this?"

'"I have a stone in my pouch," says the traveller, "which, when placed in a cauldron of boiling water, transforms it into a delicious soup."

'"Show me this stone," says the cook.

'"I have it in my pouch, if you'll let me into the warm, I will gladly demonstrate its powers to you."

'The cook tugs thoughtfully at his beard, for this was in the days when all cooks wore the beard, not just the female ones. And the cook says, "I'll tell you what I'll do. As I haven't eaten yet tonight, I'll let you come in and demonstrate your magic. If it works you can share the soup, if not, I'll kick you back into the night."

'"Fair enough," says the traveller.

'"Yeah, and one thing more, if the magic works, then I get to keep the stone."

'Well, the traveller looks doubtful about this. And he huddles in his rags. But the wind is growing stronger and in the distance a wolf begins to howl. "All right," says he. "It's a deal."

'Inside the castle kitchen the cook sets a cauldron to boil upon the Aga and the traveller takes a round black stone from his pouch. With the cook looking on, he drops it into the cauldron and gives it a stir round with a wooden ladle.

'After a while the cook demands to taste the soup. He dips in the ladle and takes a sip. Then he spits onto the floor. "It tastes of nothing but water with a stone in it," says he.

'The traveller too takes a sip. "It lacks for something," he says. "Do you have any herbs, thyme, say, or rosemary?"

'"That I do."

'"Then let's put them in."

'"Very well."

'So in go the herbs and after a while the cook takes another sip. And he spits on the floor again. "Now it just tastes like water with a stone and some herbs in," says he.

'The traveller takes another sip. "It still lacks for something," he says. "Do you have any chicken stock?"

'"That I do."

'"Then let's put it in."

'"Very well."

'So the chicken stock goes in and after a while the cook takes another sip. And again he spits on the floor, remarking that now it just tastes like boiling water with a stone, some herbs and some chicken stock in it.

'The traveller agrees that it still lacks for something and he suggests the addition of a half-eaten chicken carcass that is standing on a platter on the table.

'The cook adds this to the soup.

'"How does it taste now?" asks the traveller a little later on.

'"Better," says the cook. "But it could do with some cornflour and parsnips."

'"Put them in," says the traveller. "And put in some of those carrots you have over there, and those new potatoes."

'"What about these mushrooms?" asks the cook.

'"Stick them in too," says the traveller.

'And the cook does.

'The cauldron boils and the traveller and the cook stand a sniffing. At length the traveller tastes the soup and says that in his considered opinion it is ready for the eating, but what does the cook think?

'The cook has another taste. "A touch more salt," he says.

'The traveller has another taste and declares the soup, "Just so", adding that to appreciate it at its very best it should be taken in company with thickly buttered bread.

'The cook hastens to the bread locker.

'"And fetch a jug of wine," says the traveller.

'And then the two men sit down to dine.

'Over the soup, which they both agree to be splendid, the traveller tells the cook of the sights he's seen and the things he's heard. And the cook tells the traveller about how he's thinking of opening a small restaurant down in the town.

'The talk continues over the cheese board, accompanied now by brandy from the cook's private stock and a couple of the castle lord's cigars.

'Later, somewhat full about the belly and light about the head, the two settle down in front of the kitchen fire and fall asleep.

'On the morrow the traveller departs upon his way. The cook waves goodbye from the battlements and the last he sees of him, is the traveller disappearing over the brow of a distant hill, having stopped only once, to pick up a stone at random and pop it into his pouch.'

Omally smiled and took a drink from his new pint.

'And what happened next?' Russell asked.

'What do *you* think happened next?'

'My guess would be that the traveller went on to another castle and repeated the performance.'

'That would be my guess too.'

Jim Pooley returned to the table in the company of a pint of Large and a small gin with lots of tonic. 'Did the cook fall for it again?' he asked Omally.

'He did,' said John.

Pooley placed the drinks on the table. 'One day he won't and I pity the poor traveller then.'

'Did you get it?' John asked Russell. 'Do you understand the metaphor?'

'Oh yes,' said Russell. 'I get it.'

'I wish I did,' said Jim.

Russell turned to Julie. 'We had best drink up and set to work. I think I know what to do.'

'These will help.' Omally reached under the table and brought out two plastic bin liners. 'A change of clothes for each of you. And there's some money in the pockets.'

'Thank you, John.' Russell shook Omally by the hand. Jim stuck his out, but Russell politely declined on the grounds that things might become a little complicated and there was still a great deal to do.

They changed in the toilets. Russell togged up in the black suit with lightning-flash insignias on the shoulders and Julie into that dress of golden scales.

Back in the saloon bar they said farewell and thanks to Pooley and Omally.

'If it all works out,' said Russell, 'we'll see you both back in old Brentford. Here in this very bar. And the drinks will be on me this time.'

'I'll drink to that,' said Pooley.

John and Jim returned to their window seats and watched as Russell and Julie walked off hand in hand along the something-strasser, bound once more for the big shopping mall.

'I hope he makes it,' said Jim.

'He will,' said John.

'John?' said Jim.

'Jim?' said John.

'All that stuff about the metaphor, you wouldn't care to explain that to *me*?'

'I would,' said John. 'If I only knew what it meant.'

# CHAPTER 19

# BACK TO THE FÜHRER III

'So you know what it means?' said Julie as they walked towards the mall.

'Oh yes,' said Russell. 'It all makes perfect sense.'

'Well, I understand that you're the traveller.'

'Oh no, I'm not the traveller, I'm the stone.'

'But the stone was a fake, it didn't do anything.'

'It was a symbol,' said Russell. 'It represents the individual, the individual as a catalyst for change.'

'And the cauldron?'

'The cauldron is the world.'

'And the vegetables and suchlike?'

'Society,' said Russell.

'That sounds about right.'

'You see the stone couldn't make the soup on its own, but without the stone the soup would never have been made.'

'I thought the cook made the soup.'

'The cook is an aspect of society. He represents society's greed and its ultimate gullibility.'

'And the traveller?'

'The traveller is time.'

'A time traveller, then the traveller is you.'

'No, I'm definitely the stone.'

'And the boiling water?'

'Change,' said Russell. 'Water represents change, because water can be changed into steam or into ice.'

'Water represents permanence,' said Julie. 'You can change its form, but you can't get rid of it. So perhaps the water represents society.'

'Society is the sum of its parts,' said Russell. 'The soup is society.'

'You said the vegetables were society.'

'Yes, I meant the vegetables.'

'But you just said the soup.'

'The soup is made out of the vegetables.'

'So they can't both be society, the soup *and* the vegetables.'

'They're aspects.'

'You said the cook was aspects.'

'He is.'

'But he put the soup together, so he can't be society too.'

'Perhaps it's the castle,' said Russell.

'What do you mean, *perhaps*? I thought you knew.'

'I do know.'

'What's the wasteland, then?'

'Time,' said Russell.

'The traveller is time, you said.'

'The traveller came out of the wasteland. The

265

wasteland is an aspect of time. Endless you see, like an endless wasteland.'

'The stone came out of the wasteland. So the stone must be an aspect of an aspect of time.'

'In a manner of speaking.'

'What a load of old rubbish.'

'It *is not.*'

'What's the kitchen, then?'

'Stop it,' said Russell. 'You're giving me a headache.'

By now they had reached the Schauberger Memorial Mall.

'Right,' said Russell. 'So this is the plan.'

'You have a plan?'

'Of course. Now what I want you to do is this: go into one of the gift shops and buy a box to put the programmer in. Write out a note to go with it telling me to take the programmer to Hangar 18. Oh, and I'll be in The Bricklayer's Arms eating a stale ham sandwich when I read the note, so mention that, I recall it giving me a shock.'

'And while the little woman is attending to her chores what will her big bold man be doing?'

'There's no need for that,' said Russell. 'I have to acquire the means for us to travel back in time. Meet me in an hour outside the electrical shop.'

'Oh, you'll have got that sorted in an hour, will you?'

'I very much doubt it, but if it takes me a month to get it sorted, and I *will* get it sorted, I'll set the controls on the time device to an hour from now and I'll meet you outside the electrical shop.'

'That's very clever, Russell.'

'Thank you. Do I get a kiss?'

'I'll give you one in an hour.'

Julie gave Russell a wonderful smile, then turned and walked off into the mall.

Russell watched until she was out of sight and then he returned to The Flying Swan.

Pooley and Omally still sat at the window seat, each with a pint glass in hand. A third pint, freshly pulled, stood upon the table.

Russell sat down, raised it to his lips and said, 'Cheers.'

'Cheers,' agreed Pooley and Omally.

Russell drained off half a perfect pint, then placed his glass upon the table.

'You knew I'd come back,' he said.

'Hoped,' said Omally.

'So you know that I've reasoned it out.'

'About the metaphor?'

Russell nodded. 'Julie was the traveller and I was the cook. She's working for them, isn't she? For the bad guys. I've been had.'

'Very good,' said Omally. 'But how did you reason it out.'

'She fits the part too well. I had my suspicions the moment she took the controls of the *Flügelrad*. Then she spun me the intricate story and I wasn't sure. But she knew too much. In her eagerness to prove she was on my side she told me too

267

much. And she wasn't really surprised when we saw Bobby Boy in the mall and she wasn't really surprised when we met you. And the one thing that she *must* know, she won't tell me. And that's the end of the movie. But what clinched it, was when I told her just now to buy a box to put the programmer in and write out the note. She didn't even flinch at the thought or try to convince me otherwise, it's what she intended, it's why she landed the craft at the exact time she did. So that *I* would pick up the programmer Bobby Boy forgot to take.'

'You really *have* reasoned it out,' Omally raised his glass in salute. 'Any more?'

'Yes. I don't think she's Fudgepacker's step-daughter at all.'

'You don't?'

'No, I think she's his wife.'

'Give the man a big cigar,' said Jim Pooley. 'How did you work that one out?'

'Something she said about Hitler being a friend of the family. It wouldn't have been her family then, she hadn't even been born. And the fact that she was sheltering Hitler at the Bricklayer's. No young woman of the nineteen nineties would do a thing like that.'

'So why is she still so young?' asked Omally.

'Ah, I've reasoned that out too. She's still the same age she was in 1945. Because she came with Hitler on the *Flügelrad*, that's how she knew how to fly it, you see.'

'But if she was Fudgepacker's wife, why would she be on the *Flügelrad* with Hitler?'

'Think about it,' said Russell. 'The war's almost lost. Hitler has the opportunity to go into the future and step out as some kind of new Messiah. He may only have one ball, but would he have passed up the opportunity to nick his chief engineer's beautiful wife and offer her a voyage into the future to be Mrs Messiah? I think it was the offer she couldn't refuse. She fits the bill, doesn't she? The Aryan type, tall, blond, blue-eyed. Hitler's ideal woman.'

'Has he only got one ball?' Jim Pooley asked.

'I'll ask him the next time I see him.' Russell finished his third perfect pint of the day. 'So am I right, or am I right?'

'Right as the now-legendary ninepence,' said Omally. 'In old money, of course.'

'But of course.'

'So what are you going to do now?'

'You know what I'm going to do now.'

'And that is?'

'He's going to the Emporium,' said Jim Pooley.

'Thank you, Jim,' said Russell. 'That's just what I'm going to do.'

The Kew Road was little more than a track. No grey cars moved along it now. Cars that fly have little need for roads\*. The Emporium stood all alone in a scrubby field, a bit like a castle, rising

---

\* This isn't a metaphor, it's an aphorism.

from the waste. Russell paused before the Gothic door. He didn't have a magic stone about his person, but then he wasn't the traveller, was he? No, he was certain that he wasn't.

But did he have a plan?

Yes, he was certain that he did.

He knew what was going to happen. He'd seen it on the video cassette, with Bobby Boy playing him and being led through the secret door down into the boiler room to meet the thing. He was asking for more time. Could that be the means to travel back in time? Russell couldn't remember precisely how the words went, but if he mucked up the script a bit and got a few words wrong, would it actually matter?

'This calls for a bit of method acting,' said Russell to himself and he knocked upon the door.

After what seemed an age, but was probably less than a minute, the door creaked open a crack and Viktor Schauberger, alias Ernest Fudgepacker, looked out at Russell.

He hadn't changed a bit. He was still the same old clapped-out wizened wreck of a man he'd been back in the nineties. But just a little bit more so.

As he swung wide the door and waved Russell in, Russell noticed the way that he moved, stiffly, like an automaton. Russell smiled and said, 'Hello.'

The ancient man inclined his turtle neck. 'So it's that day already, is it?' he asked, his voice a death-rattle cough. 'I did look at the calendar, but one day is much like another and this year like the last.'

270

'Are you well?' Russell asked.

The magnified eyes stared at Russell. They were the eyes of a corpse.

'The old place looks the same,' Russell said and he glanced about the vestibule. But the old place didn't look the same, the walls were charred, the glossy floor tiles dull and cracked. Above, blackened roof timbers gave access to the sky.

'No customers now,' coughed Mr Fudgepacker. 'No-one. Just me and Him.'

'You know that I've come to see Him?'

'I don't allow Him visitors. I've never allowed Him visitors. But you are special, Russell, you gave Him to me.'

I'm losing this, thought Russell. But just play along.

'Is *He* well?' Russell asked.

'He doesn't change. He can never change.'

'That's nice for Him.'

'*What?*' Mr Fudgepacker's eyes took life. 'Nothing is nice for Him. I see to that.'

Lost it completely, thought Russell. Him and me both, by the sound of it.

'Come with me.' Mr Fudgepacker took Russell by the arm. His fingers were hard, wooden, they dug into Russell's flesh.

As they walked slowly along the aisle, Russell looked around at the stock. It was all going to pieces. The stuffed beasts worm-eaten and green with growing mould. Precious things that Russell had cared for on lunch-times long ago were now

271

corroded, worthless junk. It broke Russell's heart to see them so. One of the catwalks had collapsed, smashing sarcophagi and ancient urns. A rank smell filled the air. The perfume of decay.

Russell recalled some of the words that Bobby Boy had spoken. 'How long? How long has He been with you?'

'For all these years. I am His guardian. All this, all this in the Emporium. His doing. You can't capture time, Russell. It won't be caught. Try and hold it in your hands and it runs through your fingers, like sand.' The old man cackled. 'Like the sands of time, eh, Russell?'

Russell nodded helplessly. None of that was right, surely? That wasn't what Peter Cushing had said on the video.

They reached the small Gothic door at the end of the aisle. Russell pressed it open and the two men passed through the narrow opening, down an ill-lit flight of steps and into the boiler room.

'This way.' Mr Fudgepacker led Russell between piles of ancient luggage, old portmanteaus, Gladstone bags, towards a curtained-off corner of the room.

Russell knew what lay in wait behind that curtain. He had seen the horror, he knew what to expect.

But it didn't help. It didn't help to know. Russell hesitated. It was very strong that thing. Could it be reasoned with? Russell felt that it could not. He would have to offer something. The stone that promised magic? The Judas kiss? He would have to lie, he'd come prepared to lie. But how convincing would he be? And how much *did* it know?

Russell felt afraid. His knees began to sag, yet at the same time prepared themselves to run.

'Part the curtain,' said Mr Fudgepacker. 'But avert your gaze.'

Russell reached out to the curtain. There was still time to run. Still time to escape. He didn't have to do this.

But he would. He knew that he would.

Russell took the curtain, it was cold and damp, it clung to his fingers. Russell pulled at the curtain and it fell away like shredded sodden tissue.

Russell turned down his eyes. But his hand came up to cover his nose. The smell was appalling. Sickening. Russell gagged into his hand and dared a glance.

And then he started back and stared with eyes quite round.

It sat upon the throne-like chair. All twisted to one side. A leg tucked up beneath itself, the other dangling down, the foot the wrong way round. The hands were shrunken claws with long yellow nails. The face. Russell stared at the face.

The face was that of Adolf Hitler.

Hitler's head lolled onto his left shoulder. The eyes were open, but unfocused, crossed. Lines of congealed slime ran from the nose and open mouth, caked the chest, hung in stalactites descending to a crust upon the floor.

'Hitler,' Russell gasped. 'He's dead.'

'He is *not*.' Ernest set up another high cackle. 'He just smells dead. The filthy fucker, he's shat himself again.'

Russell took a step forward, but the stench forced him back. The once proud Reich Führer was now a shrivelled mummy, festering in his own filth. Paralyzed and helpless.

'What happened to him?' Russell asked. 'How did he get this way?'

'Your doing, Russell. All your doing.'

'*My* doing? No.'

'It's better than he deserves. The irony of it, Russell. The man who wanted the whole world for his own, now has this for his whole world. I must get a new curtain, it's months since I've been down here, the old one's all rotted away.'

'Months?' Russell asked. 'Don't you feed him? Wash him?'

'He doesn't need feeding. I spray him with insecticide once in a while. Bluebottles lay their eggs in him. The maggots eat out through the skin. See, his left ear's gone and some of the back of his head.'

Russell felt vomit rising in his throat. 'This is inhuman,' he gasped. 'Why? Tell me why?'

'You know why. He took my wife, my beautiful wife. Left me to grow old alone. But I'm converted now. Good for another four hundred years at least. And I'll spend them with him. He'll have time to muse upon his evil.'

Russell turned his face away. No man deserved such a terrible fate, not even one so vile as Hitler.

'Go upstairs,' said Russell. 'Go upstairs now.'

'You can poke him with my pointy stick if you want. But don't trouble yourself to have a go at his ball. I had that off years ago. I've got it upstairs in a jar.'

'Go,' said Russell. 'As quick as you can now.'

Mr Fudgepacker spat towards the cripple in the chair, then slowly turned and hobbled from the room.

Russell listened to the shuffling footsteps on the stairs and then the creaking of the floorboards overhead.

With a pounding heart and popping ears, Russell sought a means towards an end. He selected a length of iron pipe that lay against the wall and tested its weight on his palm. And then he walked back over to the figure in the chair.

Russell looked into the unfocused eyes. He saw there the flicker of life. He saw the slime-caked lips begin to part and the dry tongue move within. And Russell knew the words that would come.

'Help me. Help me.'

Russell spoke a prayer and asked forgiveness. Then he swung the heavy pipe and put Adolf Hitler out of his misery.

Upstairs in the vestibule, Ernest Fudgepacker stood, nodding his head stiffly to a rhythm only he heard. Russell's knees were almost giving out, but he forced himself to walk as naturally as he could.

'Did you give him a bit of a poke?' asked Ernest.

'A bit of a poke. Yes.'

'Will you come back again?'

'I don't think so. Goodbye.'

'Not so fast,' said the ancient. 'I haven't given you what you came for.'

Russell's brain was all fogged up. All he wanted was to get out. To get away from this place. 'What I came for?' he asked.

'You came for these, didn't you?' Mr Fudgepacker produced two black leather belts with complicated dials set into the buckles.

'What are those?'

'For your journey home. To get you back safely.'

'The time devices.'

'Modern technology,' said Mr Fudgepacker. 'An improvement on the old *Flügelrad*. I designed them myself.'

With whose, or *what's*, help? thought Russell. As if I didn't know.

'Just set the time and press the button,' said Mr Fudgepacker. 'But they'll only work the one way and that's backwards. Time isn't for fooling about with, Russell. It's best left alone.'

'Goodbye then, Mr Fudgepacker.'

'Goodbye, Russell.'

★　　★　　★

It is often the case that after experiencing unspeakable horror, people unaccountably burst into laughter. It happens in wartime and my father told me that when he served as a fireman during the blitz, he often came upon people sitting beside the burned-out shells of their houses, laughing hysterically. He said that he was never certain whether it was simply through shock, or something more. A burst of awareness, perhaps, that they *were* alive. That they had survived and were aware of their survival, probably aware of their own existence for the first time ever.

As Russell left the Emporium and walked back along the track that had once been the Kew Road, he began to laugh. It started as small coughs that he tried to keep back but it broke from him again and again until tears ran down his face and his belly ached.

Russell had this image in his mind. An image both farcical and absurd. But he couldn't shake it free. It was a newspaper headline, splashed across a Sunday tabloid.

It read:

ASSASSIN CONFESSES:
'I SHAGGED HITLER'S GIRLFRIEND'

# CHAPTER 20

# ARYAN 3

Russell returned to the Schauberger Memorial Mall, but he did so via a different entrance, purchased several items from one of the gift shops and slipped these into an inner pocket of his sharp black jacket. Then he strode at a brisk pace towards the electrical store and Julie.

Julie wasn't there.

Russell checked his watch, he was rather late. But she'd have waited, surely? She'd have had to wait. Russell looked up and down the shopping mall, no sign of her.

What to do? Go back to The Flying Swan? See if he could tease where to go next from Jim Pooley? Stay here? Wait outside?

Wait outside, Russell decided. This place depressed him anyway. Wait outside it was. Russell walked down the arcade, under the big golden arch and out through the glass revolving doors.

'*Russell!*' A harsh stage whisper.

'Julie?'

'Over here.'

Russell turned, Julie's hand beckoned to him

from behind one of the chromium portico columns that flanked the entrance.

Russell wandered over. 'Why are you hiding?' he asked.

'Why are you late?' was Julie's reply. 'I've been waiting for an hour.'

Russell began with the first in a series of carefully rehearsed lies. 'I was held up,' he said. 'I was only able to acquire *one* time belt.'

Julie didn't seem unduly miffed by this. 'Only one? Well, give it to me, give it to me.' Altogether far too eager. Her glance met Russell's. 'I mean, well done, Russell. I knew you could do it.'

'It wasn't easy. There's all the big celebrations going on.'

'Celebrations? What celebrations?'

'For the return of Hitler. He must have come in the *Flügelrad*. He materialized in Berlin an hour ago. There's huge rallies and firework displays. I saw it on a TV in one of the shops.'

Julie looked as bewildered as Russell had hoped she would. 'That isn't right,' she whispered. 'He's not due until tomorrow.'

'Sorry?' said Russell. 'I didn't catch that.'

'Nothing. Nothing. Give me the programmer.'

'We're supposed to do this outside the electrical store, that's the way it was done in the movie.'

'Well, this *isn't* a movie. Give me the programmer.'

Russell took the programmer from his pocket.

Julie dug into a carrier bag and brought out the gift box.

'Here, let me put it in,' said Russell, taking the box from her hands. 'I can pack it in the way I remember it being packed when I unwrapped it. If you know what I mean.'

'I do, but just hurry.'

Russell turned away and fiddled about.

'Are you done? Come on, give it to me.'

Russell turned back and presented Julie with a neatly wrapped parcel. 'There,' said he. 'Done.'

'And the time belt?'

'Yes, of course.' Russell took one of the time belts from his jacket pocket. Julie strapped the belt around her slender waist. 'How does it work?' she asked.

'I've set the time and the co-ordinates. You know what to do, go back to the date and the time. I will be in The Ape of Thoth with Morgan. Give the programmer to me and let me do the rest.'

Julie looked up at Russell and for one terrible moment Russell thought she was going to ask the obvious question: why are you doing this? Russell did have an ingenious answer worked out. But he was not called upon to use it.

'What are *you* going to do?' Julie asked.

'I can't leave,' said Russell. 'I'm trapped here. But *He* is here, Hitler. Maybe I can raise an underground resistance movement, or something.'

'Fat chance,' whispered Julie.

'Sorry, I didn't catch that.'

'I said, I hope you get *that chance*.'

'Thank you.' Russell recalled in the movie there being a bit of passionate kissing and the words 'I love you' being bandied about. Russell stuck his lips out for a snog.

But he didn't get one.

'Right,' said Julie. 'I'll be off.'

And pressing the button on the buckle of her belt.

She was.


Russell stood on his own, cocked his head on one side and listened. According to what he'd seen in the movie and back at The Ape of Thoth, the big metal clanking things with the terror weapons should now be making an appearance to chase Julie through time.

But they weren't, were they?

'No,' said Russell. 'They are not. Because that was just another trick, probably done with the Cyberstar machine, to make me trust and be protective to Julie from the very first moment. Boy, did I get taken for a sucker. But, however.' Russell delved into another pocket and brought out a package. It was identical in shape and form to the one Julie had taken back into the past.

Russell had switched them.

Russell grinned and unwrapped the programmer. Julie would be delivering the package to the Russell of the past in The Ape of Thoth, but this time, when the Russell of the past opened it, it would not contain the programmer. It would contain a nice fresh ham roll. After all, Russell had been eating that stale ham sandwich when he opened the package in The Bricklayer's Arms, hadn't he?

'I had,' Russell grinned. 'You sly dog, Russell. You have pulled it off. No programmer, no movie, you've beaten the buggers.' Russell dropped the programmer to the marble paving and ground his heel upon it.

That was a job well done.

Russell stood on the steps of the shopping mall, a smug little smile on his face. He *had* got it done, he really had. He'd stopped the movie getting made and the world getting changed. He looked up at the monolithic building, all this would soon fade away. How long? Russell didn't have a clue. But it would, he knew that it would.

So what to do now?

Another pint at The Flying Swan? That was tempting.

Return at once to the past? He still had to deal with the ultimate evil. The red insect thing in Fudgepacker's basement. But he *would* deal with that. He felt certain he would.

'No,' said Russell. 'One last look around while I'm here. There's something I'd like to see. Something that would help me out no end.'

Russell walked back into the mall and along the arcade to the electrical store. He looked in at the window, the Cyberstars stood in mock conversation, children played upon the holographic machines.

Russell entered the store.

The chap behind the counter smiled him a welcomer.

Russell smiled back.

'How can I help you, citizen?' asked the chap.

'I'm interested in acquiring a copy of an old movie,' said Russell. 'In fact, if you have it in stock, I'd like to view a bit of it. Just a few minutes. The end bit.'

'I'm sure that can be arranged, sir. What is the name of this movie?'

'*Nostradamus Ate my Hamster*,' said Russell.

'Oh sir, sir,' the chap wrung his hands in evident joy.

'One of your favourites?' Russell asked.

'Oh my very favourite. Everyone's favourite.'

'Indeed?' said Russell. Not for much longer, he thought. 'Then you have a copy in stock?'

'Probably one hundred copies.'

'That popular, eh?'

'Where have you been, sir, on the moon? The biggest box office success in the history of film making. Years before its time, you see. An Ernest Fudgepacker production, starring—'

'Just about everybody,' said Russell.

'But not just *anybody*, sir.'

'Go on,' said Russell.

'Starring Julie Hitler, sir. The Führer's wife.'

That did catch Russell a little off guard, but he might have expected it really. 'Could I have a viewing?' Russell asked. 'Just the end bit?'

'Of course, sir, of course. Oh, I'm so excited.'

'I thought you'd seen it.'

'Yes, sir, but seeing her, seeing her.'

'Seeing her?' said Russell.

'Here, sir, here.'

'What do you mean?' Russell asked.

'She was here, sir. In the store, not an hour and a half ago. Large as life and twice as beautiful.'

'Here?'

'I got her autograph. Look, I'll show it to you. But you can't touch it.'

'I don't really want to,' said Russell.

'Oh come on, sir. Just to touch her autograph, imagine.'

I've touched a lot more than *that*, Russell thought. 'I'm sorry,' he said. 'I don't understand. Why did the lovely Mrs Hitler come in here?'

'Well, sir. It seems that the Führer and she have one of the Cyberstar systems. I expect they re-enact famous movies in the comfort of their palace. Well, apparently she'd mislaid the programmer and she came in here, in here, sir, into my humble store, for a replacement.'

'*What?*' went Russell. 'And you gave it to her?'

'With compliments, sir.'

'Oh my God!'

'Whatever is it, sir? You've come over all un-necessary.'

Russell shook his fists in the air. She'd done it to him again. She'd left nothing to chance. A spare programmer in case he lost his, or *something*. All she'd wanted from him was the time belt to get back with. She'd never trusted him. He'd been stitched up, good and proper.

'Aaaaagh!'

'Please, sir, control yourself, whatever is the matter?'

Russell made fists and looked all around the shop. He'd failed. Well, of course he'd failed. If he'd succeeded, then this place would never have come to be. He'd be standing in empty space right now, or the middle of the Great West Road. He'd blown it and it was all *his* fault. He'd given her the time device. He'd laid it all on.

Russell took to groaning. There was that other Russell back in the past, that one who would watch Julie appear, would be given the programmer and would take it to Bobby Boy. That stupid lame-brained Russell who would be conned every inch of the way. Who would work until he nearly dropped to produce a movie that would reduce the people of the world to little more than slaves.

Russell shook his head. Whatever was he to do *now*?

'Sir,' said the chap behind the counter, 'if you're all right, sir, would you like to see the movie?'

Russell turned and Russell smiled. 'Oh yes,' he said. 'Oh very much indeed.'

★   ★   ★

And so Russell sat down and watched the movie, the manager was so excited that he insisted Russell watch all the way through. And so Russell did. There was so much more that he hadn't seen. But it all made perfect sense when you viewed it from the beginning to the end. The dark alien creature, always in the background, always manipulating, experimenting with this means and that to control and exploit mankind. And he, Russell, played by Bobby Boy, finally defeating the creature in a manner Russell hadn't even considered.

As the credits rolled away the manager clapped his hands in warm applause. 'Isn't it wonderful, sir, marvellous, a *tour de force*. And it's all true, you know. Well, not true as in true. It's a metaphor you see. For life. You see the Emporium represents—'

'Yes,' said Russell. 'Well I don't think we need to go into all that now. I wanted to see the end and now I've seen it. I know all I need to know.'

'If only that were true, sir, eh?'

'It *is* true,' said Russell.

The manager laughed, politely, but he *did* laugh.

'Why are you laughing?' Russell enquired.

'Because of what you said about the ending, sir. You see that's the whole point of the movie. That's part of the metaphor. The movie doesn't have an ending. Well not one, I've a hundred copies in stock and there's a hundred different endings. That's what made the movie so successful. If you go and see a movie twice you know it will have the same ending. But this one never did. Almost every copy was different. *Is* different. No-one has ever been able to work out how it was done. How Fudgepacker *found the time.*'

Russell really couldn't help but be impressed. That was *some* gimmick. That would really have packed them in. He could just picture the train-spotter types, vying with one another, seeing who could score the most endings. Why there was probably a *Nostradamus Ate my Hamster Appreciation Society**. 'Do you think anyone has seen all the endings?' Russell asked.

'Who can say, sir? That's part of the mythos, isn't it?'

'Well, thank you for showing it to me. It was an experience.'

'And will sir be taking a copy?'

'No, I don't think so. But tell me this, as far as you know, does the movie always have a happy ending?'

'Of course it does, sir, of course it does.'

Russell was relieved to hear this at least. 'That's a weight off my mind,' he said.

'Oh yes,' said the manager. 'The endings are always happy. Even the ones where the Russell character meets a grisly death.'

Russell groaned.

'Oh yes, sir, there's the version where he gets gang-banged at the bikers' barbecue, and the one

---

* And of course there was. Russell had sat on one of their benches.

where he's shot with the General Electric minigun, and the one where the cannibal cult get him, oh and my favourite, the amazing slow-motion sequence where the escaped psychopath takes this hedge-clipper and puts it right up his . . .'

# CHAPTER 21

## BASIC TIN SINK

Russell left the store and then the mall. He walked slowly back along the something-strasser, with his head bowed into his chest and his hands thrust deep in his trouser pockets.

He was down, Russell was, it had not been his day. As days went, he'd known better. For it's not every day that you're chased by a howling mob, escape in a time machine while having sex with a beautiful woman, kill Adolf Hitler and still have a moment to screw up the future of the human race.

And it was early yet. Scarcely five of the afternoon clock. Russell scuffed his shoes along the pavement. What was he going to do now? He'd have to go back and try to sort things out. But things were rather complicated. If the time belt only took you *back* in time, then he couldn't go back too far. Certainly not further than the moment when he and Julie escaped in the *Flügelrad*, when *he* escaped. If he went back further, he'd already be there. The other Russell, the one that was the 'him-then', who didn't know what he knew now. So to speak.

'I am in a state of stress,' said Russell, startling a passer-by. 'I really thought I could win this. But now I'm not too sure. It doesn't matter what I do, they're always one step ahead of me. If only there was some way. Some way.'

Russell stopped short and began to laugh. Those hysterics again? Not this time. There *was* a solution. It was a bold plan, and there was a risk of failure. A big risk. In fact the very biggest risk there could be. A risk that could cost Russell everything. His life. Everything. But it was a risk he was prepared to take. Because if there was one person capable of pulling the whole thing off, then that one person was he, Russell.

Russell took a very deep breath. 'All right,' said he. 'This time.'

Mr Eric Nelluss* was a tall imposing figure. Although now the graveyard side of sixty-five and the wearer of a long grey beard, he was still a force to be reckoned with. A major force, for he was undoubtedly the most powerful and influential film producer and distributor in the western world. In his long career he had struck many deals and invested many millions, but today, today would be the very crowning point of his brilliant career.

Because today he was having a meeting with a Mr Ernest Fudgepacker and his associates, to put

* The chap mentioned in Chapter 14.

the final seal on a film deal, the like of which the world had never seen before.

Mr Nelluss stood, his hands behind his back, looking out from the boardroom window of his towering corporation building at Docklands.

Below the hum of London traffic, above the clear blue sky.

Mr Nelluss coughed and clutched one hand against his chest. He was not a well man, he had a heart condition, the years of constant stress had taken their toll. But today. Today was going to be *his* day.

The intercom on the long black boardroom table buzzed and Mr Nelluss strode over and sat down in his big red leather chairman's chair.

'Yes, Doris?' His voice had a deep American accent. They said that he hailed form the mid-west, but no-one knew for sure. The man was an enigma. A virtual recluse.

'Mr Fudgepacker and his associates are here, Mr Nelluss. Should I send them up?'

'Please do, Doris.' Mr Nelluss sat back in his chair and smiled a pleasant smile. Before him on the table were the stacks of contracts. The rights, the residuals, the spin-offs, the series, the video games, the whole world marketing deals.

At the far end of the boardroom the lift light blinked red and chromium doors opened in the wall of travertine marble.

Before him stood an ancient fellow in a long black coat, supported at the elbows by his two

291

associates, a gaunt thin pinch-faced man in black and a beautiful blond woman in a golden dress and a fitted, buttoned jacket, also in black.

'Mr Fudgepacker, come in, sir, come in.' Mr Nelluss rose from his chair and came forward to greet his guests.

He wrung Mr Fudgepacker's wrinkly hand between his own, patted the fellow in black on the shoulder and returned the flashing smile of the beautiful blonde. 'Bobby Boy, Julie,' Mr Nelluss beckoned them in. 'Come in. Sit down. Would you care for a drink? Tea, coffee, something stronger? Champagne, perhaps?'

'Champagne,' said Bobby Boy.

'Yes,' said Julie.

Mr Fudgepacker nodded.

Mr Nelluss pressed the intercom button and ordered champagne. 'You got here all right?' he asked. 'My guys pick up all the stuff? No problems?'

'No problems,' said Mr Fudgepacker, easing himself onto a boardroom chair.

Bobby Boy limped over, pulled one out from beneath the table and sat down upon it. Leaving Julie standing.

Mr Nelluss strode around and assisted her into a chair.

'Thank you,' said Julie. 'At least there's one gentleman in the room.'

Mr Fudgepacker grunted. Bobby Boy said nothing.

'Bobby Boy,' said Mr Nelluss, 'I see you're still limping. Went a little over the top with that stunt you pulled on us at the end-of-picture party at Hangar 18.'

Bobby Boy sniffed, it had been just two weeks since the screening and him getting shot in the kneecap.

'Quite some stunt,' said Mr Nelluss. 'And quite some party. You really know how to throw a party, Mr F. Having a mock shoot-out and that guy dressed up as Adolf Hitler. And the flying saucer just vanishing in the car park. I've been in the movie game for nearly forty years and I've never seen anything like that.'

'Glad it entertained you,' said Mr Fudgepacker.

A door slid open and the champagne arrived.

'Just leave it, Doris,' said Mr Nelluss. 'I'll pour the drinks.'

After the door had shut once more, Mr Nelluss poured champagne and passed glasses round. 'You didn't bring the other guy with you,' he said. 'Your producer, Russell. Where's he today, then?'

'Russell is no longer with us,' said Mr Fudgepacker. 'I don't think we'll see Russell again.'

'Shame. I kind of liked the guy. Although all I saw of him was him wielding the prop pistol. Seemed like a crazy dude.'

'Can we just talk about the movie?' asked Bobby Boy. 'And *the money*?'

'Sure we can. Sure we can. That's what we're all

here for, after all. Now, I've got contracts drawn up and you're gonna like them, I promise.'

'How much?' asked Bobby Boy.

'For what?'

'For a start off my fee as star of the movie.'

'I thought twenty-five million,' said Mr Nelluss.

The corners of Bobby Boy's mean little mouth rose halfway up his cheeks. 'Sounds about right,' he said.

'But it's chicken feed in the ultimate scheme of things. Now, before we start any signing, I have to know, did you bring everything? Everything I asked you to bring?'

Mr Fudgepacker nodded shakily. 'Everything and I wouldn't have done so but for your reputation and your standing.'

Mr Nelluss smiled once more. 'But of course,' said he. 'I know what I'm worth and you know what I'm worth. I am *the power* behind movies. You had to choose me, you know you did.'

Mr Fudgepacker nodded again.

'So you've brought it *all* with you? The negatives, the rushes, the out-takes, the videos and the Cyberstar equipment? That alone is going to gross us more millions than, well, shit, than I've had business lunches, for God's sake.' Mr Nelluss laughed. But he did so alone.

'Quite so. Quite so. But this is an exciting day for me. If I was to tell you that I have looked forward to this day throughout all the long years of my career I would not be exaggerating. No siree, by golly.'

'Let's get the contracts signed,' said Mr Fudgepacker. 'I want to go down to your laboratories and personally supervise the copying of the negatives. It is absolutely essential that it's done under my personal supervision.'

'No problem there. We'll have them coming hot off the press and I do mean *hot*.'

'Give us another glass of champagne,' said Bobby Boy.

'Help yourself, my good friend. Help yourself.'

Bobby Boy helped himself.

'Some over here,' said Julie. Bobby Boy passed her the bottle.

Mr Nelluss rose from his big red chairman's chair and took himself over to the boardroom window. 'This is one hell of a day,' he said, flexing his shoulders. 'One hell of a day.'

'Can we get on with the signing?' asked Mr Fudgepacker.

'Yeah, sure, that's what we're here for. But hey, what are those guys down in the car park doing?'

'I don't give a damn,' said Mr Fudgepacker. 'Let's get this done.'

'No, you really should see this, come over to the window, do.'

'I'm not interested.'

'Sure you are, sure you are. Come over. Bobby Boy, you come over too and Julie, come on, all of you.'

'Oh all right!' Mr Fudgepacker struggled from his chair and limped over to the window. Bobby

Boy joined him in the limping. Julie didn't limp, she sort of 'swept'.

'Look at those guys,' said Mr Nelluss. 'What do you think they're up to?'

Many storeys below tiny figures moved in the car park. They were tossing things into a skip.

'Just builders,' said Mr Fudgepacker. 'Now let's not waste any more time.'

'I don't think they're builders,' said Mr Nelluss. 'Surely those are cans of film they have there.'

Mr Fudgepacker's eyes bulged behind the pebbled lenses of his spectacles. 'Cans of film?' he croaked. 'That's *my* film, they're opening up the cans. They're exposing the negatives.'

'By God,' said Mr Nelluss. 'That does look like what they're doing, doesn't it?'

'They're chucking it onto the skip.' Mr Fudgepacker swayed to and fro. 'They're destroying it.'

'Hey, and look at that guy.' Mr Nellus pointed. 'Surely that's the Cyberstar equipment he's got there. He's not going to . . . oh my lord, he's thrown that on too.'

'No!' Mr Fudgepacker croaked.

'And who are those?' Mr Nellus pointed once more. 'Those guys in the protective suits. Are those flame-throwers they're carrying?'

Mr Fudgepacker chewed upon his fingers. 'Bobby Boy, do something. Do something.'

'What can I do?' Bobby Boy had fingers of his own to chew. 'Look what they're doing now.'

'Isn't that gasoline?' Mr Nelluss asked. 'Surely it is. They're pouring it into the skip.'

Mr Fudgepacker gasped and tottered.

'They're lighting it up.'

From below came a muffled report, a flash of flame and a mushroom cloud of oily black smoke.

'Dear, oh dear, oh dear,' said Mr Nellus, returning to his chair. 'Now is *that* a blow to business, or what?' He perused the piles of contracts on the table before him and then, with a single sweeping gesture of his arm, he drove the lot into a wastepaper bin, positioned as if for the purpose.

Ernest Fudgepacker sank to his knees. Bobby Boy stood and made fists. Julie's face wore a bitter expression, tears were welling in her eyes.

'Why?' croaked Mr Fudgepacker. 'Why? Who did this? Who?'

'I did it,' said Eric Nelluss, suddenly losing his accent. 'It was me.'

'It was *you*? But why? All the money. Everything. Everything lost. The future lost, oh the future, the future.'

'I did it,' said Eric Nelluss, 'because my name is not Eric Nelluss. Can't you guess who I really am?'

'You're a mad old man,' shouted Bobby Boy. 'And I'll take your head off.'

Bobby Boy lunged across the table, but the Eric Nelluss who was apparently not Eric Nelluss skilfully caught him by the left wrist, snapped it and cast him down to the thick pile carpet.

'I could always take you,' said not-Eric Nelluss. 'I did ju-jitsu at night school, remember?'

Bobby Boy clutched at his maimed wrist. 'Russell?' he gasped. 'Is that *you*?'

'Yes, it's me.' Russell settled back into his big red chairman's chair.

'But how? You're old, or is that make-up? You bastard.'

'It's not make-up.' Russell took a sip of champagne. 'I *am* old. I'm more than sixty-five years old. I gave up my life for this day. For this moment. My time. I gave up my time.'

'But *how*?'

'I know how,' said Julie. 'He came back from the future with one of the time belts and he went into the past.'

'Correct,' said Russell. 'It was a one-way journey. You were always one step ahead of me. That's what gave me the idea. I would be one step ahead of you. I went back to 1955 and I took a job in the film industry. Just a humble gopher, but I worked hard. You know me, Mr Fudgepacker, I work hard and if I'm given a job to do, I do it. I worked my way up. Well, I knew which films to invest in, didn't I? But it was hard work. But as the years went by I grew more and more powerful. I only had one ambition, you see, to be top of the heap.

'To be the biggest and most influential independent film producer and distributor in the world.

298

The one you would have to bring the movie to. And you did. And now it's all over. The film is destroyed, the Cyberstar equipment is destroyed. It is all over. All of it.'

'No,' Mr Fudgepacker groaned. 'It can't end like this, it just can't.'

'But it can and it has. I agree it could have been a whole lot more exciting. Explosions going off, roof-top chases, chases through time, even. Guns, violence, all the stuff you love in your movies. But that's not life, is it? I know life is duller than art, but there's more power in the boardroom than on the battlefield. It's all over now. It's done.'

'No!' Mr Fudgepacker raised a shrivelled fist. 'I'm not done. *He's* not done.'

'I'm afraid you're wrong again,' said Russell. '*He* is done. *He* is being disposed of even as we speak.'

'*No!* That cannot be.'

'I set up a little bureau back in the Fifties,' said Russell. 'Department 23. To investigate paranormal occurrences. The data came in from police stations around the country. I called myself The Captain, investigated one or two very strange ones in the Brentford district. A crime wave caused by a man who turned out not to be a man at all, just a bundle of spare parts.

'The workings of that thing in your basement. I've kept Him under close surveillance and I've learned all about Him and all about His weaknesses.'

'He doesn't have any weaknesses. Only—'

'Only his problem with time,' said Russell. 'He lives time in reverse, doesn't he? He was born in the future, and he'll die in the past. He halts the process by absorbing other people's time. He can do that to them. Steal their time. And I know about his voice. His one voice which is many. The voice that has the power to hypnotize and control, the voice you intended to dub onto the movie so that all who heard it would be controlled.'

'He'll take you,' crowed Mr Fudgepacker. 'He'll take *your* time.'

'No,' said Russell. 'A special unit of my operatives is already at the Emporium. They are wearing protective reflecting suits. And earphones which broadcast white noise. Your creature cannot influence them. They have the time belt. I've set it for the year *dot*, as it were. I wonder how long ago that is? A million years? A billion? They will put the time belt on the creature and press the little button.'

As Russell spoke the intercom purred. Russell whispered words into it and whispered words were returned to him.

'It is done,' said Russell. 'It is all over.'

Julie slumped into one of the boardroom chairs and stared across the table at the old man who sat before her. 'You really did a number on us, didn't you, Russell? You really pulled out all the stops.'

'It has cost me my life. I have a chronic heart condition. I only have months, maybe only weeks,

300

to live. But I held on because I knew this day would come. I'm finished now, but I have stopped you.'

'Oh no you haven't,' said Julie. 'There's something you've forgotten.'

'What?' Russell asked.

'I still have *my* time belt, I can go back to yesterday and cancel this meeting.'

'No,' said Russell. 'You wouldn't do *that*?'

'Oh yes I would.' Julie opened her jacket. She was wearing the belt. She adjusted the little dial on the buckle.

'No,' implored Russell. 'Don't do it.'

'I'll see you yesterday,' said Julie. 'Except you won't see today. I'll gun you down as you cross the street. You're dead, Russell. Goodbye, and it hasn't been nice knowing you.'

And with that she pressed the button on her belt and promptly vanished.

'Ha ha!' Bobby Boy laughed up from the floor. 'You're dead, Russell. Ha, ha, ha.'

Russell smiled. 'I don't feel very dead,' he said.

'But she'll shoot you, yesterday.'

'I don't remember being shot, *yesterday*.'

'What?'

'You didn't really think I'd leave a loose end like that floating about, surely?'

'*What?*'

'I'm afraid *I* did something *yesterday*,' said Russell. 'I crept into Julie's bedroom and did a bit of reprogramming to her time belt. I think

301

you'll find she's a long way from here now. Back in the year dot.'

'You bastard!' croaked Fudgepacker. 'That was my wife.'

'The Führer's girlfriend,' said Russell. 'She played you false. She played everybody false.'

'Ah yes,' Ernest Fudgepacker rose from his knees. 'The Führer, the Führer.'

'Ah yes. The Führer.' Russell perused the golden Rolex on his wrist. 'I think just about now, on the western horizon . . . If you'll just look into the sky.'

Ernest Fudgepacker turned and as he did so a bright flash, almost like a daytime firework, lit up the western sky and then faded into the blue.

Ernest Fudgepacker groaned.

'Bomb on board the *Flügelrad*,' said Russell. 'If only he hadn't kept popping back from the future to have a drink with you. Still, at least this time he went out with a bang, rather than a whimper.'

'What do you mean?'

'I saw what you did to him in the future,' said Russell. 'What did you do, sacrifice him to that time creature of yours?'

'I would have, a couple of years from now, for what he did. Taking my beautiful wife.'

'Well, he's gone now,' said Russell, 'for ever. And that, gentlemen, I think, is it. I'm afraid the excitement has all been a little much for me, I will have to have a lie down. I can call for a paramedic if you want, Bobby Boy.'

'No thanks,' the thin man climbed unsteadily to his feet.

'And you'd best get back to the Emporium, Mr Fudgepacker,' said Russell. 'There's a lot of business coming your way.'

'There is?'

'I'm producing a movie,' said Russell. 'It will be my last. But I'll want to hire props from the Emporium. Many props. *All* the props. You'll make enough for a happy retirement, Mr Fudgepacker. I wouldn't deprive you of that.'

Mr Fudgepacker sighed. 'You've a good heart, Russell. You've always had a good heart.'

'Sadly,' said Russell, 'I now have a bad one. But you'll get your retirement fund. I'll see that you do.'

Mr Fudgepacker shuffled to the lift door accompanied by a sulking Bobby Boy, and then he turned.

'Tell me, Russell,' he said, 'what's your movie about?'

'It's autobiographical,' said Russell. 'It's called *Nostradamus Ate my Hamster*.'

# CHAPTER 22

'And?' said Pooley.

'And what?' said Omally.

'And what happened next? I suppose.'

'Well, nothing happened next. That's the end of the story.'

'Oh,' said Pooley, taking a sip from his pint. 'So that was it. Just like that.'

'Just like that.' Omally joined Jim with a sip from his own. 'But it wasn't really just like that, was it? I mean Russell gave up all of his life for just that one moment. A pretty noble thing to do by any reckoning.'

Jim nodded thoughtfully. 'It's not the way we would have done it,' he said. 'If we'd done it there *would* have been explosions going off and people running all over the place.'

'But *we* didn't do it, did we?'

Jim now shook his head with an equal degree of thoughtfulness. 'No,' said he, 'you're right there.'

'Cometh the hour, cometh the man,' said Omally, raising his glass to his companion.

Jim raised his in return and both took deep respectful draughts.

'But what do you think did happen to Russell?' Pooley asked.

Omally shrugged. 'Who can say? Perhaps he's dead now. Or perhaps all the things in the story have yet to happen. After all, I've never seen his movie, have you?'

'No,' said Jim. 'And let's face it, we've never actually met the fellow. We didn't get atomized at Christmas time and we didn't get sent into the future. The Swan's still here and we're still in it.'

'Makes you think,' said John Omally.

'It certainly does,' Jim agreed. 'And it makes you wonder also.'

'Some say,' said John, 'that he *is* still alive. In fact . . .' And here Omally gestured towards old Pete, who stood at the bar counter tasting rum, his dog Chips sampling a drips tray that Neville had put out for him. 'Some say that old Pete is actually Russell.'

'Leave it out!' Jim coughed into his pint. 'Not that surly old sod.'

'I heard that,' said Pete.

Me too, thought Chips, but he said only 'woof'.

'Others,' Omally drew Jim near with a beckoning hand, 'others say that if you were to go to Fudgepacker's Emporium and discover the secret door, go down the steps and enter the boiler room, you would find a tiny curtained-off corner. And if you had the nerve, you might draw that curtain aside. And there, there, seated on a kind of throne-like chair, you would see Russell. Still a young man and just sitting there staring forever into space. You see, some say that he was never a real person at all, that he was just a construct. A bit of you and a bit of me. A bit of everyone who cares about the borough, called into life by magical means when the need arose. Cometh the hour, cometh the man. And possibly . . .' John paused.

'Possibly what?' Jim asked.

'Possibly if you were to go right up to him and put your ear to his lips, you might just hear this little voice.'

'Little voice?'

'Little voice. And it would say . . .' John paused again.

'What would it say?'

'It would say, *Help me, help me.*'

'Urgh no!' Jim shook his head fiercely. 'That is a terrible story, John. That is quite horrible. That's not the way it should end at all.'

'No, you're right.' Omally finished his pint. 'But, of course, other folk say other things. I heard tell, for instance, that because Russell stopped all the bad stuff from happening by giving up his whole life, that he, of course, changed the future. So if none of the bad stuff could happen in the future, he would never go there, get the time belt and have to do all he did. So, in a twinkling of an eye, everything un-happened and he was a young man again, working back at Fudge-packer's.'

'I like that one,' said Jim. 'That one I like. That's

what I'd call a happy ending. I hope it happened that way.'

'Me too.' Omally rattled his empty glass upon the table. 'Me too.'

A young man now entered The Flying Swan. He was a fit and agile-looking young man, with a fine head of thick dark hair. He approached the bar and the new blonde barmaid Neville had taken on for lunch-times turned to greet him.

She smiled the young man a mouthload of lovely white teeth. 'What will it be, sir?' she asked.

The young man paused a moment, as if suddenly torn by some inner struggle, possibly regarding what blonde barmaids expect a *real* man to drink. But the moment he paused for was a brief one and straightening his shoulders he said, 'a Perrier water, please.'

'Oh good,' said the blonde barmaid, beaming hugely and beautifully, as if possibly recalling something her horoscope had said. 'Oh, just perfect.'

Omally looked at Pooley.

And Pooley looked at Omally.

'Now that,' said Jim, 'is what I call a happy ending.'

'I'll drink to it,' said Omally. 'Hey, Russell, two pints over here.'

## THE END